ABOUT THE AUTHOR

Lexie Winston has been an astronaut, rock star, princess and time traveller. In her dreams. But none of the dreams have lived up to what becoming an author has been like. She gets to live in a world of pure imagination, and her heroines get to do the things she's always wished she could.

When not writing books, Lexie is a mother of two gorgeous teenagers and the wife to a patient and understanding man. They live in Western Australia and are lorded over by a black toy poodle. She loves camping, reading and if her Kindle was stolen, her world would explode.

And you can find all links at

www.lexiewinston.com

INTERLUDE

LEXIE WINSTON

ALSO BY LEXIE WINSTON

The Collectors Division

(Paranormal Reverse Harem Series)

Guardian

Guardian's Blood

Guardian Ascending

Collector's Division Omnibus

Neighpalm Industries Collective

(Enemies to Lovers Reverse Harem)

Abandoned Girl

Broken Girl

Tormented Girl

Wanted Girl

Cherished Girl

Loved Girl

Superficial Girl - Jacinta's Story Part 1

Superficial Girl - Jacinta's Story Part 2

Neighpalm Industries Collective 1-3

Neighpalm Industries Collective 4-6

Seductive Sins Collection

(Reverse Harem Series)

Glorious Gluttony

Gangs, Guns, and Glory

Glory Glory Hellelujah

Crowning Glory

What's the Story, Morning Glory?

(Seductive Sins Omnibus)

Galaxy Circus

(Sci-Fi Reverse Harem Series)

Apprentice

Stagehand

Whisperer

Mama - Galaxy Circus Novella

Performer

Ringmaster

Interlude

A Night Most Wicked - Galaxy Circus Novella

Broken Promises

(Dark Poly Romance Series)

Secrets Kept

Lies Untold

Trust Broken

First published by Neighpalm Publishing in 2024

Interlude

Mobi format: 978-0-6459663-8-1
Print: 978-0-6459663-9-8
Cover design by Raven Ink Cover

Editing by Elemental Editing

FOREWORD

I decided not to add a glossary in this book. I had complaints whether I put it in the front or the back. So if you need a refresher on our cast of characters the main ones are listed on the next page. Everything else you can find by scanning the QR code which will take you to my website Galaxy Glossary

MAIN CHARACTERS

Lila Adams
Caspian
Link
Saxon
Xavier
Echo
Maxsim
Tirrian
Silac
Nikos
Ghosie
Brannock
Zeydan

CHAPTER ONE

Lila

I'm frozen on Silac's lap, and his arms have tightened around me in his anger. I hear him hiss aggressively, but I stare down at the beautiful, deadly man in front of me, and I'm kind of speechless. I know Bubby said he'd been acting suspiciously, but I had never considered this was the reason why. Brannock's eyes glisten with shame and guilt, and I really don't know what to say or do. Thankfully, one of the others does.

Xavier waves a hand, and Brannock is wrapped in bands of light and dragged up off the floor until he floats in the air, completely trapped. He doesn't struggle or fight, just heaves a resigned sigh at my warlock mate's actions.

"Please let me explain," he begs. Thankfully,

Link is able to keep a cool head and organize everyone around me.

"Cas, do you and the cats want to take the kids back to our place and get them settled?" In the wake of the announcement, Ghosie, Max, and Echo hurried to soothe the crying toddlers. Each of them holds one of our babies, who blink wearily, their faces blotchy with tears.

Cas and Max look torn between wanting to comfort our kids and finding out what Brannock is talking about, but Ghosie and Echo are completely focused on the little ones.

"I'll go," Ghosie offers, "if the alpha doesn't mind me accompanying his omega. You two look like you want to be involved." A rush of warmth flows over me at the bear's thoughtfulness. He really is nothing like how he portrayed himself to his brethren.

Cas bites his lip and looks carefully at the carevasta bear. He just joined us, and we don't know enough about him yet to blindly trust him with our babies, but Xavier waves his hand.

"I fully interrogated him while we were on the ship. I even dug into his mind, and he isn't hiding anything. Everything he told us about his faction of bears is true. They do love their children, and much like warlocks, they wouldn't do anything to harm them or Echo," he says to reassure the alpha and father.

"Are you okay with that, Echo?" Max asks our omega, who quickly nods his head.

"Yes, if Xavier says he can be trusted, then that's good enough for me. He also helped our mate, so that gives him points in my opinion." Echo smiles gently at the multicolored bear. There isn't a single aggressive bone in his body. He's so sweet and accepting.

"Cas?" I ask, and he stares intensely at the bear, his eyes flicking from his own lovely, stormy blue to the black of his beast. It's like they are having an internal conversation. I know the feeling well.

"Yes, that's fine, but if you do anything to hurt our babies or omega, we will eat you," he threatens in the growl of his beast, his eyes are pure black.

Ghosie bows his head respectfully. "I would expect nothing less."

Echo takes Jack from Max, as I push Silac's arms away from me. He's reluctant to let me go, but they drop away, and I give my children kisses, trying to soothe them, but they seem perfectly content snuggled into the bear's and cat's fur. I guess that is one bonus of having fur. I whisper to them to sleep well and then move out of the way so Cas can also do the same. The rest are too focused on Brannock to do anything, not to mention Saxon and Tirrian who are frozen, but the babies don't seem to care.

The five of them take their leave, and Cas and I return our focus to the Aaz'axian. Eric and William look furious and are glaring at him, but John looks sad.

"We gave you a home," he says mournfully. I think he feels disappointed. I know I am.

"Yes, and I've struggled since the moment you treated me with more respect than anyone who knew my race ever did," Brannock tells my grandpa, who has sat back down, the toll from his illness showing in the strain in his face.

"I don't understand. You told us you weren't compatible with other races and that you never finished with your wife. How can there be a child?" Xavier asks, his confusion evident in his tone, but before Brannock can answer, Link steps in and puts his hand on my warlock mate's shoulder.

"Why don't we all take a seat and talk about this calmly?" He waves at all the chairs that were pushed back and overturned in everyone's annoyance.

"Fine, but he stays contained until we get to the bottom of this," Xavier argues as the rest of us return to the seats we were in.

"What about these two?" I ask, stopping between a frozen Saxon and Tirrian, and Xavier winces.

"I think I'll leave them like that for now. Their anger is explosive, and they can't think straight. They are likely to harm him before we can get the whole story."

"They will be angry at you," Max murmurs as

he retakes his seat, the one Echo sat in next to him empty now.

"I don't envy you," William remarks, agreeing with Max, "but I think you are right. Can they still hear the story?"

"Yes, of course," Xavier answers.

"Then leave them. All that growling and aggression won't help now. We don't want to trigger Brannock's berserker mode. He seems calm and rational for now, and that's how we want to keep him," Eric says through gritted teeth. He is slow to anger, but when he does, it's like the flames of hell are fueling his rage. "Plus, it will be easier to kill him if we don't trigger it," he adds, and I'm not even surprised. My family is all about protecting ourselves, so I'm surprised nobody popped him the minute he made that announcement. Maybe we're maturing.

Xavier moves Brannock with a flick of his wrist, so that he's now floating above the table we sit around. He makes him spin slowly so he can see everyone at the round table, and I'm going to guess to also keep him slightly off balance in case he tries anything. He looks like he's not going anywhere though—Xavier's bands of light are tight.

"Start with the child, and we will get back to Smith," William demands.

I sit down, this time in the chair next to Silac that Ghosie had been in. I take his hand and give it a squeeze, because he keeps hissing violently and flaring his hood. I hadn't even noticed he changed from his two-legged form to his half form. His large snake body is curled up under him, and his scales rustle restlessly in agitation.

I look around the table. Cas sits with Link on one side and Max on the other. Tirrian and Saxon are frozen in place, their chairs tipped back behind them. My grandpas are on the other side of them, all seated with their arms crossed and glares on their faces. That just leaves Xavier, who doesn't look as angry as I thought he would. In fact, he seems to be concentrating on something. In the past, he said Brannock's mind was like a vault, very hard to get into, and unless he gave Xavier a reason to suspect him, he wasn't going to intrude. I guess this is exactly what he was waiting for, but it looks like maybe Brannock has given him full access, because he just appears resigned.

I watch my warlock husband as his face runs the gamut of emotions. I know he seems like he's cold, calculating, and unfeeling to the world, but that's an act. This man feels it all, and in front of the people he loves, he isn't afraid to show it. His frown slowly eases as he digs through Brannock's memories. Occasionally, he scowls, but then he finally sighs and closes his eyes.

"I understand now." Xavier opens his eyes and nods. "Tell them," he demands before taking a seat on my other side and grabbing my hand, giving it a squeeze.

"Caspian was the only one who wasn't present when we talked about this, but Aaz'axians are not compatible with any other race," Brannock begins. "We have barbs on our cocks that pierce a female's inner walls and lock in. It's only when I get close to my peak that the spikes activate. A female Aaz'axian secretes an enzyme that numbs their inner walls, allowing the barbs to pierce and cause pleasure, setting off the female's orgasm and allowing her to release an egg. In any other race, that would create excruciating pain."

Cas winces, but the rest of us have heard this already.

"So while I was married and had sex with my wife, I could never reach completion."

"She never knew?" Link sounds skeptical, and Brannock grimaces.

"I got very good at faking it and always made sure she orgasmed so she was distracted and didn't notice that I hadn't."

"So how did the child happen?" Silac hisses aggressively, and I shake off Xavier's hand so I can climb back onto my snake's lap and run my hands over his scales in an attempt to soothe him. His body undulates, and I'm wrapped up in his tail. I actually really love how it feels, especially when it's a little tight. It makes me feel safe and secure, kind of like a weighted blanket.

"I loved my wife very much. Seven hundred years is a long time to be alone, and I took a chance to grab some happiness where and when I could, but this was the first time I married, and she desperately wanted a child. I knew it would never happen, though, so I kept mesmerizing her to forget about it."

"Wait, mesmerize?" I ask. Why haven't I ever asked about his powers before? I mean, I know he has berserker mode and can glamour, but that's it.

"Yes, like the Vilaxian can," he responds, and Link takes over.

"Aaz'axians and Vilaxians are distant relatives. Vilaxians can compel people, and so can the Aaz'axians."

"Do you drink blood?" I ask, because I'm sure everyone else knows the answer.

Brannock kind of shrugs as much as he can while still wrapped up in Xavier's light bands. "We can, but it's for fun, not for nourishment like the Vilaxians. It kind of works like alcohol on our system and makes us drunk."

"So you compelled your wife to forget about wanting a child?" Cas asks, trying to get the conversation back on track.

"Yes, but for some reason, the compulsion would wear off, and I got tired of seeing her cry every time she got her monthly bleeds." There are tears in his eyes. "So I agreed to IVF, knowing it wasn't going to work, to appease her. The enzyme a female secrets is essential in the conception of a child. Not only does it numb their walls, but it strips the sperm, for lack of a better word, of its protective coating, making fertilization easier. Prior to the plague that struck all our women, we were an extremely fertile bunch."

"Strange that the plague only targeted women. It sounds very similar to what happened to the carevasta bears," Max points out offhandedly.

"Hmm, yes, you're right," Link muses, rubbing his chin. "He said theirs was caused by a vengeful goddess who felt insulted."

Brannock's eyes widen. "It was said that the gods were not happy with our leadership trying to take the orb from the Una's and that it was our punishment."

"You know what? These old gods are popping up quite a bit, aren't they?" William looks thoughtful. "Maybe they didn't disappear like people thought, and they are pulling strings from the background instead of being front and center."

"Back to the traitor," Silac hisses. I feel him become even more agitated when we veer off track.

"So we entered the IVF program. It was hard to hide the fact that my cum looked nothing like a human's, but I found a warlock on Earth who spelled me so it would appear normal."

"A warlock? Which one?" Xavier asks quickly, but I can tell he already knows the answer.

"The same one I helped capture—your cousin, Xane."

"He knew you were Aaz'axian?" Eric asks, leaning forward, but Brannock shakes his head.

"No, I glamoured myself to appear Vilaxian. He didn't question it. Of course a Vilaxian would want their blood-red cum to appear normal."

"What color is yours?" I ask, unable to help myself, and I hear Cas chuckle as my grandpas groan. Xavier smirks at me.

"The same color as my body," Brannock says with a small smile, and my eyes widen. Oh yeah, nope, that would be hard to explain, all opal and glittery.

Silac gets us back on track again. "But this IVF worked?"

"IVF is a process that allows the doctors to directly fertilize the egg in couples who are having trouble conceiving on their own," I explain to him, stroking my hand over his body.

"It shouldn't have, but it did. My wife was thrilled, but I was completely horrified," Brannock admits, not meeting my eyes. "It's not that I didn't want kids," he continues quickly, "but I wasn't sure how I was going to be able to continue to hide what I was from my wife. I also had no idea what our baby was going to be—human, Aaz'axian, or a crossbreed."

"How were you going to explain you weren't aging?" John asks quietly. "You must have had a plan for that."

Again, Brannock sighs heavily. "I was going to fake my own death."

I gasp, horrified for his poor wife. "That's awful," I scold him, and he nods in agreement.

"I know, but I was going to make her a very wealthy woman. I'd been living on Earth since we escaped the war, and you tend to build up a lot of wealth in that period of time. I thought it would make up for what she was missing out on, and I was going to suggest adoption when the IVF failed."

"But it didn't fail," Cas says gently, and I know he's rolling all the information around in his brain.

"No," Brannock says tearfully, "it didn't."

"How did your wife die?" Link asks, and I see Brannock shudder.

"Aaz'axian pregnancies are very much like Vilaxian ones," he explains.

"The babies take nutrients from the mother?" Link asks, and Brannock nods.

"Yes. It's the only time we drink blood like a Vilaxian—or the mother does at least. It helps nourish our babies inside their wombs."

"But your wife wasn't Aaz'axian and wasn't drinking your blood," Max surmises, and Brannock confirms with a jerky nod and a sob that escapes unbidden.

"I begged her to terminate. She was already getting sick within weeks of conception. The doctors told her she had some rare blood cancer, which was the only thing they could attribute her symptoms to, and she refused."

"How did no one notice on the scans? I'm sure an Aaz'axian baby looks different during an ultrasound," I ask, still trying to wrap my head around everything he told us.

"When she refused to terminate, arguing she wanted me to have someone when she passed, I begged Madam Aura to let her Celestian mate care for my wife. I mesmerized her into thinking she was having scans and seeing doctors. In the end, there was nothing Savannah could do. My wife wasn't actually sick, so she couldn't heal her. All she could do was transfuse blood until the babe was formed enough to be born. My wife slipped away as our daughter was born. She never even got to hold her." Tears stream down the male's face, and the wave of agony and sorrow I feel resonating from him is enough to have me hunching in on myself. I shouldn't be able to feel it in my normal body, but it's like these feelings are so strong, my warlock nature takes over and draws them into me.

"Let him down please," I beg Xavier, unable to stop the sob from escaping my mouth. I can see Xavier is just as affected as I am by this creature's emotions. Tears sparkle in his eyes as he lowers Brannock to the ground and removes the bands. The two of us get to our feet and embrace the man as he shudders, crying as he sags into our embrace.

CHAPTER TWO

Lila

Brannock shudders as the two of us drain his sorrow and grief, freeing him from the horrible burden. We don't remove it completely, but enough for him to be able to continue his story.

"I'm so sorry for your loss," Eric says, and when I look around the room, I notice that all the others are affected, except for the two who are still frozen.

"What happened to your child?" William asks gently. "Did it survive?"

Xavier and I release Brannock, and he shakes himself but doesn't sit down as Xavier and I return to our seats.

"Yes, she did, and she was born looking perfectly human, if not a little small." He smiles with a parent's love that is blinding.

"So that's why Aura and Xane didn't know you were Aaz'axian. I did wonder about that. They acted like they had never seen you before," Xavier says, crossing his legs and leaning back in his chair.

"That's because they hadn't. I always appeared in my Vilaxian glamour. They questioned how I could handle the Las Vegas heat and where I got my blood from, but I told them I mostly stayed inside and had a couple of other aliens that I knew who regularly donated."

"This didn't make them suspicious?" I ask skeptically, and it's John who answers.

"Probably not. At any given time, there are hundreds of aliens living normal lives in the United States. Smith made it seem like they were always deporting people, but they really weren't. Before they were killed, Marcus and Alina facilitated a blood service for any aliens who needed it. There were many willing volunteers happy to help out. Someone else took that on when they passed."

Brannock nods. "John's right. If you know where to look, you can find anything. Earth is set up to cater to the needs of extraterrestrials, because then there is less chance of them getting caught."

"So your daughter is human?" Link asks, leaning forward. He's dying for knowledge.

"She was perfectly human for the first three years, but then, one day, not long after her third birthday, she was frightened, and it triggered her Aaz'axian genes and she changed forms. I'm assuming her human form was just a glamour she had been born with. It was hard to explain to a curious little girl about what she actually was and that no one could know about it. Up until then, I hadn't shown her my real form either. If she was going to be completely human, I wasn't going to bother, and I couldn't have Savannah do any tests because then they would know I wasn't from Vilax like I claimed."

"God, that must have been so incredibly lonely for you." My mouth drops open at Cas's words. Instead of focusing on how he betrayed us, he's choosing to understand why he did. Everyone is taking this so much better than I thought. I'm almost tempted to have Xavier unfreeze the two terrors, but I'll wait until we get to the orb part of the story. Saxon would probably be okay now that he heard about Brannock's child, since he would do anything for ours, but Tirrian still might turn him into Aaz'axian BBQ.

"Unfortunately when Chloe changed forms, it was in a shopping mall. Although I wasn't a hundred percent certain anyone noticed, I was quick to cover her up. I decided I wasn't risking the EAA catching wind of it, so I sold my place and bought a cabin in the Alaskan wilderness, and we moved there. There wasn't a soul around, and the only way we could get supplies was via float plane so I could hear them coming a mile away. There, she was free to just be, and I was able to teach her how to glamour. I didn't learn to until I was in my teens, since there was no need, but I knew she would need to know sooner rather than later."

"What happened?" Maxsim asks, completely engrossed with the tale.

"Her changing didn't go unnoticed, but it took them a while to figure out where I moved to. You don't spend seven hundred years changing identities without learning a thing or two, but it was much easier when technology was nonexistent on Earth. It got a lot harder the last thirty years. It was about eighteen months after we moved to Alaska, and I guess I had become complacent. I was invited to Vegas for a meet-up with the men from my old unit. It was something we did every year, but I hadn't been since Chloe was born, and they were starting to get suspicious. Instead of blowing it off, we went. I stressed to Chloe how important it was to stay in her glamour, and she understood and was really good at holding it. I thought we'd be safe. I booked us a room at a hotel and hired a babysitter for the night. Chloe was going to bed, and the sitter was just going to be there in case she woke up."

"You can hold your glamour in your sleep?" Xavier asks, and Brannock nods.

"Yeah. It's easy to do, and we practiced for weeks. It's only alcohol and extreme emotions that affect it, so I went to the bar and all hell broke loose. Betrayed by my own teammate, I was tranqued, and when I came to, they had Chloe and I had that collar on. There was nothing I could do but cooperate so they didn't hurt her, including deporting me so I could look for the orb. If I don't find it, they will start experimenting on her. In fact I wouldn't put it past them to already be doing that now that I'm not on Earth to demand to see her."

His anguish is bitter and unpleasant, and I wrinkle my nose, trying not to gag. Xavier waves a hand and frees our two frozen friends. Saxon immediately backs off, but smoke still continues to blow from Tirrian's nose in agitation.

"You should have told us immediately." He points a finger at Brannock.

"Yes, maybe then we could have helped you rescue your daughter immediately," William agrees.

"You'll have to forgive me for not thinking clearly. They have my child, and I knew nothing about any of you. For all I knew, you could have been as bad as they were." Brannock's form flashes, his body changing color, the normal opalescent shimmer bleeding to green while his shoulders, spikes, and head turn red.

"Whoa, settle down." Eric leaps to his feet and holds out his hands. "It's okay," he reassures the angry alien. "We're on your side."

"Sit down, Tirrian," Xavier orders. "You are setting off his berserker mode."

I watch with fascination as Brannock's body shudders, and his color flashes back and forth. Silac slowly slides us backward out of firing range, but

Brannock manages to get himself under control, and his body changes back to normal. Silac relaxes slightly underneath me and moves me back to the table.

"Did Smith say why he thought we had the orb?" John has stayed relatively calm this whole time, tossing everything we learned around in his mind.

"Yes. Smith said the Syndicate had credible information from a source. When I questioned the reliability of the source, he bragged that it came directly from an Adams."

A rush of fear flows through the room, and I see my grandpas' faces turn ashen.

"Lili?" William asks, and Brannock shrugs.

"I'm assuming, but I can't confirm either way. Smith said it took a long time for them to crack her, which is why they only had this information for the last few months."

"God!" John gasps, horrified. "What have they done to her?"

"Why keep her alive and in stasis then? I would think they would dispose of her now that they have the information they need," Tirrian asks without tact, but he's not wrong.

"They didn't want to risk the Adams brothers dying before they could locate the orb and in case they needed a hostage to exchange," Brannock explains.

"You knew all this before we even went to

Rilu?" Cas is the one who asks this, and I feel like I've been hit over the head. Did he know?

Brannock is quick to shake his head. "No, I was instructed to contact Smith while we were on Z68, before Lila's meeting with the halla harvester. I demanded answers during the conversation. I told him I wanted to know why they think it's on the ship, because I haven't been able to feel or see any sign of it, and he was happy to gloat. He also provided my weekly check-in with Chloe so I know she's still alive to encourage me to continue seeking the orb. I knew it was time to tell you all everything though. I've seen how you work so hard to help one another, and you've been nothing but kind to me."

"Of course we will help you," John replies, but he still looks distracted.

"Is it true?" Max suddenly breaks the silence, looking at my three grandpas.

"Is what true?" William hedges.

"Is the orb with the circus?"

John and William start to deny it, but Eric scoffs and holds up a hand. "Enough. People's lives are on the line. It was different when it was just a rumor, but now we need to go into damage control." He turns his attention to Xavier.

"Can you make it so nobody can talk about it, even under torture?" He looks green as he asks this. He must be thinking about what my grandma had been subjected to. I don't know much about the galaxy yet, but I'm certain torture is a common and disturbingly creative process.

"Yes, absolutely." He waves his hand in the air, a couple of my former marks lighting up on his body. He weaves a spell in front of us, one way more complicated than I know. Suddenly, he claps his hands together, and a blast of lavender light blasts out from the impact, the shockwave rolling through the dining room and covering everyone before pulsing through the walls. "That will carry to Echo, Ghosie, and the children, as well as Broderick," Xavier assures my grandpas.

"Yes, we control the orb of power. We have since the Una's disappeared. Their final act was giving the Adams family control. It is why the circus was founded. Although the orb is contained by a special barrier, which they promised us would keep its power signature safe, they recommended we never stay in one place for a permanent amount of time," he tells the four who weren't already in the know.

Various looks cross their faces, but it's Maxsim's low growl that has me worried.

"What's wrong?" I ask the alpha.

"We are never going to be safe as long as that orb exists," he snarls. "Even if we take care of the Syndicate, now that the rumor is out there, It's not contained any longer. My omegas and our babies are in danger."

Of course that's his first thought. I feel the same

way about my own children, but I have no other suggestions. I brace myself and make him an offer that I really don't want to, but I'm not selfish enough to keep him in danger.

"If you and Echo would like to return to Iceen for the time being, I would understand," I tell him.

"No, Lila," Cas protests, but Link nods his agreement, knowing it's only going to get more dangerous from here on.

"Will you come with us?" Maxsim asks, and I blink with shock. "You are part of our streak. We won't leave you in danger," he growls like he's insulted I suggested it, and I melt a little.

I wriggle in Silac's grip. He's been mostly quiet since he calmed, and I'm worried he's one wrong word away from striking Brannock down, but he stays where he is while I hurry over to give my alpha a hug.

"You know I can't. I have to stay here," I tell him, running my hands through the fur on his back as he grips me tightly. His worry and anxiety are almost as bad as Brannock's now. "But I promise to be careful."

"Then we will stay too," he declares, his own arms tightening around me before he releases me. "I will help deal with the Syndicate so it will be safe for our family."

"I'm not sure we're ever going to be safe. I think it's time we considered a new home for the orb. If we could destroy it, we would have already," William tells us.

"What about dropping it in one of the volcanoes on Fluxx?" Tirrian suggests, an occasional puff of smoke still billowing from his nose.

"It would only blow up the planet, and the orb would survive," John tells him, shaking his head.

"What about in the cavern where we got the flamegem from?" Link asks, but it's Xavier who shakes his head this time.

"No, we already know that there are ways in and out of it. They proved that with Liliana."

I've been listening half-heartedly to their suggestions and have an idea of my own. "What about the warlock home world?" I ask my husband. "That isn't even on our plane. Nobody would know it was there, and nobody could access it. Only people bonding with their intimate and you and your parents can ever go there. Let's face it, intimate bonding is enough of a distraction that nobody will be thinking about the orb."

My grandpas' eyes widen with the promise of a solution, but Xavier shakes his head.

"No, there is still a warlock race that lives on that planet, and we wouldn't want them getting their hands on the ultimate power. Warlocks are power hungry, so I can't imagine what the originals are like. We would be giving another plane of existence our problem."

"How do you destroy it?" Silac asks quietly. "Can we do that?"

Eric shakes his head. "Not without wiping out a good portion of our galaxy. It's why it was never destroyed in the first place. The Una's were remorseful that their experimentation created such unlimited but unusable power."

"Why is it unusable though?" I ask, not entirely sure why. "If it's an unlimited source of energy, then why not make it available to everyone?"

"Because if it was manipulated in the wrong way, it would become a power vacuum with the ability to destroy planets in the blink of an eye," John explains, but I feel confused.

"But how?"

"Kind of like the Death Star." Eric uses terms I can understand. "A focused beam of laser through the orb increases the power a million times, which will destroy planets. It's what started the war. Originally, the Una's gave the power to planets throughout the galaxy. They placed a spark from the orb in a centralized location on each planet, and it produced unlimited energy, powering everything, such as vehicles, homes, machines, and technology as well as making crops abundant and keeping animals and plants healthy. Even the beings on the planets were healthy. It had godlike powers. Planets and realms thrived, but of course some races couldn't leave it at that. They wanted to know what else they could do with the spark, so they started experimenting."

"And that's how our leaders discovered that if you concentrated a laser beam through the spark that you could destroy a planet. They experimented on one at the far edges of the galaxy—an uninhabited moon. They tried to keep it a secret, but not everyone involved with the project was interested in subjugation, and word got out," Brannock explains, his firsthand knowledge invaluable. "The Una's gathered the sparks and returned them to the mother orb, declaring it was too dangerous. Most of the galaxy agreed, but the leaders of my people were not happy, and we went to war. It was five years of hell, but unbeknownst to us, our leadership had prepared for such an occasion. Every Aaz'axian was implanted with a control chip at birth, a gift from some cyborg entrepreneur who was enamored with one of the Aaz'axian kings. Either we fought or died."

"God, that is barbaric." Saxon scowls. "Vilaxians are a warrior race too, but we would never force our people. Once you've done your two years of mandated service, you can do whatever you choose."

"Is that still a possibility? You being activated?" Link asks, and Brannock shrugs.

"I guess. I don't know what happened to our leadership. As far as I know, they were all killed, and I'm assuming that technology was lost, but someone could very well have it in case any of us reappear."

"And Smith knows about you. This is a problem," Xavier points out.

"I will scan him and see if we can remove that chip," Link offers.

"I would appreciate it." Brannock nods his thanks. "When they did it, we were told it wasn't possible, but it was a long time ago, so hopefully something has advanced enough to be able to."

"Well, I guess that means we will be returning to Earth sooner rather than later." William stands up, stretching.

"Oshan said he had an Una partner. I think we need to speak to them and revisit our options about dealing with the orb. I refuse to put our family at risk any longer," John suggests, and from the murmuring around the table, I think we are all in agreement.

"Okay, but first, Grandma. It's late, and we need to be at Z68 for the harvester recruiters. How about we all try to get some sleep?" I suggest. "We have a lot on our plate, and we need to tackle everything one at a time, otherwise, we are going to get overwhelmed."

"Agreed," Cas says, getting to his feet. This cues a mass movement from everyone. "Shall we meet back here at six in the morning?"

"Sounds good, we can finalize the plan for Husadavia."

"I will offer to give Broderick a break. We still need to get this ship to Husadavia as well, so we are ready to send Ghosie when you get where you need to go," Saxon says.

"Aren't you tired? Do you need some blood?" I ask my mate, and he shakes his head.

"I'm fine. I require less sleep than most. I also won't take your blood just before you go on a dangerous mission, and I am still full from Link," he replies, reminding me of what they were doing to maintain their cover.

"But I don't know how long I will be gone," I argue.

"I am happy to offer up my neck again," Link says quickly, and Cas chuckles.

"I will help out as well if he needs it. Are you going to be okay only being able to feed from Xavier?" he asks, biting his lip with concern.

"I would gladly offer up my vein for Lila," Brannock volunteers, blushing slightly, "so that she doesn't weaken the warlock."

I feel a rush of warmth at the thought of drinking from this gorgeous creature despite him keeping secrets. Xavier chuckles quietly, obviously able to feel my emotions.

"Thank you, that would be appreciated by both of us," he replies.

"I will be observing from above if you have need of me as well," Tirrian reminds us gruffly, crossing his arms.

"Yes, we know you will, dragon, but you still have some ass kissing to do," Xavier reminds him, and it's my turn to blush. We haven't really discussed what's happening between us, but once again, that's a future Lila problem.

Tirrian grumbles but doesn't argue with my warlock.

"Okay then, we will see you in the morning." John comes over and gives me a kiss on the cheek. "I can't wait for you to meet your grandma."

"She's going to love you," Eric says as he gives me a quick hug.

William approaches. "Get some rest," he suggests before grimacing, "and everything else you need to be in tip-top shape tomorrow. We don't know how long you're going to be on Husadavia, and not only is it dangerous, but you're going to have to use your mimic powers a lot, so you need to be at full strength, because you'll only have Xavier to pull energy from if you need it."

His reminder has me freezing. Fuck, my mimic forms are powered by sex, and I will only have one of my mates with me if I need to power up. I think about whether I can take any of the others, but there's no option. Saxon is a possibility, since he has the skills to be an asset, but he will require blood as well. Cas and Link aren't fighters, Maxsim won't be useful in the temperature, and both Nikos and Echo are completely out. Silac would possibly be an asset, but he isn't my mate, and we can't do anything about it until he resolves things with his fiancée.

"Ah, yeah, sure," I stammer, not wanting to look at my grandpa, but my eyes slide to the dragon. He claims I am his mate, but he doesn't want it. I can't force it just so I'll survive our journey. I want him to want it. I straighten my spine and hug William. "I'll be fine. I'm getting stronger every day, and if I don't have to mimic too often, everything will be okay. Hopefully the being is willing to help us," I say, and he looks as doubtful as I feel, but we have no other choice.

They take their leave, and a weird silence falls over us all. Thankfully, my cyborg is ready to come to my rescue. "Why don't you go down and check on Nikos before going to bed?" he suggests, and I jump at the idea.

"Yes! Good thinking," I blurt out, and Xavier, the shit, snickers, feeling everything I am—anticipation at seeing my can of tuna, unrequited lust for the dragon, my longing for the snake, and my curiosity about Brannock. I have to face the fact that my mimic self wants them all, and my Lila self is not opposed to being a Pokémon keeper either, even if I won't admit it out loud.

"I'll see you in the morning," I say to the three men who won't be in my suite tonight, and then I give each of my present mates a kiss before hurrying out of the dining room in the direction of the pool.

A swim to cool off sounds pretty damn good.

CHAPTER THREE

Lila

My mind is a chaotic mess as I hurry in the direction of the Aquilian level, trying to process everything we learned about Brannock, my feelings for the snake and dragon, and my nerves about our mission to Husadavia. Our plan is thin, but we don't really have any other options at this stage. I refuse to leave my grandma behind. My grandpas have been through enough, and they deserve to be happy, but between Xavier and me, we have some pretty impressive powers, and Brannock will be an asset. We are going to nail this and be on our way in no time.

The doors open to the pool room, and I quickly strip off my clothes and dive into the pool, allowing the change to wash over me. I haven't spent a lot of time in my Aquilian form, mostly just when we rescued Nikos and the swim previous to that, but it feels good to be in it again. I take a big breath, and the water running through my gills seems to wash away some of the fatigue I've been feeling. Down here, it's easy to forget your troubles and just be. I flick my tail and start to swim towards Nikos's little home. I'll check there first. Link said he was still sleeping a lot because he was still recovering from his father's horrific treatment.

The water rushes over my body as I move toward the tunnel at the bottom of his house. I swim past all sorts of weird and wonderful sea creatures, nothing I recognize having come from Earth. They dart here and there, cognizant of a bigger predator in the pool, but quickly return when they realize I'm not interested in them. I got my fair share of hunting when I was pregnant with the babies, and I am in no hurry to repeat the experience—or not for fish, at any rate. I still feel like gagging as I recall catching and eating them raw on Skar.

When I get to the tunnel, I swim up it, but I know before I even get there that he's not in the house, which means he's swimming, but judging by the size of him, that's not an easy feat in his condition, so I'm guessing he is in the pretty jeweled cave that I used as my own refuge.

Spinning around, I head back in that direction, a small ball of nerves sitting in the bottom of my stomach. Nikos's and my relationship has been bumpy, to say the least, and I was horrible to him after what happened with the babies. I feel guilty now knowing that he probably couldn't control his reaction any more than I could. I'm also nervous because I'm seeing him alone. We had Link as a buffer when we first brought him back to the ship. I should have asked Cas to come with me, but that's just me being a chicken shit.

Flicking my tail, I swim deeper into the pool, still blown away by this whole level and the fact that we're on a starship in the middle of space. I could easily be swimming in a tropical reef in the Caribbean. The water is temperate, the artificial sun shines brightly above, and the serenity below the surface is a surefire way to calm one's emotions.

The ball of nerves in my stomach grows the closer I get to the little cave. I run my hand across it in an attempt to alleviate it, but of course it does nothing.

I hear something. It sounds like singing. It's soothing and calming, and it makes me feel warm and cherished. I stop at the entrance of the cave and stare at the sight before me. Nikos no longer looks listless and dull. Instead, his scales sparkle like gems in the mysterious light the cave produces, and his golden hair, which had looked unwashed and stringy, is shiny and full as he strokes a comb through it. He's wrapped up by the anemone that lives in here, and he sings softly, his attention on his round belly, running his other hand over it in small circles. I can't help the grin that crosses my lips. He looks sexy, and he's glowing like an expecting mother—or in this case, father. I feel a rush of relief and gratitude toward my cyborg mate.

He finally senses me, and when he looks up, his eyes widen, and he tosses the comb to the side. I expect something ridiculous to come out of his mouth, but he just smiles.

Hello, Lila, he says in my mind, and I blink a couple of times, shocked that he's using my name instead of a ridiculous pet name. He smirks at my reaction. *I thought I should probably drop the bimbo act since we are going to become parents. I need to set a good example for our babies.* He lovingly strokes a hand over his stomach, and I'm speechless, my mouth opening and closing a couple of times.

He chuckles and shifts slightly on the anemone, patting the space he made next to himself. *Come sit. We have some things we need to talk about.*

I swim toward him, still trying to wrap my mind around this incredibly normal person. What happened to my ridiculous can of tuna?

It isn't easy to get comfortable sitting with a fish tail, but eventually, after a couple of attempts, I find myself reclined next to a very pregnant Nikos. We're both stretched out, facing one another, with his baby bump between us.

Hi, I say to him shyly, my gaze swinging

between his eyes and his belly that I'm trying hard not to reach out and rub my hand across.

I owe you an apology, he says, dragging my attention back up, and I see shame in his eyes. Before he can continue, though, I reach out and put a finger against his lips.

No, you don't. Nixie explained everything to me. If anything, I owe you one. I was horrible to you, but in my defense, I was blind with worry for my babies.

Nikos nods, and his hair flows around us. I tied my own back before I got in the pool, knowing it would be annoying while swimming. *Of course you were. I never would have put them in danger like that if I'd been in my right mind, but the minute you changed into your Aquilian form, I was mesmerized. The mating daze overcame me, and nothing else mattered. I am also very sorry for biting you—again, another effect of the daze. Will you ever forgive me?* he asks, looking despondent.

Why me? I ask him, not answering his question yet. *I was told that you don't have fated mates, so you could have chosen anyone you wanted in Aquilia. I'm sure you had no shortage of potential mates. I mean, look at you.* His lips turn up slightly at my comment, and he preens. Ah, that's more like it. I feel relieved at seeing my ridiculous peacock again.

Because of exactly that, he admits, shrugging his shoulders. *I could have anyone, and it was boring. I wanted a challenge, not someone who accepted that ridiculous act that I put on just because of who I was. They wanted the crown prince of Aquila, the future king, not Nikos the merman who likes to raise phadolls and collects ancient weapons. You didn't though. You called me out, and I was the most turned on I've ever been in my life. Every time you slapped me down verbally, I thought my cock was going to burst out of my slit and wave around.* He chuckles.

So you're into degradation? I ask him, raising an eyebrow. I'm confused about all the things he just told me, so I grab onto the one thing I can make sense of.

No, not really. I just liked that you didn't take any crap and all those ridiculous pet names I came up with. It made me feel seen, and it was intoxicating. I mean, you're also gorgeous, so it wasn't hard to fall for you.

Just like that? I ask, still skeptical, and he finally reaches out and takes my hand, pressing a kiss to the back of it.

Yes, just like that. Many species and races are quite primal in their instincts, Lila. It isn't uncommon for quick courtships, not to mention fated mates like blood roses and intimates, as well as a person's animal insisting on a mate, like Caspian.

Or Tirrian, I murmur, and his eyebrows jump in surprise.

The dragon prince believes you're his mate? You really do have some very powerful people in your mating circle. But then you will need protection, because my father is not going to be the only one who has nefarious plans for you.

I scowl as he reminds me of that slug of a man, and I'm not sad at all that Cronus dealt with him. He's my favorite father-in-law at the moment, though I have no doubt that Murphy would have done the same thing.

So we're half mated? I ask him, gesturing to the scar around my nipple, and his eyes drop from my face to my breasts. I have to give him credit, it's the first time it's happened since I arrived, which is very unlike Nikos, especially since I didn't bother to cover them with scales like I have before. One side of his mouth tips up in a smirk as he nods, staring at his mark with smugness. He drops my hand and trails a finger around his teeth marks, and a shiver runs down my spine as my tail fins quiver. He doesn't miss it but stays where he is, though he shifts his body slightly like he's uncomfortable.

Yes, again, I underestimated my control while under the mating daze. You see, mers don't have sex in this form unless they are with their committed partner. I miscalculated how incredible it would feel doing that with you. He points at his rounded belly. *I also did not expect this to happen, and when I realized it, it was too late, and I was too far gone to stop it.* His cheeks darken, and I realize he's blushing.

I look down and reach out hesitantly. *Can I?* I ask, and he quickly nods his head, grabbing my wrist and pulling it so I can run my hand over the smooth section of his skin.

I almost moan, and I bite my lip to stop it from escaping, even though my pussy throbs and my kraken roars inside my head. Fuck me, that's sexy. I kind of want to fuck his brains out in celebration.

Do I have a breeding kink, or is that my kraken? It's hard to tell these days, but I promised I'd be open-minded. There's also a primal part of me that isn't going to let this man get away from me. He's *my* can of tuna, and I'll kill any bitch who thinks they can take him from me. I feel a possessive thrill, knowing I'm the only one he's ever fucked in mer form before and I rocked his world so much that he couldn't stop himself from becoming pregnant. Those are some mad sex skills, and there is no way I am letting him go now.

Before I can overthink any more of this, I feel my mer teeth form, and I launch myself at him to return the favor. My lips latch around one of his nipples, and I bite down until I feel his blood pour into my mouth. I expected him to taste fishy, but his blood has a smoky bourbon flavor. I release my teeth and suckle at the flesh around his nipple. I feel his body stiffen under me as his hands come up and grip my hips, our tails brushing together slightly, but his belly prohibits us from getting too close.

Oh God! His shout of surprise turns into a moan of pleasure, and he throws his head back, all that beautiful, golden hair surrounding us, giving us an illusion of privacy.

My hands drift over his body, caressing his stomach before sliding lower. I want to show him that I am all in, and there's no better way than lavishing his body with pleasure. I lick the teeth marks and pull back, admiring my handiwork. He and I now have a matching set of mate marks, and I couldn't be happier.

You mated me? He blinks, unable to hide the shock he's feeling, and despite being in the ocean, his eyes glisten with unshed tears.

Of course I did, you silly can of tuna. You're mine, I growl, my kraken making herself known despite being in my mer form. He looks shocked for a moment before a blinding smile crosses his lips.

Oh, I knew it. I knew that my little starfish wouldn't be able to resist me after we stroked our tails together. No one can resist my beautiful tail once they get their hands on it. He winks, and I giggle at his ridiculous act, realizing I missed it, before growling and grabbing a handful of his hair.

Nobody better be putting their hands on your tail but me. That's my hard cock and sexual slit to play with, I tell him, and I watch as his pupils dilate and he shivers. Hmm, maybe he has a kink we can explore. *Look at my little slut, all round with my babies and still begging for my mouth.* I look down and see his cock wiggling around under his belly behind his scales. His slit hasn't opened yet.

I wish I had something to restrain him with so I could have my wicked way with him. The moment I think this, the anemone tentacles slither around his arms and capture them, bringing them over his head, then wrap around his tail as well, spreading him out below me, his stomach on display.

You can use your warlock powers in mer form? He sounds surprised, and I wince.

That's not a mer thing? I ask, checking even though I was fairly certain it wasn't, and he shakes his head. *Yeah, it seems like I may be a special snowflake.*

I run my finger down between his nipples and over his belly until I get to his wriggling cock. He grunts as I move farther down to look at it.

Will the slit stay closed unless we're swimming? I ask him, running my finger over the squirming mass, and he shakes his head, his voice turning husky inside my head.

It's activated by the enzyme your scales produce.

So if I slide my tail back and forth like this? It's not easy, because his stomach is so big and I'm not all that experienced with my tail yet, but I manage to brush it back and forth across the base of his, our flukes touching. He squeezes his eyes closed and moans quietly, but then I slide farther down, bring my mouth in line with a small gap, and lick around it. He groans even louder.

Oh my little slut likes his slit licked, does he? I growl, my nipples rock hard as an ache burns deep within me. He shivers, deliciously responsive to my words. *Now be a good boy for me and let me devour you.* I hold his hips still and go to town on the small gap that widens with every pass of my tongue. I spear in and out, like I'm fucking it, and he moans and thrashes his head back and forth, his voice turning hypnotic, begging so beautifully for me. It finally opens wide enough for his cock to be released, and as it pushes through, I take it into my mouth, hollowing my cheeks and sucking. His back bends up off the soft bed of the anemone as he shouts.

Oh my god, please, Lila, I'm going to come, he calls, his voice pleading in my mind. His cock moves on its own, and it wriggles inside my mouth, tickling my cheeks as I lavish it with attention. I lick and suck at the same time I praise him. Telepathy makes it possible to do both, and it's pushing all of my buttons.

Such a good boy, so pretty and compliant for his mistress. I love listening to you beg me. Do you want to come, my little slut? Tell me what you want, I order him.

Please, I want to come. Please let me come, he begs just like I wanted him to, and my core throbs with need, but I don't think there's any way I can fuck him while he's pregnant, so I'll settle for making him feel good then make one of my other mates relieve my need when I return to our suite.

I take him down as far as I can, the suckers in the back of my throat assisting me as they ripple around him. He stiffens and shouts, bubbles coming from his mouth and floating up to the ceiling of the cavern before he floods my mouth with his cum. I drink it down, his cum tasting like the finest of bourbons just like his blood. It's heady and deli-cious, and I can't get enough. His cock writhes and throbs as I tell him what a good boy he is, stroking my hands over the rest of his body. I feel smug that I've pleasured my merman so thoroughly.

CHAPTER FOUR

Lila

I allow the tentacles to recede and rub my merman's wrists and arms before stroking my tail across his, trying to get some of the circulation back into them. My desire still thrums through my body, but I want to make sure my pregnant merman is okay first and that what I did wasn't too much for him.

I wrap my arms around him and nuzzle into his neck. *Are you okay?* I ask him. He's had his eyes closed with a look of pure bliss on his face, but he now opens them and smiles at me.

So okay, he tells me, reaching up to stroke his hand over my face, our bodies as close as they can be with tails and a baby belly in the way. I'm actually looking forward to him being able to shift again so I can get him in my bed in our suite.

We lie together for a moment, enjoying being with one another. I want to ask so many questions, since there are things I'm dying to know about my merman, but before I can get my mind in some semblance of order, Nikos grunts and curls in on himself, and I panic.

What's wrong? I ask. *Did I hurt you or the babies?* I ask him, worried that maybe he shouldn't be having sex while pregnant. I just remembered how horny the pregnancy hormones made me. *Should I get Link?* I'm frantic, but as I go to leave, he grabs my hand, chuckling.

No, my precious jimble gem. He drags me back to him and rests my hand on his stomach. I can feel our babies moving around inside him, and when I look down, I see a small tail press against the inside of his stomach. My mouth drops open. *Our children are very active. Strong and fierce, like their mama.* He sounds proud, and when my eyes meet his, he's looking at me with complete adoration.

I melt into his side. *Whoa.* I'm mesmerized, feeling no small amount of awe. It's weird being on the other side of the situation, but I'm not hating it, which is kind of a relief because I have another pregnant husband as well. Then, something horrifying occurs to me. *How, exactly, do you give birth to them?* I ask him.

You have to cut me open with your teeth and assist them out, he tells me with clenched teeth.

I have to do what? I screech, and he winces before he can no longer hide his mischievous smile.

Just kidding, he says, and I smack him with my tail fluke. *The same slit that my cock comes through births the babies. My cock retracts deep into my body, and the slit opens up so I can expel them into the water column.*

I guess it's a little like a seahorse from Earth. *Well, that's good to know,* I mutter, and he just gives me a squeeze. *I'm so glad you are feeling better,* I tell him. *I will have to let Nixie know, she was so worried about you.*

My father was an asshole. I'm not sorry he's dead, Nikos says without looking at me, so I grab his chin and make him.

Hey, it's okay not to be sad. Can't say I am either, and if Cronus hadn't killed him, I would have done it myself, or Cas or Xavier. Nobody treats our can of tuna like that, I tell him, smiling, and he rolls his eyes, but he cheers up slightly. *What is a phadoll or a jimble gem?*

He said both of these things earlier, and I have no idea what he meant, but I want to know so much more about him than I do now, and it's a great way to start.

Those are jimble gems, he says pointing to the gorgeous, brightly colored stones in the cavern of the walls. *Well, that's certainly my favorite of all of his names. As for a phadoll, you met one. Sweetpea is a phadoll.*

He's talking about his turtle seal cross creature

that my kids have had so much fun chasing around the tank. We left her back on Aquilia at Nikos's request. He said with the new babies coming and moving into our suite that she would be better off with his sister.

Are you sure you're okay with moving into our home once these babies are born? I ask him, putting my hand over his bump again. I smile when I get kicked. *I was told you didn't socialize with the crew very often. Are you not comfortable on two feet?*

It makes me so happy that you want me to be a part of your family. I will probably have to come for a swim every day, but I am just as comfortable without a tail as I am with one. Despite my father's prejudice, a lot of mers had dry homes below the ocean and spent a lot of time without fins. My rooms in the castle were like that, and so were mother's and Nixie's. It ensured we didn't need to spend much time with Father because he abhorred legs, said it was a sign of weakness.

Well, as long as you're comfortable. We have a pool in our room now, but I'm not sure it's going to be big enough for five krakens and three mers to regularly take swims, let alone Tirrian's water dragon. I think about the size of the dragon I saw back on Fluxx, and I'm pretty sure it's even bigger than my kraken. *We'll probably all need to make use of this pool. Maybe it's not such a bad thing that there isn't going to be a mer show anymore.*

This gets a reaction out of him, and he flicks his tail and swims upright. *There won't be? Why not?*

Well, with the fallout on Aquilia, your mother wasn't

willing to commit to sending any new merpeople yet, and we're going to have the babies. Once Grandma Liliana is rescued, I am going to arrange for auditions. My grandpas told me it's part of my job now.

That isn't right. I will speak to my mother as soon as the babies come. It's advantageous for the Aquilians to have an act in the circus. It shows the galaxy we aren't as secular as they believe we are. It definitely helped my father, not that he would ever admit it.

That's fine, but I'm still going to audition more performers just in case. It won't hurt to have a couple of new acts as a draw, especially because I don't know what's going to happen with the Vilaxians either. We have to go to Vilux and sort out Saxon's clan dissolution as well. I don't think his brother and his two clan mates were willing to join the circus permanently. It was just as a favor for the queen.

My poor little coolmy, you sound like you are going to be very busy. He sounds sad and wears a pout with puppy dog eyes.

Don't worry, I will make sure to see you every day, I promise him, *and as much as I'd like to stay and cuddle, I need some sleep. We're busting my grandma out tomorrow.*

Yes, Link told me you found her. That is wonderful. I am so happy for the Adams brothers. Make sure you are safe and come back to us. I don't think it will be long before our babies are here, he warns.

How will you know when they are ready?

I will get contractions just like a normal pregnancy. Link has left a communicator in the bottom of our house so I can let him know as soon as it happens.

Okay, good. I flick my tail and give him a kiss. He looks surprised, and I realize we really haven't done much kissing. I can't give him an open-mouthed kiss in the water, so instead, I press my lips to his and kiss him a little more forcefully before pulling away.

I can't wait for you to get your legs back so I can kiss you properly, I tell him. *Now be a good boy for me and get some rest. I'll check on you when we return.*

He still looks surprised, but a grin creeps across his face as I swim away. I feel a sense of relief that Nikos and I have started sorting everything out. It's one less thing to worry about, though there is still the matter that we're going to be parents any day now. Grandma first, new babies second. Shit, I didn't ask how old they will be and how rapidly they will develop. We will need more clothes and beds and everything. Hopefully we can source these. I might give that job to Echo, since he's already doing it for his babies. It's not like Nik can do it underwater.

Seriously, how did my life become this? I'm not upset, but it's a lot, and sometimes a girl just needs five minutes to breathe and down a couple of shots of tequila.

I allow the change to wash over me once I get to the surface, where I grab a towel out of the basket kept near the elevator and dry off before putting my clothes on again. I take it with me to throw in the laundry basket at home. It's getting pretty full now that there isn't any crew to do the washing, so

I'll probably have to ask someone where the ship laundry is and do a few loads. Then again, maybe I'll just ask Xavier to show me how to use our warlock powers to clean everything with magic. God, I love magic.

When I return to our family suite, I find Link, Cas, and Xavier sitting around having a drink.

"Hi, how did it go with Nikos?" Link jumps up and hurries over to our fridge, grabbing a bottle of rilaxious before returning and dragging me to the couch to join them. He pops the top and hands it to me.

I take a long drink before sighing and wiping my mouth with the back of my hand. "Thanks, I needed that," I tell him, even though I have a craving for a Jack and Coke. Hmm, I wonder why? "Nikos is good. He looks so much better, and we were able to have a little chat about a few things."

"Hmm, I believe chatting was not all you did, *phoeall*." Xavier has an annoying little smirk on his lips.

"It's rude to read other people's emotions without permission, or that's what you keep telling me." I glare at him, and he shrugs.

"But we are one now. Your feelings are my feelings, my beautiful intimate," he says without shame.

I huff. "No, you're right, I bit him so the mating wasn't one-sided," I tell them, waiting for their reactions, but none of them show any sign of distress.

"We had no doubt, sweetheart," Cas says,

swinging an arm around my shoulders and tucking me in closer to him.

"But that's not all, right?" Xavier pushes, and I narrow my eyes on him.

"You know, just because there are a lot of people in this mating circle doesn't mean I need to share all the details with all of you," I say, baring my teeth.

He nods his head in acknowledgement but doesn't look like he's sorry. "No, but when I can feel how horny you are and some of us are in the position to fix that needy ache, I'm not going to keep quiet about it."

I groan, because he's not wrong. The needy ache inside hasn't disappeared. It's this constant pressure, which I now know are my mimic powers making themself known. I shifted forms, so now I need to refuel. "Ugh, Nikos's belly and our tails are not conducive to pregnancy sex, so I took care of his needs. I remember how horny I was while I was pregnant."

"Nothing's changed," Link says, chuckling, and my glare turns from Xavier to him, but he holds his hands up. "Hey, we know you can't help it, and we love it, so there are no complaints, believe me."

"Not at all, and I'm glad you have a lot of mates to keep your voracious appetites satisfied," Cas adds, brushing a lock of damp hair back from my face. "And none of us will be upset if you decide to add a dragon and snake to the roster.

You and Silac looked pretty cozy during the meeting."

I don't hear a hint of jealousy, just curiosity from my kraken. "He declared his intentions to pursue me if he can get his situation sorted out. I told him I was interested, and I enjoyed sitting in his lap. I love being wrapped up by his snake body, it's soothing."

"And the dragon?" Xavier can't help but push boundaries.

I down the rest of my drink before putting the bottle on the table and pulling my legs up under me, snuggling against Cas. "Who knows?" I really have no idea. We'll see what happens.

"And then there's Brannock and our new friend Ghosie as well. Your marks appeared on them," Link says cautiously, knowing I'm pretty close to losing my shit.

"Yes, but we all know that mimic Lila is a slut," I grumble, feeling my cheeks pinken slightly with embarrassment.

"Aw, babe, don't say that about yourself. That's an Earth concept. The galaxy isn't like that." Cas gives my shoulder a squeeze.

"My mimic powers are basically a Pokémon trainer. She wants them all." My grumble turns into a whine, and I don't look at any of them as I bury my face in Cas's chest. His arms wrap around me, and he gives me a hug.

"And we love you and don't care if you add

three more or thirty more," Xavier says, and I lift my head off Cas's chest to gape at him in horror.

"Thirty? Let's just hold a funeral for my poor vagina now. Even my magic Skarrian vagina powers won't be able to handle that many men. RIP, Lila's vagina." I know I sound slightly hysterical, but wouldn't you be? "It's like a porno in the making. *Lila Does the Galaxy*, or *Lila's Alien Gang Bang*, or *Lila Fills All Her Holes*, or *Lila's Bukkaki Party*." I know I'm rambling, but give a girl a break. I'm tired, horny, and hungry, and not necessarily in that order.

"Bukkaki? I don't think that's a term I know," Link muses, and I groan and drop my chin against my chest.

"Of course that's the one thing you pay attention to. Look, all I'm saying is how am I ever going to give all of you the right amount of attention?"

"Baby, you have so much love to give, and with the circus and our rapidly growing family, there will always be someone around to love on the babies or help you out with the show or the cast, and I promise we all know to come to you if we are feeling neglected, but you are handling this wonderfully." Cas presses a kiss to my forehead as I sag against him again.

"How about we take care of all your needs so you are in peak condition for Husadavia tomorrow?" Link suggests. "You too, Xavier. You need to have a power boost, and I know Lila gives you everything you need now, but it won't hurt for you to be extra topped off." Link stands up and offers me his hand. When I take it, he pulls me up, and we start in the direction of the bedroom.

"You coming?" he calls to Cas and Xavier over his shoulder, and I hear them scramble to catch up.

Well, I do like this assertive side of Link. Apparently I'm getting my freak on, and I am not going to argue. I can't wait to see Link and Cas together again, and this time, I want to be involved. A certain scenario that I've been fantasizing about for a while floats through my mind, and I hear Xavier start coughing behind me.

"Are you okay?" Cas asks him, and when I look over my shoulder, my warlock mate is smirking at me.

"I am very much okay, just a little surprised by what Lila wants." I feel my cheeks heat again, but he shakes his head. "Oh no, my dirty little intimate. I didn't say it was a bad surprise. I would very much like to see it too."

When we get to my room, Link opens the door, and we all pile in. We reach my massive bed, and he turns around with an eyebrow raised in question.

"Well, are you going to share?"

CHAPTER FIVE

Xavier

I watch with amusement as our mate's cheeks turn a rosy pink with her embarrassment. I almost couldn't believe what I read in her mind. I wasn't actively searching it, but she was practically shouting her thoughts. I knew she was kinky, but this is delicious.

"Well, are you going to share?" our cyborg asks her with a raised eyebrow, and I feel her panic.

"*Phoeall*, don't be embarrassed. I think your idea is delightful," I assure her, and she glares at me. I know she doesn't really mean it, but I feel like Lila needs to be pushed sometimes. Earth's puritanical ideals still influence her decisions and thoughts, and pushing her out of her comfort zone will be freeing.

"Stay out of my head." She stabs a finger in my direction, and I hold my hands up in defense.

"You were practically shouting those thoughts. I think subconsciously you wanted me to hear them so I would push your boundaries," I say, walking toward her and dropping my hands to her hips, pulling her flush against my body so she can feel how hard I am at her idea. My cock throbs with need, and I feel the tip of it weep.

I lean down and press a kiss against her soft, lush lips before whispering, "I can't wait to see you rail them."

She stiffens in my arms when I say this, but I spin her around and make her face her other two mates, holding her back flush against my front so she can't get away.

I grip her chin in one hand, forcing her to meet their eyes. "Now tell your husbands what you want to do to them." She practically squirms in my hold, and I can't stop the low chuckle from leaving my mouth. "Now, Lila," I order her, knowing she needs to be pushed.

"I want to…" The last bit is mumbled, and I can tell Caspian and Link didn't hear her, so I swat her across her ass.

"Lila, don't make me spank you," I growl. "Tell your husbands what you want, or I will do it for you."

"Fine, ugh, you are so annoying." She stomps a foot. "I would like to use my cyborg cock to peg both of you," she says calmly, even though her body is practically vibrating with excitement.

I couldn't believe it when I saw that picture inside my head—Cas and Link lying on top of each other, their cocks pinned between them while Lila used a double cock to fuck them. I almost came in my pants. I project the stolen image into their brains, because both of them are speechless, and I can feel Lila retreating into herself at their lack of a reaction.

"Oh," Link says, adjusting himself, and Cas grins once he sees the memory play through his mind, their lust thickening the atmosphere.

"I do love your devious mind. Baby, your wish is my command."

I feel Lila's hesitation and realize I'm going to have to be the conductor of this orchestra, so I wave my hand and remove everyone's clothes. Lila's heat against my skin is delightful. I feel her intake of breath against the hand I'm holding around her, and Link just rolls his eyes.

"Well, I guess that was easy," he says as he runs a hand over his erect cock. I'm not the only one who liked the picture Lila conjured up. He climbs up on the bed, his skin shimmery in the artificial light. He's perfection, his cyborg body designed to be the ultimate desire. Muscles ripple just below the surface of his skin, every dip and definition drawing your eye. Lila and I watch as Cas joins him, his blue skin a stark contrast against Link's shimmery perfection. Cas is bigger and bulkier than our cyborg but no less desirable. The two of them on the bed together are delicious.

"Now kiss," I command them, telling them in their minds that we're going to give Lila a little show to tease her. I already know she's needy and aching from the fun she had with her can of tuna, but I want her so turned on that she won't overthink any of this.

I feel her body tense in anticipation as Cas and Link roll toward one another and start to make out, their thick lengths rubbing together as they lazily thrust their hips. Lila moans quietly at the sight as I allow one of my hands to slide south and lightly circle her clit. Her knees practically buckle with the first swipe of my finger, the tight bud slick with her desire. I circle it while nibbling on her ear and neck, using the other hand I had banded across her chest to pluck her nipples. Cas's and Link's hands roam all over each other's bodies, and I feel Lila getting needier. I sip on the desire and lust in the air, and my eyes roll back in my head. Fuck, that's good. Although my intimate's emotions and feelings can sustain me now, and Lila is very powerful, it's always so much tastier when her mates are involved. It's like pure ambrosia. I'm wondering if it's a product of our mating—me getting some of Lila's mimic powers in the form of needing to feed on her mates, much like Cas's kraken is suddenly okay with sharing her and themselves with us.

We watch as Link slides down Cas's body and takes his thick length into his mouth. Cas's cock is so fun with all those suckers on it. Link bobs up and down as Cas threads his hand through Link's silver hair, his head thrown back as he enjoys what Link is doing to him. It's so fucking decadent. I love watching, and I know Lila does too, but I can tell she's ready to join them.

"Do you want to play with your husbands now? Are you ready to have some fun?" I ask her and feel her nod. "How about you show me how you grew a cock? I'm dying to see it, and you're going to need two if you want to fuck them both," I remind her, and I put the image of my now dead harem member, Mithus, in her mind. He had two cocks, which were perfect for double stuffing.

She growls at the reminder of my harem member, and there's a stab of jealousy in her emotions for a moment, but when I reach down to brush her clit again to distract her, I'm surprised to find it gone, and in its place are two fully functioning erect dicks. Whoa, I wasn't expecting it to be that quick. I bring both hands down to stroke them, and Lila's head drops back against my shoulder as she moans.

"Fuck, that feels good," she tells me, turning her head and biting into my skin, and I shiver because her fangs are out, and now she's sucking my blood with big, deep draws that make my cock pulse as her venom runs through my body. I groan, and my knees shake slightly as I thrust against her, painting her back with my cum, unable to stop my orgasm.

"Fuck," I mutter and rest my chin on her shoulder. I can feel her smug satisfaction.

"You shouldn't tease your wife," she says, swiping her tongue across the bite mark to seal the punctures.

I continue to slide my hands up and down both cocks before releasing one and fondling her testicles. Gliding my cock through the mess I made, I bend my knees and slide it up and down her ass crack, pushing against her puckered hole. Lila's smugness slides away, replaced with another wave of roaring lust.

"You shouldn't tease your husband," I tease her. I pull back and survey the mess I made, feeling pretty primal because my seed is all over her. I'd have preferred it to be in her, but we can work on that. We have plenty of time to have babies, and our family has grown enough for now.

"Go stand by the bed in front of your husbands," I direct her, and she quickly obeys just like I knew she would. Lila is so wonderfully multifaceted, our sex life is never going to be boring. I saw in her mind how she dominated her can of tuna and how responsive he was. That's going to be a fun dynamic to watch grow, but she's just as happy to take instructions like now.

When she gets to the bed, I catch the guys' attention by putting an image of what I want them to do in their minds. That way, Lila will get to enjoy the anticipation of not knowing what's about to happen.

Link and Cas break apart and turn their attention to her. I watch a shiver flow over her spine as they crawl down the enormous bed before they each take one of her cocks into their mouths. She moans loudly, and I see her knees buckle so badly that I have to leap forward to steady her.

I wrap my arms around her, supporting her once more. I remember what it was like getting my first couple of blow jobs and how hard it was not to come the minute their warm, wet mouths wrapped around my length. Double that, it must be twice as bad. I look down over her shoulder and watch as they lavish her cocks with attention, using their tongues, lips, and hands to bring her as much pleasure as possible. She moans and mutters curses, but I can feel how much she's enjoying it.

"Don't your husbands look so pretty sucking your cocks?" I whisper into her ear, but when I turn my head, she has her eyes squeezed tightly shut. I grab her chin and force her to look down. "Open your eyes, Lila," I command, and she does as ordered. "Aren't they such good boys, pleasing their mistress?"

That's it, Lila is done for. I feel her entire body stiffen, and she starts to thrust her hips, which I had been holding tightly. Her hands dig into their hair, and she fucks their mouths with abandon before shouting and spilling her cum into their mouths. Link was expecting it, but Cas is surprised, so some of it dribbles out of the side of his mouth. I release Lila and bend over, licking the cum from Cas's mouth. When I look back at my wife, her eyes are glazed, but she's staring at me.

"Mm, delicious," I tease, licking my lips.

"She really is. It's kind of fruity," Link says, licking the length of the cock he'd been sucking.

Lila shudders and pushes his head away, and I chuckle. "How about we attempt to make Lila's fantasies come true?" I suggest, running my fingers through Cas's hair. It's sticking out all over the place from Lila's fingers. He practically purrs and leans against me. I slide my hand down his chest and tug on one of his nipple rings. Cas groans, and his eyes flash to the black of his beast for a moment. I smirk before releasing it.

"Link, lie on your back." I nod to the middle of the bed, and he quickly slides his body back and lies down. "Spread your legs a little," I tell him, and he does. I snap my fingers, and a bottle of lube appears in my hand, pushing Cas a little and putting the picture of what I want into his mind. He quickly joins Link, assuming the same position. I want to put on a little show for Lila while she takes a moment to recover from her first orgasm, so I crawl up onto the bed and shuffle over until I'm in between them. I squirt some of the lube into my palm before dropping the bottle—I'm going to need more of it later. Rubbing the lube between my hands, I reach for their cocks, stroking my slick palms over each of them.

Link's cock is long and thick but incredibly smooth with a large head. There's a bump in the middle of the head he must use to give Lila extra pleasure, like a piercing. I know he can change its shape to whatever he likes. Cas's suckers tickle my palm as I stroke up and down. His cock is shaped more like an actual tentacle, thicker at the base and more tapered at the top. I'd like to know what both of them feel like deep inside me, and I send Lila a picture of that idea. Her mouth rounds, and her eyes widen as she watches a clip of me being fucked first by Link and then Caspian. Her breathing gets a little heavier, and the lust in the air spikes. She is completely entranced, which is what I wanted. I had to get her out of her head.

I remove my hands from their cocks, both of the males now breathing heavier from my ministrations. "Lie on top of Cas," I tell Link. He's the slighter of the two, and Cas shouldn't be completely squashed. Link gets up and does as I said, their fronts pressed together and their cocks sliding against one another, the lube making it nice and slippery.

I watch as they take matters into their own hands, and Cas kisses Link again, holding his head slightly sideways to give himself a better angle. Lila's eyes are now on them, so I conjure up a cock sleeve, and while they make out, I magic it to slide over their cocks so they will slide together with every thrust. I crook a finger at my wife and gesture for her to join us.

Lila's eyes are wide, kind of like a junky on a high, and she doesn't take them off the couple in front of her. She is delightfully obedient, however, and does what I ask. I watch her shuffle up the bed, her luscious tits jiggling with every movement, and my mouth waters. When she gets closer, I bend down and take one of her tight nipples into my mouth. She groans and clutches my head with one hand, the other going to one of her cocks and tugging.

"It hurts," she whines, and I chuckle, pulling away to lavish attention on the other sweet nipple. All the while, I take constant sips of the lust circulating between us, until I'm practically drunk on it. Shaking my head, I pull back and kiss her. Our tongues tangle, and I bite and nip her lips. She's so reactive, giving as well as she takes.

I pull back and grab her head, making her look me in the eye. "I'm going to fuck your ass while you fuck them, okay?" I ask, knowing Lila's not going to complain.

"Like a train?" she mutters incoherently, and I realize she's drunk on lust too, despite not being in her warlock form. Lila really is a special little snowflake. I can't believe how powerful our wife is. She shouldn't be able to access other forms' powers unless she's in that form.

I smirk at her question. "Yes, you dirty girl, like a train."

She eagerly nods, and I magic the bottle of lube to my hand, liberally applying it to her cocks before pouring a little in her hand.

"Make sure our boys are nice and prepped," I tell her, dragging her closer and helping her spread the lube over Link's and Cas's holes. They both start to squirm as we eventually stretch them with three fingers. "That's good, Lila," I praise her, and she shivers. "So good, looking after your husbands. Such a good wife. Now, why don't you use your new appendages to make them feel good?" She turns her head, looking at me. Lila is flying high, so I grab her arm and help her shuffle forward.

"Hold your cocks, Lila," I instruct her. I saw my former harem member use his two cocks, so I can help her with this. I watch as she fists one in each hand before she lines them up and starts to push forward. "Go slowly," I tell her before I tell Cas and Link, "Bear down, boys."

Their mouths part, and I watch as Lila slowly works her cocks into their asses. Their moans and grunts are such wonderful sounds to hear, both of them drunk on the lust I've been pumping into the room too. I fist my own cock, rubbing lube all over it. I still need to prep Lila, but I'll wait until she's balls deep. She gently glides in and out until she's fully seated. Her hands are on Link's hips, and I can see her white-knuckle grip.

"Oh my god," she rasps, and her head drops forward. "It's so tight and hot."

I brush a hand over her head and push a sweaty lock of hair from her face, leaning in to kiss her. "You are doing such a good job, baby. You look fucking sexy. Now lean forward for me," I encourage, giving her a small push on her back. She does as I ask, and I slide behind her, nudging her knees apart. Cas and Link both grunt with the movement.

I dribble some lube down her ass crack and use two fingers to prep her. She moans at the intrusion, her tight little hole squeezing my fingers, but as I work them in and out, it gives slightly. I praise her the entire time, telling her she's such a good girl and that we're going to make them feel so good. With my other hand, I massage the remainder of my cum into her back, loving how her skin glistens with it.

Finally, I line myself up and slowly push forward.

"Fuck, fuck, fuck, fuck," Lila mutters through clenched teeth before groaning loudly.

CHAPTER SIX

Lila

I clench my jaw and close my eyes. The pressure of Link's and Cas's asses on my two new cocks is exquisite, and added to the full, stretched feeling of Xavier in my own ass, it's taking all my nastiest thoughts not to bust a nut before we've even started. Madovian snake lady, carevasta bear guts splattered all over the room, Eric getting it on with his sex bot. Yup, that's the one that does it. Gag.

"You okay?" Xavier's voice is husky with strain as he caresses my tits. I'm lust drunk, but I feel freaking amazing, so I nod my head as he tweaks one of my nipples.

"Yup, I'm good, I'm ready to ride this train. All aboard, toot toot," I call and slap Link's perfectly round ass. I'd love to bend down and bite one of those delicious globes, but alas, I can't reach. Link grunts and turns to look at me, and Caspian giggles like crazy.

"Xavier," Link growls.

"Giddy up, boy!" I shout and go to slap Link's ass again, but Xavier's hand stops mine.

"Lila, hang on tight, because it's going to be a bumpy ride," he whispers into my ear, and I giggle again, but Link's still glaring at us. Poor robot boy, now I need to try really hard to make him feel good. I think about the cock that's in his ass, and I make a lovely little bump that's going to brush against his prostate with every stroke.

"Okay, I'm ready," I tell my warlock, and I grab Link's hips, while Xavier grips mine. I basically don't have to do anything, because Xavier is the maestro of this orchestra. He slides his cock out of me, which has me doing the same for Cas and Link before thrusting forward, and I follow suit. The moans are loud, with mine possibly being the loudest. Their asses grip my cocks tightly, and Xavier feels incredible in my own ass, stuffed to the brim. It feels different from when I have a woman's body though—not less amazing, just different and more intense. It only takes a couple more strokes from Xavier before I'm on the edge again.

"Oh my god, it's so good," I call out, dropping my head forward against my chest. I crack my eyes open to see how my boys are faring.

"Fuck, that cock sleeve started vibrating," Cas

yells, and I turn my head to look at my warlock who is smirking with glee. He picks up the pace, and I lose track of what's happening and drift into the sensations. Xavier's hands roam over my body, tweaking my nipples and holding my hips with a hard grip all while fucking my ass, and all I can do is hang on. Both Link and Cas have gotten very vocal, their moans and groans music to my ears, and I feel my balls tighten and my toes curl. Xavier swirls his hips in a different direction, and I'm done.

"Fuck, I'm coming!" I cry out, and he picks up the pace, hammering into me. I drive into them, the pleasure so exquisite it's bordering on painful as I fill their channels with my cum. Link's ass cheeks tighten, and he and Cas cum in unison. Xavier's motions stutter, and it's his turn to fill my ass as well. I feel his heat paint the inside of my channel as he stops moving and holds me firmly against his chest, resting his head on my shoulder as we both drink deeply of all the lust in the air. I can feel his power become painfully strong as it practically crackles around me.

"Such a good girl taking care of your mates," he coos behind me, petting me, and I sink into his hold. I'm exhausted, but I've never felt so fucking powerful. I'm like a tick that has gorged on its host, and I pity the person who tries to stop my warlock and me from trying to get my grandma.

Our breathing finally settles, and Xavier pulls out of my ass. I feel his cum dribble down the backs of my legs. He helps me disconnect from both guys, and I watch with no short amount of pride when my own cum dribbles out of their holes as they slowly close back up. It's all filthy and nasty, and I did that.

Link reaches between them, and I see some movement. Cas grunts before he pulls out the cock sleeve Xavier gave them, and then Link rolls off my kraken. Their stomachs glisten with their release, and I climb up onto the bed and lap at each of their cocks, cleaning the mess, before Xavier waves his hand and the four of us are instantly cleaned.

"Thank fuck, I don't want to move," Cas mutters, an arm draped across his face. He's flat on his back, so I snuggle into him, reaching over so I'm also touching Link.

A snore from Link has me stifling a giggle. He rolls over and wraps his arm around Cas's waist, snuggled into his opposite side.

"You wore the cyborg out, *phoeall*. That really is an achievement." Xavier chuckles, his body curling around my side.

"Double cocks for the win." I hold my hand up, making a fist, and Xavier doesn't let me down—he reaches around me and bumps it. I drop my arm and wriggle my body so Xavier snuggles even closer. Our sex life is off the fucking charts, but I love this part just as much, knowing that when I wake up, there is always going to be someone I can snuggle with.

"How are your power levels?" Xavier asks as Cas's eyes flutter shut. I can tell when he falls asleep because his breathing evens out.

"I feel fucking incredible, like there's a live wire running through my veins, but I'm fucking starving," I reply.

"For blood?" he asks, and I think about it.

"Yes, but it's not as urgent as food. I don't actually remember when I ate last."

"How about we get up and get you something to eat?" he asks, rolling off me, but I put a hand out to stop him.

"No. Stay here and get some rest. You need it too. I'm going to go get something to eat, and then I'm going to go sleep with the cats. I kind of feel like I need to hang out with all my mates before I do this. I've seen Nikos and now you three. I need to check in with them, and I'll probably use Saxon as a Slurpee tomorrow morning before we leave."

He frowns at me and reaches up to push a piece of hair behind my ear before drawing a finger across my lips.

"Are you nervous?" he asks, and I shrug, trying to play it off, even though we both know he can feel exactly what's wrong with me.

I think carefully before I answer. "For the mission? A little, but I'm pretty confident between you, Brannock, and me that we'll be okay, not to mention our air support dragon, but mostly, I'm worried about making sure all my mates get equal attention and don't feel left out. I'm feeling pretty fucking guilty because although Skarrians have multi people marriages, I'm pretty sure none of you thought we'd be seven in with another possible two to go."

"Two or four?" Xavier asks, and I feel another wave of guilt.

I throw my hands into the air. "I don't fucking know. I would love to say none, but if Tirrian's dragons truly think I'm his mate, and Silac's snake says the same, then who am I to deny them?"

"You know Ghosie and Brannock don't have fated mates," he counters, and I wince.

"No, but both of them have no females in their race. I'm literally their only option. I can't say that makes me feel amazing."

He frowns at my admission. "Lila, don't be like that. I'm sure that isn't the reason either of them are attracted to you. I can search their minds if you want. Hell, you could search their minds if you really wanted to know how they feel about you, but you do have the attraction marks already, so I would say their feelings are fairly obvious."

I sigh and crawl over him, getting off the bed. I look around for my clothes but remember Xavier had poofed them away, so I head into my closet for a robe. Pulling on a big, fat fluffy one, I fasten the belt and return.

"Yes, but I'm worried that once you all get to know me, you're going to regret what fate has unkindly taken out of your hands. It's my biggest worry after making sure that Cordy, Cally, and Jack are safe and loved and looked after. While I'm not failing at that yet, I'm not exactly winning a mother of the year award. I'm basically an absent parent with everything that has been going on."

This conversation got way deeper than I wanted it to. Xavier's eyes soften with sympathy, and he gets up and comes over to me. Despite all my concerns, when he's walking toward me with that gorgeous lavender skin on display, I say a little prayer of thanks to whoever blessed me as his intimate. Fuck me, he's sexy.

One side of his mouth kicks up in amusement. Damn warlock powers. "Lila, honey, you are an amazing mother. Sure, you may not be attached at the hip, but they also have seven fathers to make up for when you can't be there. They are by no means neglected, and once everything settles down, you will have plenty of time with them."

I scoff. "I'm about to take over for my grandpas, so I very much doubt there is going to be any down-time. With Link's predictions, they will age rapidly, and I'm going to blink, and they will be teenagers with all the drama that's going to come along with that. Fuck me, I don't envy the girls trying to have relationships. I thought I'd have a good fifteen to sixteen years before I needed to have the sex talk with them, and that's going to happen so much sooner than I want." I'm spiraling, and Xavier knows it. He takes my arm and leads me out of my bedroom to the kitchen. There, he helps me into a chair at the island counter and goes over to the replicator, pushing a few buttons. While he's waiting for that to work, he goes to the fridge and pulls out my favorite drink, popping the top and placing it in front of me.

"Take a deep breath, *phoeall*. We will deal with everything as it happens. I'm sure you will deal with it with as much grace and patience as you have dealt with all the other major changes in your life over the last couple of months." The replicator pings, and he goes over and pulls out whatever he prepared for me. I take a sip of my drink, and my eyes slide to his ass. He's still naked and very distracting. Turning around, he returns and places a big plate of food in front of me. The smells hit my nose, and I just about start drooling. It's a huge plate of some kind of pasta with garlic bread on the side.

"Eat this and then go snuggle with your kitties. When you wake up, we'll have a big breakfast, and you can drink from Saxon. By tomorrow evening, we'll have your grandma, and things will start to look a little better without her rescue hanging over our heads. One step at a time, okay?"

I pick up my fork and wind the fettuccini around the tines before blowing on it and taking a bite. I moan as the flavor of the creamy tomato sauce hits my taste buds. It's delicious, with a slight kick of chili, the bacon adding a delectable smoky flavor to the perfectly cooked shrimp.

"Oh my god, this is so good," I mumble as I eat, and Xavier chuckles.

"Good, now can I get you anything else?" he asks, and I swallow before shaking my head.

"No, thank you, this is perfect and just what I needed. How did you know?"

He winks before stating, "Because I'm attuned to everything about you. It is my greatest joy to be able to provide for my intimate."

My heart melts, and I fall even more in love with him. How did I get so lucky? Despite everything being out of my control, the universe has picked perfectly for me so far. Each and every one of my mates is wonderful, even my silly can of tuna. I can't wait to get to know him better, and I'm excited for the impending arrival of our babies, even if I worry I can't give them the attention they need. Xavier was also right, though, when he said they have seven daddies to pick up the slack, not to mention three devoted great-grandpas. I'm excited to see what their great-grandma is like. Hopefully she isn't too traumatized by her time in captivity, and if she is, I'll have a discussion with Xavier about having those memories removed and give her the option.

Xavier waves goodbye and leaves me on my own, retreating to the bedrooms. I wonder if he'll join the other two in my bed or if he will escape to his own private space. I know he can sense that I need some alone time, even if it's while I finish this meal to decompress and get myself ready for tomorrow. Thankfully, this doesn't upset or annoy him like it has a few of the previous men I've dated in the past. Fucking Earth men are so needy and insecure, or at least all the ones I dated were.

CHAPTER SEVEN

Lila

I finish up my dinner and get a big piece of pecan pie with whipped cream to round it off, as well as coffee after I finish my Relaxious. I haven't been missing coffee, but I had a sudden craving for it. I think it's probably a comfort thing. I would go to a late night diner not far from my bar job and have this exact thing quite often after work. Maybe I'm just craving a reminder of when life was a lot simpler—boring but simpler.

Once I'm done, I slide all the dishes into the dishwasher and turn it on. We're practically using it daily, sometimes twice a day, with how many people are in our family. Maybe I should have had them put in two. Turning off the overhead light, I retreat to the bedroom area. I'm still only wrapped in my robe, and my feet are bare, but I'm going into the cats' domain. They still have a den-like bedroom, and although this one doesn't have snow-covered tundra to cross, it will be considerably colder, and I'm not exactly dressed for it.

I could shift, but I'm reluctant to because I want to save all the power I just absorbed until I need it. I don't know how long I'm going to have to hold my earth elemental form for, and there won't be time or an opportunity for a quickie. I consider returning to my room to grab some shoes, but I'm exhausted, so I decide that I'm just going to be quick. Once I get to the nest, Echo's and Maxsim's body heat will be enough for me. I get to their door and press my hand against the sensor. It slides open, and a rush of cold air hits me, causing goosebumps to erupt all over my skin.

"Shit, it's cold," I mutter, regretting my laziness. The lights are dimmed, but I know their nest is on the far side of the room, with a small living area in front of it so they can hang out in the subarctic temperatures when they need to. I step in, and the door closes behind me, my teeth start chattering as I navigate the room. I bash my hip against something and grumble, rubbing the spot.

"Lila." Maxsim suddenly appears in front of me, and I squeal in fright.

"Fuck, you move so stealthily," I tell him to make up for my moment of shock. He smiles, but I can see concern in his eyes when he looks down at where I'm rubbing my hip.

"Did you get hurt? Why didn't you turn the light on?" he asks as he leads me through the rest of the furniture to the sunken nest bed. The light is even dimmer back here, but my eyes suddenly adjust, and I can see Echo curled up amongst all the soft furnishings.

"I'm okay, but I think my eyes just shifted," I say and glance around. Sure enough, I can see everything clearly now, but as my body shakes with a shiver, I realize that it was just my eyes.

Maxsim swoops me into his arms and jumps down into the nest. His fur already chases away some of the chill, but once he lowers me down and Echo snuggles in, being cold is a thing of the past.

Echo nuzzles my cheek as Maxsim snuggles into my back. "Hello, pretty mate. You smell like you've been well taken care of." Echo's eyes sparkle with interest as he takes a deep breath in through his nose. "Very well taken care of." His tongue flicks out and swipes up my neck, and I wrinkle my nose.

Maxsim reaches for the belt of my robe and strips it off, leaving me completely naked. The two of them crowd closer until I'm completely surrounded by their bodies, and then Echo reaches for the blankets and pulls them up. Before long, I'm toasty warm, and I jolt in surprise when I realize I'm purring with pleasure despite not having shifted.

"Why aren't you changing?" Maxsim grumbles in my ear.

"I need to conserve my power for our trip tomorrow. I will only have Xavier if I need to refuel," I remind him.

His arm tightens around my waist. "I don't like it," he murmurs, and I smile at his concern.

"I know. It isn't ideal, but I'm hoping it won't take too long."

"Make sure you use the dragon if you need him. It's about time he pulled his head out of his ass and properly joined this family," Maxsim replies, and Echo's eyebrows jump in surprise.

"Really?" I can hear the disbelief in his voice, and I share it. Maxsim is usually pretty damn possessive, so I would have thought the alpha in him would have balked at the alpha vibes Tirrian puts out.

He sighs heavily. "I am aware that this family is going to continue to grow due to Lila's mimic nature. How can I be angry at something she can't control? That would be supremely unfair. Does this mean I will sometimes need you all to ourselves? Yes, but I can see the benefit in having all these powerful men to protect my omegas and our young."

"That's very mature of you." Echo leans over me and gives his alpha a quick kiss. "I'm proud of you," he says, and I watch as they nuzzle each other's noses, and I smile. Echo nuzzles mine next before he pulls back, and I give him a kiss. Now that I'm warm and surrounded by them, I feel my eyes grow heavy. "Sleep, our pretty mate. You need your rest so you can rescue the Adams brothers' wife tomorrow. Don't worry about anything here on the ship. We will take care of the babies."

I reach out and press a hand against his stomach. There is a tiny pooch developing there. "How are you feeling?" I ask him, and he smiles.

"Really good."

"I went and saw Nikos earlier," I tell him, and he nods.

"Yes, I can smell him on you."

"Can you maybe get together with him and ask him what kind of things we are going to need for his babies? I know he births them in the water, but I'm not sure how long they stay there, or when they are going to shift, and how old they are when they are born. All of the really important stuff. Also, order it all so that when it's time for them to leave the water, they'll have a place here in our home."

"Of course I can. I'm glad the two of you sorted everything out and that he is starting to feel better. I will be happy to help welcome him and our new babies to our family. The room next to the pool is still available. We left it because we thought he would end up as your mate. There is a door between the two rooms. I'll make sure we order two more children's beds and have them delivered to

Fluxx. That's where we are going next, right? To rescue Silac's family?"

"Just have the warlock conjure them," Maxsim rumbles, adding his two cents.

Echo rolls his eyes and sighs. "Expecting parents like to have input. Nikos may like to decide what he wants for his babies."

I feel a pang of guilt, and I can't hide my wince from Echo. "I'm failing at parenting 101."

He shakes his head. "No, Lila, you aren't. We know you have a lot of responsibilities. Maybe on the trip back to Fluxx, we can all sit down together and browse some catalogs. Despite Xavier's spell, our kids will grow quickly, so we need to order more clothes for the kraken babies. You can help with that."

"Okay, yeah, that sounds good."

"You know what we do need?" Maxsim says. "A large play area for them. They need to be able to run off their energy."

"Will our kittens have trouble with warmer temperatures?" I ask, thinking we could create a big ball pit with a playground for them on one of the levels. I'm sure there is space somewhere to accommodate it.

"I don't know. Having some of your genes may make them more tolerant. Our bodies do adjust to normal temps, it's just any excessive heat or humidity where we feel drained and sluggish." Echo shrugs. "I guess we'll find out once they are here."

"Enough talk. Sleep now, and all of this can be dealt with later." I hear the finality in his tone. Our alpha has spoken, and we must obey. I'm incredibly tempted to be a brat and disobey, but I am exhausted, and when they both start purring, I drift off.

The next morning, I'm up bright and early, even before both of my lazy kitty cats. Echo groans as I move and rolls over. I giggle and give him a kiss. I remember how exhausting it was growing new life-forms. Maxsim scoops me into his arms and leaps out of the nest with me, so I don't have to shift to do it. Now that I am no longer pregnant and have my vampire genetics, I can make the leap on my own, but I think he likes to feel needed, so I don't complain. I love any excuse to be in his arms.

"Be safe," he tells me, giving me a kiss as he wraps my robe around my body and ties the belt. He's not unaffected by my naked body, but he also knows I don't have time to play knot the omega. I'm sure Echo will benefit from it though.

"I will. Go make Echo's morning a very good one." I nod down at his erect cock, and he smirks.

"Oh, I plan on it." He kisses me before turning

me around and slapping my ass. I squeak and glare at him, but I don't hang around because it's freezing, and I'm still not wearing a lot.

I leave them with a pang of longing, but I need blood, and I know my vampire will take care of all my needs. I just have to find him. I head out into the living area and find Cas, Link, Xavier, and all three of our babies.

"Mama!" Cally catches sight of me and holds her hands up. She is strapped into her high chair and is having what looks like purple pancakes for breakfast. I go over and pick her up, smothering kisses all over her little body. She grabs my cheeks and returns my kisses. Yup, whatever she's eating is very sticky, and I am now wearing some of it.

"My turn," Jack demands as I place her back in her seat.

"No, my turn!" Cordy shouts, picking up her sippy cup and lobbing it at her brother. I gape in shock, too surprised to do anything, but thankfully Xavier's reactions are on point, and it freezes midair.

He drifts it back to her tray. "Cordelia, that was not very nice," he scolds her, and she pouts, crossing her arms and glaring at him.

I pick Jack up and give him his cuddles while watching what's happening out of the corner of my eye.

"We don't throw things at people. Use your words."

"Jack, you are a bum head," Cordy says and sticks her tongue out at her brother. He just laughs and claps his hands as I set him back down.

"Wow, what's happening here?" I ask, looking at my three mates for some answers.

"I think Cordy climbed out of the wrong side of the bed today," Link says, sighing. "I think maybe she should go back to bed."

I go over to my third child and look down at her. She's still glaring at both Jack and Xavier. I see dark circles under her eyes. "Are you sure that's all?" I ask, picking her up, and she snuggles into my side, wrapping her little arms around my neck.

She starts to cry, and I'm shocked. I don't think I've really seen any of them cry, except for a few tantrums. They are the most even-natured cheerful children.

"Can we do a scan of her and check? I'm worried that with all my changes while I was pregnant I may have damaged them. What if this is a result of that?" I ask, and I can see Link purses his lips in thought, but it's Caspian who answers. He comes over and wraps his arms around me so he's snuggling both of us.

"I'm sure they are fine, baby. Stop worrying about them."

"She might be onto something," Link says, and I think my heart skips a beat.

"Fuck." I can't stop the swear word from leaving

my mouth, and I wince when I hear Jack shout, "Fuck, fuckity fuck."

"Good job, Lila," Xavier rolls his eyes, but I can see him trying to smother a grin.

"Are they getting blood?" Before they shifted, they were getting it in the form of the fish they would catch to eat, but they aren't eating like that anymore.

"Yes, they do when we swim," Cas replies.

"But not as much as they were. A Vilaxian baby gets its blood from its mothers milk when they are breast fed, and then they get it in their drinks until their fangs grow in at the age of five," Link explains.

"They don't get fangs until they are five?" I ask.

"No, because could you imagine a bunch of fangy, grumpy toddlers running around?" It's Saxon who answers, and when I look up, he's standing in the doorway of the suite. He looks tired. He must have spent all night on the flight deck, relieving Bubby.

"Yeah, that wouldn't be fun," Xavier agrees as the door closes behind Saxon, and he joins us in the kitchen.

"Put a little bit of Lila's blood in their bottles today. It won't hurt them," he suggests, taking Cordelia out of my arms. "Is daddy's little girl grumpy?" he asks, rubbing his cheek against hers, and she and I both melt.

She mutters something incoherently as she

snuggles into his arms. I pull out of Cas's embrace, go over to the fridge, and pull out three already prepared bottles. I also grab a bag of my blood and proceed to divide it between the three bottles. "Is that enough?" I ask Saxon, and he nods.

Cas nods in agreement. "Yeah, that's good. It shouldn't hurt them. They are shifters, and shifters don't mind a bit of blood."

I put the bottles in the microwave to warm them slightly. It has a bottle setting, so it never gets too hot. Once done, I hand them out to my three toddlers, each of them reaching for one.

"They might be having a growth spurt. Don't be surprised if they are sleepy after their bottles," Saxon warns. "Or at least that's what happens with our children."

Link nods, and I can see him making notes on his arm screen. "This is all very helpful. Thank you, Saxon."

"As long as they are not suddenly teenagers when I return. Then I'm going to cry," I warn them, and Saxon chuckles.

"They won't be teenagers, I promise," he says as we watch the three of them guzzle their bottles. It's like an instant fix. The dark circles under Cordy's eyes disappear, and her skin starts to shine ever so slightly like Saxon's does.

"Well, I guess these three did end up with some of your DNA in the change." Cas slaps Saxon on the shoulder, no jealousy in his tone.

"Oh my god, it's just one more thing we have to worry about—blood sources for them. What do children do for blood?" I ask him, not sure if it had been discussed or not.

"Exactly what you just did, and when their fangs come in, we teach them to bite. They don't get venom until they are older though," he explains.

"But who do they bite?"

"People in their clan. That's why we have them. Everyone supports one another. They only need to feed once or twice a week until they hit maturity. That's when it kicks into overdrive, the venom starts to work, and they feed daily. By then, they have usually started to establish their own clans. It's part of their schooling. With the kids being predominantly shifters, though, they probably won't need to feed every day, and clans really won't be possible here in the circus."

"Ah, let's not count our chickens before they are hatched," Link warns. "I'm certain these three are going to have unexpected traits. The other babies will probably have them too, since Lila's eggs were fertilized."

"Our kids aren't going to have any friends except for each other, but they are all blood relatives, so when they get to the age to start looking for mates, clans, streaks, and possible family groups, they are going to leave us," I wail, knowing this isn't going to be the usual eighteen or so years like it is on Earth.

"Well, maybe we need to start employing acts that are made up of families. We could add a school as well as a playground. Let's face it, there's still a lot of space on this ship that isn't needed," Cas points out, going over to Cally and taking her bottle out of her hand before she drops it. Her eyes drifted closed three quarters of the way through it, and she's out like a light. Jack is fighting it, but both he and Cordy look sleepy too.

"Don't forget there's also the academy," Xavier says, taking a sip of his mug. He's taken to drinking coffee just like I do.

"The academy?" I seem to be the only one in the room who doesn't seem to know what he's talking about.

"There is an elite school located on the planet Vizzar that fosters intergalactic and interspecies relationships. I attended," Xavier explains. "A lot of royal families and upper echelon send their children there to learn to be diplomats."

"As did I, but obviously a lot earlier than Xavier," Saxon says, reminding me of the fact he's a lot older than I am

"What about you two?" I ask Link and Cas.

Cas shakes his head. "No, I did my schooling on Fluxx with the rest of my family."

"I attended the academy for a year, before my mother decided to drag me home saying that the education wasn't up to her standards," Link says with a frown.

"Tirrian and Nikos both did too. Tirrian was in my year, that's how I know him, and Nikos and Nixie were a year or two behind us, but they didn't attend for long either."

"That doesn't surprise me. Their father was an asshole. So at least there are options, but I hate the idea of them going away to school. I guess they will all be close in age, though, and have each other to lean on." I feel a pang of sadness at the thought that they will grow up too soon for my liking.

"How about we take these ones and put them to bed and then go have a discussion with your grandpas about it? I'm sure they could use the distraction while they wait for you to return," Link suggests. "You three go top off your power levels, and then Brannock will be waiting at the teleporter at eight. The harvester call-up is at nine. It will give you a chance to get a lay of the land."

"And take out any of the competition," Xavier says gleefully, rubbing his hands together. Trust him to be happy with the idea of maiming and killing.

I look at the clock on the wall, and it's only seven. I have time to drink from Saxon and take a shower before we need to leave.

"Okay." I give my babies kisses on their soft little heads before Link and Cas take them to bed. Their care quite often falls to both of them, but neither seem to mind. I'm sure Maxsim and Echo will be here soon enough to relieve them, and they'll probably take them to see my grandpas when they wake up. The three of them will keep them suitably distracted while they wait.

"Love you all." I wave as they disappear, and I'm just left with Saxon and Xavier.

"Hungry?" Saxon asks, scooping me up in a flash.

"Very," I tell him, my core starting to throb as my fangs drop down.

"Let's go fix that then," he says before raising an eyebrow at Xavier. "You coming?"

"Not yet," is his reply.

CHAPTER EIGHT

Saxon

My wife's hand is warm in mine, and my nose tickles with the scent of the lightning cats she spent the night with. It isn't an awful scent, just strong and electric. There's also the slightest smell of sex. I don't think it was with the cat's this morning, though, because it would be a lot stronger, so I'm guessing it's from last night. I can make out three distinct scents, and I'm happy that my fellow husbands took care of our wife and made sure she has everything she needs for the coming mission. Now, it's my turn.

I open the door to my room. I want to do it in here because I want her scent all over my sheets while I rest. I shouldn't need one after I have blood, but I will take an hour or two to nap so I'm rested to do whatever is needed of me—whether that be to look after our babies or beam down to the surface in case everything goes to shit. That's the contingency plan. Silac and I are on call if we need to extract the others, both of us able to cope with whatever the planet can throw at us. From what I understand, although Cas and Link both have some defense training, it isn't enough for this mission, and while the cats could be handy, they are not built for the temperatures. As for the bear, he only just joined us, and it wouldn't be fair to ask him to get involved in our fight.

Originally, we considered going with them, but I am fairly recognizable across the galaxy due to my status as the queen's nephew and being a general in the armed forces in my own right. The naga is also probably too identifiable due to the near extinction of their species. Xavier could have glamoured us, but it would have taken some of his power to do that. We don't know what conditions they'll be facing on the planet, so we decided a smaller force to start with was optimum. The teleporter will be primed to beam them back or us to them if we need it.

"We arrived at the space station a little while ago, but we haven't docked. We will teleport you aboard when you're ready to go," I tell them as I drag Lila over to my bed.

"What about our prisoner still in the cells?" she asks, stripping off her robe and letting it fall to the floor. I'm momentarily distracted from her question by the sight of all her luscious, golden skin. Becoming part Vilaxian didn't make her pale at all, it just gave her the same kind of luminescence we all possess, and she looks like sparkling gold dust. She's beautiful.

"We should probably take him with us. I can make it so he can't warn the others of our identities, or you could compel him to do the same," Xavier says, sounding amused by my distraction. Like he can talk, he's always distracted by our wife, not that either of us are complaining. There's just something about her that is magnetic beyond her powers.

"But weren't you going to glamour yourself as him?" Lila asks the warlock as she approaches me and lifts my shirt, dragging it up and over my head. "I don't want you having to split your focus on trying to control him and whatever we're doing. Leave him behind, and we can let him go once we're done."

God, it's sexy how she's starting to come into her role. I love how she made a decision instead of just going with our suggestions. "Yes, ma'am," I say when her hands go to the waistband of my pants.

She looks up at me, her eyes sparkling. "I like that," she says, leaning forward and taking my mouth with hers. Her unique flavor tickles my senses as she scrapes her lip along my fangs, allowing her blood to pool in my mouth. She smirks when she pulls back and runs her tongue over the small cut on her lip.

"She really likes that," Xavier chimes in, sitting on a chair I have in the corner of the room. He projects the memories of her time with the can of tuna into my mind, and I almost groan out loud at seeing her all bossy and filthy.

She pulls my pants down my legs, taking my underwear too, and now I'm naked in front of her. Instead of standing up, though, she licks a line from the base to the tip of my cock, and I have to lock my knees so they don't wobble as she lavishes attention on my dick.

"You're not joining us?" I look over at the warlock, running my hands through Lila's luscious mane of multi-hued hair, trying to distract myself from the suckers in the back of Lila's throat. Her mouth is hot and wet, and added with the suckers, it's no easy feat to stop myself from coming.

"Nope, I had my time with her last night, and I'm very happy watching. Lila looks fucking hot on her knees, and you are giving off such delicious, lusty vibes. You know the two of you together is one of my favorite snacks. Show me how you can fuck her mouth." His voice is husky with his desire, and a shiver flows down my spine. It's no wonder I would prefer to feed on him than my clan. He's pure temptation in a sexy package.

My hands tighten in Lila's hair, and I thrust my hips. She takes my cock to the back of her throat beautifully, and I moan and watch as Xavier fists his own cock and strokes it.

I feel Lila scrape her fangs along my length, and I grunt before dragging her mouth off me. If she bites me now, I'll lose it, and I really want to come in her pussy. My cock throbs at the thought of filling her with my seed. I know she said she doesn't want any more babies yet, but I really want to see her round with my baby, and it doesn't require any special ceremony or spell like it does with the warlock. I should probably mention it to her, and if she asks, I'll tell her the truth.

She slides up my body, placing kisses along her skin until she stands on her tiptoes, straining for my mouth. I smirk and lean down to kiss her. I love our size difference. It amuses me to have to bend my head to kiss my wife. Vilaxian women are usually as large as the men. Lila's not a short woman, but compared to me, she's dainty, and I like feeling like I can protect her from the world. I reach down, grab her thighs, and lift her. She wraps her legs around my waist and her arms around my neck as we kiss, biting and sucking blood from our scrapes, her delicious flavor making me want more. She grinds against me, her hot pussy sliding over my cock.

"Fuck me, please," she mutters when she breaks our kiss.

"Slow down, sweetheart. I'm going to give you exactly what you need, but let's give our warlock a little show," I whisper in her ear, and she quickly nods, her lips turning up with glee.

I walk her over to the warlock, his hand still wrapped around his cock, and slide her down my body. Spinning her around, I press on her back to make her bend, then she places her hands on his knees.

"Hello, pretty girl." He smirks as I line myself up and slide into the hot, wet channel of Lila's cunt. It's tight and has those internal suckers that make it very hard to keep from coming. She moans, and I feel her ripple around me.

"How about you suck on our warlock's dick while I destroy your pussy?" I tell our wife. I know how much she loves to have everyone involved, and while Xavier would have been happy watching, I don't like to leave him out or disappoint her.

She licks and sucks him, and I hold still, watching her make his cock wet and sloppy before she takes it all the way down, her nose pressing against his pelvis. He shouts with surprise. I don't think he was expecting her to do that so quickly, and I watch as his eyes widen. I know she injected him with her venom, because he grabs her head and holds her in place. I slide in and out of her pussy, moving slowly before really pounding into her. To anyone else, it would look like we were abusing her, but she loves it. Xavier comes hard, and Lila swallows it all down, her venom doing exactly what it's designed to do by making someone feel good.

She pulls off, and a small amount dribbles out of the side of her mouth. I grab her head and pull her back so I can lick it from the corner of her lip, enjoying the sweet taste of our warlock's cum. Lila says it tastes like something called Twizzlers, and I know she loves it, but now that she's feasted on him, I'm ready for her to feast on me.

I pull out of her and spin her around, sliding her back to sit on his lap before thrusting into her. I lean forward and kiss Xavier next to her head, and I hear her intake of breath as she watches. She's very happy to allow her mates to share one another, and all of us are very grateful she's so generous.

She moans loudly as I pick up the pace, her ankles coming up to hook around my back. I break my kiss with the warlock and kiss my wife instead. Her mouth tastes like Xavier, and my fangs throb at the thought of popping through her skin and drinking her blood, so I break the kiss and slide my fangs into the fat vein on her neck, allowing my venom to flood out as I pound into her with my cock. She screams when she can't hold back her pleasure any longer, my venom triggering her release. Her pussy tightens and pulses as I fuck her through her orgasm, her juices flooding my cock just like her blood fills my mouth, and it's all I can do to hold back my own orgasm. Xavier's hands caress her breasts and pinch her nipples as he whispers words of praise into her ear. I didn't drink too heavily, just enough to tide me over while she is gone. I know she can afford to lose it, she's made for me, but I don't want to chance weakening her, even slightly. I swipe my tongue over the holes, sealing them as I swirl my hips lazily. All the bumps and ridges hit all the right spots inside her, and she continues to moan.

"Bite him, Lila. It's time for our vampire to cum too," Xavier tells her through her lust haze. Her eyes open, and they glow red as she peels her lips back, her fangs dripping with her venom. I've never seen her look more ravishing as she strikes, burying her fangs in my neck, before sucking hard. Every draw of blood feels like it has a direct link to my cock, and I can no longer hold back. My hips hammer into her as she holds me in place. I hear her gulping my blood, her throat working hard as she swallows me down, just like she swallowed Xavier down. My seed explodes, filling her hot, tight channel with my cum, and again, I briefly wish that this time might lead to a baby.

Xavier obviously hears my thoughts, and he chuckles. *I'm pretty sure she would castrate you if that happened right now,* he tells me inside my head.

I know now is not the time, but I can't help but want it, and unlike you, we don't require some kind of magical woo-woo to get it done. It could have already happened, I reply, and I feel a pang of sympathy.

Actually, no, it won't. Lila had Link inject her with a

temporary conception inhibitor after the wedding party. She was worried about all the sex she'd been having, both with you and Link. Link told her cyborg conception is slightly different than normal reproduction, and he's not even sure the two of them can have kids. Though with her control over the nanobots he gave her, I have a feeling that isn't going to be a problem. He projects an image into my mind of what she did to Link and Caspian the night before.

I choke out a cough of surprise, which has Lila pulling back and looking at me with concern.

"Are you okay?" she asks, the lust haze clearing from her eyes, and she licks over the fang marks, sealing them up.

"He's fine. I was just showing him what you can do with your nanobots for future fun and games," Xavier assures her while continuing the conversation inside my head. *But unlike the rest of us, you don't require anything other than fertilizing her eggs, and she isn't ready to add any more babies until we get the orb situation fixed.*

That's smart, but a guy can hope. It's okay, I'll just continue to lavish love on the ones we do have, I assure him when he cocks a questioning eyebrow.

I lean in and kiss my wife, and she responds enthusiastically, but I gather her into my arms.

"Did you drink enough?" I ask, and she smiles lazily.

"Sure did," she responds, slightly blood drunk.

"Well, let's clean you up and get you dressed. You need to leave soon." I move in the direction of the door leading to our shared bathroom, and I hear Xavier follow behind.

His clothes hit the floor of my room, and I grumble, "They better not stay there."

"Relax, I'll move them, but I need a shower too."

"Yay!" Lila cheers, and I shake my head with amusement.

"No more playtime. You need to sober up and get moving. You have a grandma to rescue." I give her a squeeze, and her bottom lip drops into an adorable pout.

This has her squirming in my arms, but I don't put her down until we step into the shower, the water turning on automatically as we pass the sensors. I lower her to her feet and grab the soap so I can wash her. When I step back and get a look at her, she is practically glowing with power.

"Wow," I mutter, and she looks confused.

Xavier joins me and whistles. "You're not wrong. Lila, you are putting off some major power vibes. You practically crackle with it."

She heaves out a sigh of relief. "Thank goodness, because I have a funny gut feeling we're going to need it."

I look at her warlock mate and notice he's also glowing with the same kind of light, and I've never felt him so strong.

"You too," I tell him, and he smirks.

"Of course I am, I'm *the* warlock."

I roll my eyes at his lack of humility. I hadn't expected anything less.

"Come on, let's get clean. I still have to assume my earth elemental glamour, and you need to take on the corn man. Brannock will be waiting for both of us."

"Ah, yes, the Aaz'axian." I start to run the soap over Lila's body. "Are we still going to trust him?" I hadn't wanted to bring it up earlier, but I'm on the fence.

"He gave me full access to his mind. I don't think there's any reason not to trust him," Xavier says as he leans against the wall and watches as I wash our wife.

"Lila?" I ask her as she steps under the stream of water to rinse off the soap. I throw the bar to Xavier, and he starts to lather up his own body.

"I want to trust him. It must have been awful for him to stay hidden. I would have done the same thing if any of our babies were on the line. I plan on annihilating Smith when we return to Earth," she growls, "and tearing that base apart. If Earth wants to continue to benefit from our visits, then they will cooperate. I also want Aura and their family to return. Whether Mark and Susie go with them, I'm not sure, but what happened to them wasn't fair."

"Okay, I will support the two of you, but if he so much as sneezes in the wrong direction, I'll snap his neck faster than he can blink." I'm hoping they are both right, but someone needs to be wary, and I guess this time it's going to be me.

"Good, I'm glad someone is being a little less emotional about the whole thing. Thank you." Xavier slaps my shoulder before grabbing Lila by the hips and shuffling her out of the water.

"Hey, you know there are six different heads to stand under, so why do you need mine?" she complains, and he just leans in and kisses her silly, completely distracting her. I laugh. Life is certainly never going to be dull in this family. I'm happy both of them are full to the brim with power, but it isn't going to stop me from worrying.

CHAPTER NINE

Lila

I feel fucking amazing as we walk from our suite to the teleporter room. I kissed Saxon goodbye and patted him on his cute little butt as he climbed into his bed.

"Be safe, my blood rose," he called as we walked out the door. "You too, warlock." Aww, look at my husbands playing nice with one another. He's going to nap while we travel to Husadavia. It's a two day trip from Z68, and the galaxy ship will tail the harvesters' transport, cloaked so they don't know they are being followed. Then, Saxon and Silac will be on call if shit hits the fan and we need them on the surface.

We don't take the sideslip elevator because I wanted to take the ten minute walk to get my mind on the next job. I've spent plenty of time working out with Xavier and Saxon, trying to get my powers under control, and I think I mostly have a handle on the earth elemental form, but I'm still nervous for what's to come. Our plan is weak at best.

We arrive at the teleporter room and find Brannock waiting for us as well as Bubby and my grandpas.

Eric studies me closely before turning his attention to Xavier and nodding his head. "You both look pretty powered up. Good."

Bubby presses his fingers to the touch screen. "I've programmed this to deposit you in the docking port of the station. From there, you are going to have to find your way to wherever you need to be."

"The creature we captured told me recruitment happens at the same bar we originally met at. I pulled all the information I needed out of his head, so no one should suspect that I'm not him," Xavier tells him as his body shimmers ever so slightly and he appears in front of me as the corn man. I blink, trying to get my brain to catch up with my eyes. I reach out and poke at his corn kernel chest and marvel at how real it feels.

"Wow, it's almost like it's not even a glamour, like you've mimicked him."

Xavier's mouth drops open, and he runs his own hands over his body.

"It's still a glamour, but it's almost impossible to see through." Brannock steps up and narrows his eyes before poking like I did. "It's practically seam-less. I don't even think the most powerful of beings will know. I can only just see a glimmer of what's real."

"Is that one of your powers?" William asks before I can do the same. "We don't know much about Aaz'axians except you are killing machines when in berserker mode."

Brannock gives him a quick nod. "Yes, as well as having our own abilities to glamour." His body shimmers, and he takes on the human form I remember him wearing in the cell on Earth. "We have the ability to see through other glamours, and like Vilaxians, we have enhanced speed, strength, and senses. Unfortunately, we can't fly like them though," he grumbles adorably.

"Well, you did get glamour powers," I remind him. "I'm sure they wish they had those."

He nods before continuing. "I can mesmerize or compel, I guess, and I can launch my spikes as weapons, and they contain a paralyzing toxin." He points to the spikes on his back, joined by the whisper thin membranes. When I look closer, I see they have claws at the end of each long protrusion. Maybe that's what gets launched. "In berserker mode, I can project thorns out of my skin." I watch with fascination as his whole body shimmers, and Xavier grabs my arm, dragging me out of the way as my grandpas also take a step back. Bubby is the only one who doesn't move, and from the way he's smirking at us, I'm guessing he's seen this already.

Brannock's entire body changes shape. The spines on his back and shoulders recede into his body as his skin changes from its blue opal sheen to a bright red and green. The spikes coming out of his head remain, but they are red, and so do the ridges and spines all over his body. He's also gotten way taller and wider.

"Easy," William cautions with his hands up.

"I'm fine," Brannock rasps, his voice slightly different, and when I look closer, I see he has fangs now. "I'm not going to slaughter you, that's a rumor we didn't discourage. Berserker mode is just an alternative form which allows us to do this." He turns and faces one of the smooth walls of the transporter room, and I watch as projectiles launch from various surfaces on his body and thud into the metal walls.

I push past him, careful not to touch his body, and check out what he just did. They are large, two inch thorns which have sunk deep into the side of the room, going through like it was rubber instead of solid metal.

"Instead of just being able to project through the spines on my back, I can now do it through my whole body." He holds out both hands, and again, thorns launch out of them before hitting the wall next to me.

I screech and leap out of the way. The rest of the guys laugh when I glare at Brannock.

"Whoops, sorry," he says a little sheepishly, running a hand over the spikes on top of his head. I'm curious how they feel. They seem to bend when he touches them, but I'm not curious enough to reach out and have a go myself… yet.

"Aren't we worried that if you go like that, they will be too scared to hire you?" John is looking a little better today, but he's still a little too pale for my liking.

Xavier shakes his head. "I don't think they will. In fact, I got the feeling they would probably hire him on the spot, even if it's for protection. They lost too many harvesters on the last trip and are feeling a little jumpy."

"The shrouded figure isn't instilling much confidence in his workers. That's not good for business," Eric points out.

"I get the feeling he isn't actually the boss, just someone else who is being paid to be there. He never speaks or interacts with any of the crew, nor does he help harvest. There is no sign of them ever seeing what he looks like either—or at least this guy didn't anyway." He points to his glamoured form. "It's only assumed he's there to keep the inhabitants of the planet away. I hate not having all the information. If someone had only seen what he looks like under the cowl, we'd have a better idea. For all we know, he's a Seiomann, and we're all going to be screwed."

That sounds familiar, but I can't quite remember what it is. "What's a Seiomann?" I ask, and it's Brannock who replies.

"A race of aliens that can make it so a being can't access their powers. They also have the ability to freeze a person in stasis."

"Ugly fuckers," Eric chimes in. "They appear like they are floating, draped in a dark cloak, with their only discernible features being three red eyes."

I shiver, but Xavier shakes his head. "No, this being doesn't float, and there is no sign of red eyes, so I'm hoping we will be okay."

"Do you think one of them was used to put Grandma in stasis?" I ask, and William nods.

"Probably. They aren't exactly the most welcomed race, so people tend to avoid them, worried their own powers will be nullified. Though I'm under the impression that being in their vicinity doesn't do it. They have to actively use their powers to nullify, but it's made them pariahs and, in turn, bitter. They will do anything if the price is right."

"And without any visible cues, it's hard to pinpoint exactly what the overseer might be. I may be able to feel more when we are within his vicinity." Xavier sounds frustrated, and I know it's mostly because he's worried about me.

"Okay, Lila, we need you to take your elemental

form, and then you are good to go," Bubby announces as the teleporter hums its readiness.

I nod. "Okay, turn around, because I'm about to get naked," I announce, untying the belt to my robe as the men in the room whirl around. The only one left looking at me is Xavier, and I raise an eyebrow at him, nodding toward his new form.

"You aren't going to explode into kernels of popcorn if I get naked, are you?" I ask, and he chuckles, shaking his head.

"I may look like the corn man, but it is still a glamour. I don't have his abilities or anything."

I drop my robe, the fabric pooling at my feet, and wink at my corncob husband before picturing the earth elemental form in my mind. My mimic powers sparkle with excitement, and I'm enveloped in the shimmery haze. I feel my body start to change, getting smaller and lighter, as I try to hold onto my personality, allowing it to meld with the elemental nature that attempts to take over. I've gotten better at it, but it's still a struggle sometimes. Thankfully, the earth elemental is less volatile than the fire one, so the fight isn't as difficult.

The haze clears, and I find myself looking up at the corn man, but the smirk on his face is so Xavier. I'm about waist height, and I know whatever is about to come out of his mouth is going to be dirty.

"Look at you, so tiny and dainty and the perfect height for me to—"

"Xavier!" William snaps, cutting my dirty

warlock off. He doesn't look repentant at all as he hands me a little elemental dress to pull on over my naked form.

I flutter my wings and lift into the air. Thankfully I managed to master flying in both elemental forms, but I don't get very high before my body starts to feel heavy, and I sink to the ground, groaning as a wave of nausea washes over my new body. I wrap my arms around myself and squeeze my eyes closed, laying my cheek on the cold floor as my head starts to throb.

"Lila!" Xavier reaches for me, but in the form he's in, he can't bend over. Brannock scoops me up into his arms as everyone else gathers around me.

"What's wrong with her?" I hate the worry I hear in John's voice, but I'm in too much pain to reassure him.

"Rick, call Link to get his ass here," Eric demands, but before Bubby can react, Xavier reaches out to stop him, groaning and rubbing a hand across his own head.

"Don't, I can feel what's wrong. She's an earth elemental who hasn't had any contact with her element in a long time."

"But isn't metal an earth element?" William argues. My eyes are squeezed closed against the light, so I can't see anybody. I only listen to them discuss me. Brannock's body is soothing against mine, his skin slightly cold, and surprisingly, none of his ridges or spikes hurt me. It's like everything smoothed out when he held me against his body.

"It is, but it's been sustaining her for so long that it's starting to become ineffective. I scanned both elementals' minds before I let them go so I would have all the knowledge I needed to train Lila. The earth elemental she mimicked had been in space for an extended period of time and was waiting for a transport to a planet so they could refuel their power stores."

"But they were radiating off her when you guys walked in," John argues. "Where did it all go?"

I almost feel Xavier shrug. "That power fuels her mimic abilities, allowing her to change and hold this form, but she will still be susceptible to the form's weaknesses, like her need for blood like a Vilaxian or emotions like a warlock."

"But that's different, she's mated to both of you, which essentially changed her DNA. This isn't like that," Eric protests.

"It kind of is." I feel Brannock's chest rumble as he gets involved. "Lila becomes a new species every time she mimics someone. I bet if the cyborg ran her DNA now, she would be a mixture of every species she's mated to or mimicked. It's no surprise she has their weaknesses too. We need to get her in contact with a different earth element, or she's no good to us at all."

"There's the horticulture level, with plants and

soil up there. It isn't exactly the same, but it might help," Bubby suggests.

"Yes, it will boost her power until we can get to Husadavia at least. Once there, she should have no problems rejuvenating," Xavier agrees with him. "Wait here, we won't be long." I feel him put his cobby hands on Brannock and me, and that disorienting feeling of teleporting washes over me, not helping how I feel one little bit. I groan, and my head flops back.

"Easy, little one," Brannock murmurs as we arrive at our destination. I want to snort with amusement, but I don't have the energy. No one has ever accused me of being little.

"Put her down here," Xavier tells the Aaz'axian, who seems reluctant to let me go, but he places me gently on the ground. I groan as I feel grass below me, and I roll over, my hands turning to claws I instinctively burrow into the soil. My headache starts to ease up, as does the rolling nausea in my stomach. The aches and pains in my limbs melt away, and I can open my eyes and look around.

I feel my mouth drop open in shock. I haven't been to this level before, even though I had been told about it. It looks like a massive community garden. It takes up the entirety of this level of the ship. I see beings tending rows of crops, watering, deadheading, and pruning different plants and bushes. There is a grove of fruit trees on the far side of the space, my elemental eyesight making it easy for me to see despite the distance.

"I didn't think there was anyone on the ship," I point to the workers.

"They're automatons," Xavier explains. "That way the ships crops are always tended."

I turn my attention to the area closer to me and find myself in a small park. There is a little pond with a bench next to it. Beyond it, there's an open grassy space with a soccer ball lying abandoned on it.

"Wow." I roll over into a seated position, my wings fluttering behind me as I continue to soak up the energy from the soil below me. "I had no idea this was here," I tell the two males who are watching me carefully. My gaze lifts, and I watch clouds drift across the sky as I feel warmth on my face. "How is it doing that?" I ask, nodding toward the clouds.

"Same way we control the climate in the Aquilian level and the Iceen tundra," Xavier says, and when I look at him, he still seems worried, his little corncob mouth all pursed with tension. "How are you feeling?"

"A little better. The headache and nausea are disappearing, and I don't feel so heavy." I pull my hands out of the soil and look around in shock. The grass around me has all died, like I pulled out all of its life force. "Is that normal?" I ask, and I see the two of them exchange a glance.

"I don't know if it's a result of you being so low or not. I would assume that most elementals don't kill the things that help them survive. I didn't pick up on anything like that in the mind of the one you mimicked. We'll have to do some research." Xavier sounds a little worried.

I struggle to my feet, and I waver a little. Brannock's hand shoots out to steady me, and I smile up at him. The two of them tower over me, so I flutter my wings and feel myself rise up so I'm now head height with them. "Okay, I think I'm good to go," I reassure them when they both look at me with concern still evident in their eyes.

I see them exchange a glance. "Maybe you should stay behind," Brannock suggests bravely, and when I look at my warlock husband, I see he agrees, but he is happy for Brannock to deal with my wrath.

"Absolutely not." I cross my arms stubbornly and glare at them. "I'm fine and will be even better when we get to the planet, where I can soak up all it has to offer. I mean, poisonous, venomous, man-eating plants have to have some major power boost properties, don't you think?"

They still look unconvinced, but neither of them argue with me, which I appreciate more than I can express. "Fine, Lila, but don't get too far away from either of us," Xavier says, pointing between me and Brannock. "I'm not going to be much help in this glamour. It's cumbersome and awkward," he says as he steps up next to us, and I have to smother the chortle of laughter that wants to escape. He's not wrong, he kind of waddles. "If I have to, I'll drop the glamour, but I don't want to until we can ascertain whether you can mimic the creature that repels all the danger. We want to stay under the radar as much as possible."

"Okay, I'll stay close. Let's get this show on the road." They still look unconvinced, but Xavier puts his hands on us again, and we shift back to the transport room.

"Oh good, you're back." John heaves out a sigh of relief, which is echoed by William and Eric.

"And you look much better." William scans my form and looks relieved.

"Yup, feeling pretty good," I reply, although it's not the complete truth, but I know if I admit I'm still feeling weak, then the mission will be aborted, and I won't do that. I'm sure once I get to Husadavia, I'll be at full power in no time. I wonder if, as an earth elemental, I'll be able to control the plant life on the planet. I'm sure they've probably tried that, though, so probably not.

"Are you ready to go now?" Bubby asks, looking between the three of us.

I don't wait for any of the questions or arguments, marching up to the platform with Xavier and Brannock following behind. "Let's do this. Engage!" I shout and see Bubby press a button, and as we disappear, at least Eric has a smile on his face at my antics.

CHAPTER TEN

Lila

The three of us reform in the docking bay of the station, and all around us, lifeforms are rushing back and forth. There are a few smaller vessels inside the bay, and the noise is quite loud.

Let's get moving. We don't have long until harvester sign-ups, Xavier says inside my head, so he doesn't have to shout. I can tell he projected it to Brannock as well from the nod he gives him.

Screams of horror sound out, and I use my wings to whirl around, looking for the danger, but I realize it's us. We're the danger—or the spiky red and green man next to me is. People are freaking out at the sight of Brannock in his berserker mode.

"Shit, change of plan." Xavier waves a hand, and everyone in the docking bay instantly freezes. I can feel the tingle of his magic at work, so I'm assuming he's wiping all their minds of what they saw. That was not the low-key kind of entrance we were planning. We want to be as forgettable as possible.

"Ah, maybe it would be better to change back to normal or assume a glamour. Otherwise, there is no way we are going to get hired if this is the kind of reaction you get," I mutter to him, and he chuckles.

"I thought there would be enough time since the last war that people would have forgotten our reputation. I guess that's not the case." He sounds disappointed. I guess I would be too if my appearance caused that kind of reaction without even getting to know me. Brannock's body shudders, and I watch with interest as the red and green is replaced by his pretty sparkly blue opal color. His back and shoulder spikes also reappear, pushing out of his skin in a gruesome display that must be uncomfortable if the grimace on his face tells me anything. His whole body shakes, and he sighs, stretching out a little, before it shimmers and the pretty, sparkly man is replaced with another corn man.

"Good thinking," Xavier says. "This race is in tune with plants that bear fruit. It's why this one was hired in the first place. We'll say you are his brother. That fits his narrative." My warlock husband's ability to pry someone's brain open and get all their knowledge is an incredibly scary yet handy power to have. He waves a hand and unfreezes everyone. It's funny to watch how confused they are, but they quickly shake it off and continue on about their business prior to realizing a predator was amongst them.

"Come on, we need to get moving. It's about a ten minute walk from here to that bar, and we're running out of time." Brannock stumbles as he starts to move. "Fuck, this isn't easy," he grumbles as he catches himself. I'm not even sure how they move, to be honest. There are no visible legs, they kind of just shuffle. At this rate, it's going to take us forever.

I fly ahead of them and spy a travelator, so I wave at them. "Over here." If we continue at the rate they are going, we will never get anywhere. I'm going to have to keep an eye on both of them so they don't get chomped on by anything on the planet. They certainly can't run out of the way.

It's all I can do to keep a straight face as I watch the two of them move clumsily to the travelator. They both heave a sigh of relief as they make it there, and it starts moving them along the halls of the space station.

I flit above them, still feeling weary, but at least I'm not incapacitated. I didn't really get a good look around the station last time, and it's a fascinating blend of weird and wonderful. My eyes tend to linger on the more inhuman aliens that are all kinds of shapes and sizes, but as we move along, I spy someone I know.

"Glup, you motherfucker!" I shout at the Gurko who is talking to another of his species. I dart down so I'm in his shocked face.

"You messed with the wrong fucking girl," I growl at him, and he looks confused before snarling back at me.

"I don't know who you are, little fairy, but you better get out of my face before I eat you." He bares his teeth and snaps them at me, then I remember I'm in a different form, so there's no way he's going to remember.

"Does the name Lila Adams ring a bell?"

His snarl drops, and his blue skin turns pale as his eyes dart around. "No, I don't know anyone by that name," he mutters as he sighs when he doesn't see my original form.

"Oh, I beg to differ. I know exactly what you did to her, and now it's time for a little payback." My fury is righteous, and I allow my elemental form to shift into her more primal counterpart. My limbs grow, getting thicker and larger, fur sprouting out of my skin as I feel my head grow and my teeth lengthen, my antler style horns hardening to weapons. The wings on my back grow bigger as I set down on the ground and reach for the little troll who is a lot shorter than me now. I hear him whimper, and I feel a rush of excitement. I know that this form is technically an herbivore, but it also seems to have a slight penchant for destruction.

I lift Glup up into the air, and the other Gurko he was speaking to comes at me with his taser-like baton at the ready, but I just kick out a leg, and he goes flying across the room. I hear a loud thud as he hits the wall, but I don't bother to turn around, my focus on the being in my hands. I roar loudly in his face, and he squeals like a small child. A rush of adrenaline flows through me, and I smile, displaying all of my very large teeth.

"Put me down, put me down!" he cries, his terror obvious as he bangs his fists against my furry forearms, but I barely feel it. I shake him like a Polaroid picture, amused to see the way his eyes roll and his head snaps back and forth before slamming him down on the ground, WWE style. I use my foot to pulverize his face into the metal floor. I know that if I push just a little harder, I could pop his skull like it was a grape. As much as I would like to kill him, I don't, because that would draw too much attention. Instead, I haul back and wave a hand. The metal floor shimmers and glides up, responding to my bidding, surrounding Glup in a cage barely big enough for him to sit up in.

I lean in and whisper, "Lila's coming for you, so you better watch out."

He blanches and wraps his hands around the bars of the cage, trying to rattle them, but they are solid. Hopefully they can find another earth elemental or someone else with metallurgy abilities to remove him, otherwise he's going to be an interesting exhibit for all the station visitors.

I turn and walk away, allowing my primal form to recede, and a wave of tiredness washes over me as I catch up to Brannock and Xavier, who were stuck on the travelator, unable to get off to come to my assistance. They are almost to the end, and I see them both heave a sigh of relief when I fly into sight.

I wait for them at the end of the moving walkway, and when they get to me, Xavier—or I think it's Xavier, since they are basically identical—snatches me up and runs his hands all over my body to check that I'm okay. The hands linger slightly on my small breasts. Yup, it's Xavier. I slap his hands away. There's no time to have fun in this form. It's actually something we haven't tried, playing in my other forms, so I must remember to suggest it when we have less important matters to attend to.

"Who was that?" Brannock asks, looking back at the crowd of people who have gathered around the makeshift cage.

"That was the motherfucker who handed me over to the carevasta bears."

Both corn men's faces turn cloudy, and they start to head back in the other direction, but I grab their leaves with both hands and stop them. "We don't have time for revenge now. I put the fear of Lila in him. He's going to be constantly looking over his shoulder if he ever gets out of that cage," I tell them, smirking at my ingenious idea.

Xavier chuckles with approval. "Vindictive, I like it."

I have to tug harder on Brannock's leaf to get him to relent.

"I will kill him for you, Lila, to save you from having to do it yourself," he offers, and I can see he's trying hard to hold his glamour. It keeps shimmering. I look around, hoping nobody notices, pushing him up against a wall and grabbing his head between my two little hands.

"Brannock, look at me," I demand, his gaze locked on the Gurko in a cage. I shake him to get his attention, and his eyes finally drift to mine. I feel Xavier tuck in behind me to block us from sight, my tiny form definitely not enough to do that. "Hold it together."

There's a vicious rumbling sound coming from deep inside his chest, and his form flickers slightly. "He gave you over to be a sex slave. He will die," he grits out, his form still flickering.

"Lila, if he loses his shit, we are in big trouble. If his berserker mode activates, he will slaughter anyone in sight."

"Wasn't he in berserker mode earlier?" I ask Xavier, and he shakes his head.

"No, he had just taken that form. Berserker mode flips, and it's like they lose all sense of reasoning, like a rabid animal. They only come out of it when everyone around them is dead. It's what made them so formidable during the war."

"Formidable? I would say downright terrifying. Fuck, okay, we need to distract him." I don't wait for Xavier to make a suggestion. Instead, I press my lips to his, kissing him hard. The rumbling cuts off abruptly, and his eyes widen in shock, but it doesn't take long for him to respond, and he kisses me back. It's a little strange, my tiny mouth on his big, bubbly one, but we make it work. His arms drift up until he clasps my waist, and he pulls me toward his body.

"Well, I guess that's one way to distract him," Xavier comments behind me, sounding amused. I'm kind of lost in the kiss, though, and the way his hands feel on my body. He has fat, stubby fingers that would feel amazing pushing in and out of my pussy.

"Whoa." I pull back in shock, surprised that my thoughts went there. I blink to clear the foggy lust and look at the man in front of me. His glamour has stabilized, and he's looking back at me with wide-eyed amazement.

"You kissed me." A finger drifts up to his lips, and I feel my core throb at seeing the thick stubby thing. I need to pinch myself. *Bad Lila.*

"Ah, yeah, I mean you were pretty damned focused on killing Glup. I don't think that would have done us any favors." A rush of embarrassment prickles at my skin. I can't believe I just forced him to kiss me.

Phoeall, *you didn't have to try very hard, trust me,* Xavier reassures me. *He enjoyed it very much.*

Brannock is still staring at me with wide-eyed surprise—or as wide as the little piggy eyes they have can get. "You kissed me?" he repeats, sounding bewildered, and my embarrassment rises. Time to go.

"Ah, um, we should get moving." I break away and fly the rest of the way to the bar, waiting for the two men to reach me. There seems to be a large crowd of people hoping to get hired on to be halla harvesters.

When they catch up, Xavier doesn't wait at the back of the line, instead pushing through the crowd like a bulldozer. I allow the two of them to take the lead, and I follow behind—flying above the crowd is faster anyway. We make it to the front where there are two people sitting at a desk, talking to prospective employees.

"Why is it so busy?" I whisper in Xavier's ear.

"Because the amount they pay far outweighs the perceived danger. People are idiots, and greed plays a big part in the decision to be a halla harvester. It's what the brewers are counting on. It's also why halla mead is so expensive."

The two beings sitting at the table are a species I recognize. "Didn't you have one of these in your harem?" I say quietly out of the side of my mouth, and he gives me a wink. I glare at him. Both of them are like human trees, with foliage for hair, and their skin looks like bark. The one on the left's eyes brighten when they see Xavier.

"Dopnoo! Finally, someone who knows what they are doing. We haven't had many people return from the last outing." He exchanges a nervous glance with his counterpart.

Xavier scoffs. "Oak, Elm. Good to see you both. Is it any surprise? We lost four harvesters. I would say people are starting to wise up."

"Shh," the other one hisses, looking wildly around the room in the hope nobody heard Xavier's comment. "Let's not make that common knowledge. We need to double our crew this trip, and you'll scare off the prospects."

"Well, I'm here, and this is my brother, Dipee, and our little friend Vika." He points first to Brannock and then me. He makes "little friend" sound suggestive, and the two tree dudes eye me skeptically. Right, do the corn dudes even have dicks? I mean, I can't see anything that looks like one.

If I had the ability to mimic like you, I could show you, Xavier muses inside my mind, and it takes all my control not to roll my eyes with the attention of the two overseers still on me.

"Excellent. Earth elementals are always welcome. You did warn her that she wouldn't be able to control the plants though." Oak looks at Xavier who nods, or I guess bows, really, in acknowledgement.

"Yes, but she's been in space for too long and

needs to be one with her element. She's aware of the danger."

"Right then. Sign here, and welcome to the crew." Elm slides a tablet over, which looks like an indemnity form releasing them from any responsibility should we be maimed, injured, or killed on the job. The three of us sign our aliases, and Oak and Elm give us instructions to meet them at their ship in the docking bay in an hour.

We get pushed to the side as the next person steps up, and we make our way back through the crowd of aliens, returning to the outside of the bar.

CHAPTER ELEVEN

Lila

"Right, so we have an hour to kill. Should we find a few more aliens for you to mimic?" Xavier says, rubbing his stubby hands together and looking around.

"Probably shouldn't," Brannock grumbles, not meeting our eyes. "We need her to save her strength for Husadavia. She would use up a lot of energy shifting back and forth between forms, and then she would have to refuel." His words trail off as if he's embarrassed to remind me that I need sex to refuel.

Xavier eyes the Aaz'axian, mulling over his words before a sly smile crosses his lips. "I mean, that's not a problem if you're willing to help out."

Brannock and I have exactly the same reaction.

Our mouths drop open in surprise, and we stare at my warlock husband in shock.

"Seriously?" I ask, sounding a little miffed, and he shrugs—or this glamour's version of a shrug, which almost looks like a jump.

"Look, we both know you're attracted to each other, and honestly, I don't know why you're dancing around it. As far as I'm concerned, we're killing two birds with one stone. You get more forms to choose from, and Brannock gets to fuck a woman who he is compatible with. For God's sake, Lila, the man hasn't finished inside a woman in over six hundred years. Take pity on the poor guy."

I'm speechless, but Brannock isn't. He glares at my husband, and his glamour flickers again. "I don't need a pity fuck," he growls.

Xavier rolls his eyes. "Hardly a pity fuck. She's into you, and you're into her, so what's the big deal?"

What the actual fuck? I can't believe this male. Is he really this fucking clueless? I know warlocks are blasé about sex, but he should at least know me better than that by now. I mean, yeah, I'm most definitely attracted to Brannock, and I know he feels the same way, but I kind of want it to happen organically, like maybe go on a date and see how that goes. That might be a little naïve, considering all but one of my relationships has been forced, so to speak, but a girl likes to be wined and dined and not just sixty-nined…Well, I mean, the sixty-nine is a lot of fun too, but not essential until maybe like the second date.

Anyway, I digress. I want to throttle Xavier. If he had a neck, I would wrap my hands around it and squeeze while I watched him turn even more purple than he normally is.

Brannock and I look to be on the same wavelength, if his glare is anything to go by, but Xavier just huffs and changes the subject. "Fine, it was just a suggestion. You don't have to get pissy." Now he appears like he's sulking.

We head back the way we came, an awkward silence falling between us. I keep looking at Brannock out of the corner of my eye. I want to make sure he knows that I wasn't rejecting him so much as the timing.

He won't even look at me now, and that pisses me off. We pass a little alcove, and I push him into it, leaving Xavier to continue on his way, not even noticing we stopped.

"Whoa!" Brannock teeters a little but manages to stay upright. I wince, because I forgot they aren't very mobile in this shape. It still blows my mind that the glamour is solid and not just an illusion on top of their normal forms. I reach out to help steady him. "What's wrong?" he asks, looking around for danger. His form flickers once more in agitation. He really struggles to hold his glamour when he's emotional. I remember him saying alcohol affects it too, which is no surprise.

"Nothing's wrong, I just wanted to take a moment to talk to you without the other asshat adding his galactic two cents."

The flickering settles down, and his breathing slows, but there's still a wary look in his eye, and he crosses his arms. "Okay?" I can feel how defensive and hurt he is, even in this form.

Now I feel awkward as fuck, but I'm going to pull up my metaphorical big girl pants and woman up. "You do know I'm attracted to you, right? If we ever have sex, in no way will it ever be a pity fuck," I tell him, and I think I surprise him. "But I also don't want the first time we have sex to be about powering me up like a Super Mario mushroom."

I'm rambling with my nerves, and I can tell by the little crease between his eyes that I lost him with that reference.

I sigh. "Look, I think you're sexy as fuck and would really like to take you for a spin in whatever form you want to. If that means your cock treats my inner lady walls like a pin cushion and tears me to shreds, then so be it…" I trail off and think about what I just said. Oh my god, now I want to slap myself. What the fuck just came out of my mouth?

Luckily, Brannock's mouth twitches like he's trying to stop himself from laughing. His hurt is gone, replaced with amusement and no small amount of lust. "That's a very generous offer, Lila, thank you."

"Okay, cool, just so we're clear." My wings beat

faster as I prepare to escape this absolute clusterfuck of a conversation. How did I think I could make the situation any better? If anything, I just made it worse. Before I can leave, though, his hand shoots out and grabs me, slowly pulling me against his bumpy, corn kernel body. He pushes my long green hair back behind one of my little pointed ears, his fingertips brushing against a horn, causing a shiver to run down my spine, and leans in.

"When I tear your pussy to shreds, you will be begging for it," he whispers before releasing me and waddling off down the hallway in the same direction Xavier went in, leaving me panting with suddenly wet thighs. It's super unsexy watching him walk away, but I imagine what he normally looks like, and that's way better.

"Holy fuck!" I didn't think Brannock had it in him, but that was hot. I wave my hand in front of my face, trying to cool myself off with very little success. Well, at least I know we are both on the same page.

When I leave the alcove, I see the two of them waddling together. Xavier must have stopped and waited for us. I'm grateful he gave us a moment to chat without adding his damn commentary to the conversation. He winks at me when I get to them, and we keep moving.

We maneuver through the crowds milling around storefronts and dining establishments. This space station seems to be popular. One of the guys told me it has a more unsavory clientele than the other space station, X69. My eyes don't know where to stop as I look over the different beings, but there's something on my mind that's been plaguing me since I saw the tree men at the sign-up, so I drop down to ear height with Xavier so I can ask him a quiet question.

"Did you fuck all of your harem members?" I ask him as I bite my lip, unable to hide my worry. He frowns and looks at me with a raised eyebrow.

"Why do you ask, *phoeall*?"

I guess I wasn't doing a good job of controlling my anxiety. "Because I'm worried that our sex life has been fairly vanilla if you're used to fucking different alien species." Sure, his harem girls were all warlocks, but the men were a collection of weird and wonderful creatures. I'm worried that he's going to start looking elsewhere for the spice, and it's not like my guys are all that different. He said he can feed exclusively from me now that our intimate bond is established, but I'm sure it's probably tastier when it's kinky.

"Should I be shifting into my alternate forms like this so that you can have some fun?" I ask him, waving at my little fairy body. I'm almost certain Xavier will split me in half with his cock in this form, but I'd still be willing to take one for the team. I think about my other forms. There's the Barcoa, but I'm pretty sure neither of us want to fuck like that. There is also my necro form, which I avoid using because it's slightly terrifying being able to communicate with the dead, and I'm pretty sure my Madovian form would kill Xavier as quickly as fuck him, since she's the hardest to control, and to be honest, Madovian sex is fucking disturbing.

The confusion on his face clears and is replaced with a smile and sympathetic understanding. "No, baby." He stops, spins, and holds up his arms to catch me. They aren't long enough to reach me, so I drop down, and he gathers me into his embrace, holding me against his bumpy torso. I relax into him, enjoying a moment in my husband's arms. My insecurity slowly drifts away. "While I would have fun playing with whatever form you want, I don't need or crave it. You are everything I could ever want or need in a sexy, curvy package. The fact that you allow me to play with your other mates as well is more than I could ever wish for, and I am so very grateful that you are such a generous, loving woman."

"Well, I mean, they are your mates too, right? That's what being married is about. What's mine is yours, and what's yours is mine." I pull back and wink at him, feeling relieved, and he chuckles, giving me a quick kiss before letting me go.

"Indeed, I like your way of thinking."

I flutter my wings and rise, taking the lead before asking something else that has been plaguing my mind.

"So, I was wondering, when the grandpas first

told me I was Skarrian and what being mated was about, they said I could gain powers from my new mates, and they could get them from me, but so far, I seem to have gained everything and you guys nothing."

"I wouldn't say we've gained nothing," my husband quickly argues. "In fact, you could say we have all gained so much more than boring old powers."

"Aww, and this is why I keep you around." I blow him a kiss, and he grabs it from the air. I like that I can see him—or a version of him. If he was in his warlock form, he would be all shrouded in mystery. I mean, I get it, it gets strong reactions, fear being the greatest, but I like being able to look at him, even if he does resemble a shuffling corncob at the moment.

"Didn't you mate most of them in their own species' way?" Brannock asks, and I think about it. Cas, Xavier, Saxon, Echo, Max, and Nikos all mated me in their way. Link is the only one who mated me the Skarrian way.

"Yeah, so does that mean there isn't a crossover? Why isn't Link showing any signs of my mimic or whisperer powers?" I ask the Aaz'axian.

"I don't know for sure, but I'm going to guess that's why none of them have gained your powers. As for Link, it's probably because he's a cyborg. Magic, which I guess is what Skarrian power is at its core, doesn't work for them."

Xavier cuts in. "Their nanobot abilities, which you have shown remarkable control over" —he winks— "is purely technologically based. There's nothing magical about it but pure science, so he wouldn't be able to wield your powers anyway."

I mull over the two explanations, and that seems to make sense. "Yeah, okay, I guess I can see what you're saying. I just kind of feel like maybe they all got the short end of the stick." I hadn't realized how much it had been bothering me because I've been so busy, but now that we're talking about it, I realize it really does. I don't want them to resent me further down the line.

Xavier opens his mouth to argue, but Brannock gets there first, scoffing loudly. "Think about it this way. If they mated their own species, it wouldn't be any different, would it? They wouldn't have gained any extra abilities. I think they are lucky and extremely thankful for their beautiful and loving mate." I can see the longing in his eyes before he turns away from me.

"Also, if Caspian mated a fellow shifter, especially a kraken shifter, he would have been expected to ignore his bisexual urges. How unhappy would he have been locked into a relationship like that because that's what his animal requires? The man's soul would wither, and he would end up resenting that mate." Xavier shudders at the thought, because he was in the same boat.

"He told me that his kraken wasn't interested in

men prior to our mating but is super happy to have fun now that we are mated and have the babies."

Brannock nods. "That's no surprise. Most alien species are primal, and survival of the species is definitely a major need. Once that need has been met, then they tend to relax a little."

"Okay, I guess I can understand that. I just worry I'm not going to be enough, that the lightning cats need more cats in their streak, Xavier's kinky side is being stifled, and there isn't enough of me to go around with the seven mates I have now, not to mention three babies with four more on the way, let alone the males my mimic side is pressing me to seal to us." I wince at how desperate I sound.

"From what I know about you, Lila Adams, I would say those worries are unfounded. I have spent the last few weeks watching you with your mates, and I can confidently say every single one of them is happy and having their needs met. I haven't ever seen such a joyful and flourishing mating circle as yours, and that's with all the added stress you've been under. Remember, I'm as old as dirt and recall a time when mimics were more common. Relationships are hard work, but you seem to be coping wonderfully."

My heart thuds hard inside my chest at Brannock's words, and my mimic powers pulse erratically. It's all I can do to stop myself from tackling him, riding him to the ground, and buttering his corncob. My mimic side wants this man with a fierceness that is hard to control, and I'm certainly coming around to the idea.

Damn it, Lila, if you don't mate that man, I might have to do it for you, Xavier says in my head. *Who would have guessed he was so in touch with his emotions?*

"Thank you, Brannock. I really needed to hear that. It has been a whirlwind since I arrived at the circus."

"Don't forget you don't always have to be strong, Lila Adams. The universe gave you so many mates for a reason. Use them to lean on when you are doubting yourself, and you will never go wrong." He starts walking again, leaving Xavier and me to exchange another look.

"Seriously, if you don't ride him like a pony, I will," my husband growls and tries to stomp off, but he fails and falls on his face instead, rolling until he hits the wall of the hallway. Colorful curses pepper the air as I watch him struggle to right himself. I take pity on him and fly down, grabbing his hand to pull him back to his feet, my elemental form so much stronger than it appears.

He glares at me before muttering, "Thank you," then adds, "I mean it, Lila, you husband that man up and make him a part of our family. We need someone else with emotional depth, and he has it in spades. Who would have thought an Aaz'axian would be so thoughtful and caring?"

"It doesn't hurt that he's sexy as fuck in his real

form." I arch a questioning eyebrow, and he rolls his eyes.

"No, it doesn't hurt at all, but remember, none of us will be able to play with him, Lila, not with his spiky appendage. This is all about you." He sounds defensive, and I didn't mean to do that to him.

"I'm sorry, I was just messing around." My apology doesn't seem to appease his mood.

"Not all of us are bisexual, and you need to remember that. A good portion of us are, but Brannock and Tirrian haven't ever shown any sign of it." He sounds grumpy as fuck as we follow the Aaz'axian who has gotten a little farther ahead of us. "Don't assume I'm encouraging you to add mates for my benefit, because I can assure you, that's not the case."

"Whoa, wait, I'm sorry. I never thought that was the case," I apologize, feeling guilty. I never thought that, but I guess my joke may have made it seem that way. He heaves out a sigh and waves a stubby hand at me.

"No, it's fine. I'm sorry too. I guess I just want you to be happy, and I can feel what you feel for him, not to mention the snake. There's also your attraction to Ghosie, and despite his asshole ways, Tirrian, so in my mind, mating them all is the key to your happiness. An added bonus is that having all these powerful and dangerous men around you would help ensure your safety, because we know people will be coming for you." I stare at Xavier in astonishment. I had no idea he was so worried about everything. He certainly does a good job of keeping a wall up around his emotions.

I stop and throw my arms around my warlock and snuggle against him. "I love you. I promise I'm working on it all. Stop hiding how you're feeling from me. I know it's still a reflex from your harem, but I'm your mate. I want it all, the good and the bad," I tell him, and his relief is visceral as he practically sags against me. I give him a few quick kisses and stroke my hand over his nubby head before pulling away. "Okay, let's get our minds on the job. We have a grandma to rescue and a planet of bloodthirsty creatures to thwart. We will worry about my thirsty mimic side once this is done, I promise."

We're just about back at the space dock, and I see Brannock inside, waiting for us, so we break apart and make our way to him. Xavier will lead us to whichever ship belongs to the harvesters.

CHAPTER TWELVE

Lila

The two day trip to Husadavia feels like an eternity, and I can feel my form getting weaker. There's still no sign of the mysterious hooded figure from Dopnoo's mind, but when there was a crew meeting once all the hires were on board, we were told to stay clear of the top level of this ship.

All hundred of us are confined to the bottom level, which contains shared lodgings, the flight deck, and a cafeteria. The cafeteria is loud and smelly, and I decide that spending my trip in our assigned space is much preferable. The three of us stay in a shared room, and I decide to switch back to Skarrian form just so I can be comfortable. Once I'm no longer in my earth elemental form, the weakness disappears. I stay behind closed doors, but Brannock and Xavier do some recon. Xavier switches from his glamour to his usual mist so he can snoop on the top level, but he finds a barrier that wouldn't allow him to pass.

"I can't believe I couldn't get through that barrier. The elevator door opened, and it was like I was trying to pass through a solid wall. There wasn't a single crack to be found for me to get through it." He's running a hand through his long dark hair, his glamour dropped in the privacy of our room.

Brannock and I watch him pace back and forth, muttering about being one of the most powerful beings in the universe and what could possibly be more powerful than him.

"A blow to his ego, isn't it?" Brannock mutters out of the corner of his mouth, his eyes sparkling with amusement. I can't stop my giggle, and Xavier whirls to glare at us.

"Comments from the peanut gallery are not welcome. If you want to be heard, say something that might actually be helpful," he sneers at Brannock, whose eyes narrow. Brannock drops the amusement and becomes serious, crossing his arms and leaning back against the bed he commandeered as his own.

"Your magic is powerful, very powerful, but you are still very young, and despite what you think you know, there are more powerful beings in the universe—beings who have faded from most races' knowledge."

Xavier stops pacing. "Like what?" he demands, his arrogance and annoyance making him forget what we had been speaking about previously.

"You're talking about the old gods, right?" I ask him.

Brannock nods. "Yes. I was around prior to the war, and I remember when the galaxy used to worship the gods."

Xavier takes a seat on his single bed and leans back, finally calming. "There were six, correct?"

"Yes, life and death as well as four elemental gods. Each of them was responsible for creating life throughout the galaxy. For example, Aaz'axians were created by the goddess of death, same with Vilaxians. Una's come from the goddess of life. Obviously, each elemental species comes from one of the corresponding gods. Aquilians are from the water elemental god and so on."

"Okay, and each of these deities were worshiped by their creations. So what happened? Why did it stop?" I ask, fascinated by this new piece of history.

"And where did they go?" Xavier is less fascinated and more suspicious. "If they were so powerful, then how could they have disappeared?"

"Nobody seems to know. It was right before the Una's orb of power became common knowledge and war broke out. With that happening, I guess the knowledge of the gods was forgotten, and when the war came to an end, the council was formed."

"They just disappeared? Poof." Xavier makes an exploding motion with his hands. "They couldn't have been all that powerful then."

Brannock shrugs, the membrane floating between his spines, rippling prettily with the movement. "Maybe without worship, their power diminished, or maybe they were sick of this galaxy and their wars and petty jealousies, so they left our realm in search of somewhere else to colonize. I guess we'll never know." He side-eyes Xavier and smirks. "Or they could be hiding in plain sight, waiting for the right moment to reveal themselves to the galaxy again."

Xavier blinks then scoffs. "You think an almighty god with the power of creation would lower themselves to be a creature repellant for some greedy entrepreneurs? Not likely."

Brannock chuckles. "No, it's not likely, but it made you stop and think. The galaxy is huge, and we really don't know everything that's out there. Warlocks came from another dimension, so what's to say there isn't another powerful race somewhere out there who did the same thing?"

This has Xavier frowning as he takes in what Brannock just said. "Fuck, I had never considered that," he admits, rubbing a hand over his chin in thought. "We managed to rip a hole in the fabric of the realms, so I'm sure there are others capable of doing the same."

"Exactly."

"Which means Lila is in more danger than I thought. Maybe we should abort this mission," he suggests, looking at me, and I see the worry in his eyes.

"Uh-uh, no way. This mission is a go," I argue with him, shaking my head. "We aren't turning around now, my grandpas would be devastated. Look, we have Tirrian following us in the air, and Saxon and Silac on standby to beam down if anything goes sideways. Ghosie is ready to do his thing with the stasis box. We have this. I'm going to mimic this repelling creature, and we're going to go into the heart of the death forest and bring my grandma back. I've been thinking about it, and if worse comes to worse, I'll assume the necro form and suck out the souls of everything that comes at us. These things may be dangerous, but surely they aren't unkillable."

I watch him roll my argument around in his head, but he finally nods. "Okay. You're right. We can't leave Liliana trapped forever, but don't take any risks, Lila. Your grandpas would be incon-solable if anything happened to you, not to mention your mates would be shattered beyond recognition."

I agree to his requests, liking my life a little too much to risk it to such extreme degrees. If we have to abort, then we will come up with another plan, but I have to at least try this first.

Brannock and Xavier decide to wear their glamours and continue mingling with the rest of the crew to see if they can get any more information on the planet—mostly how far away the halla fields are from the death forest. I decide to nap. There isn't anything else to do while we wait, and we still have one more day of travel. I just hope the galaxy ship on our tail is cloaked.

I drift off to sleep, and my dreams are weird. I see flashes of beautiful, glowing creatures creating worlds and watching over them like benevolent overseers. Their creations are happy and thriving, and I instinctively know that the earlier conversation about creation gods must have triggered these dreams. These are most definitely godlike beings, but then little by little, the mood of the dreamscape starts to change. I feel envy and jealousy pulsing from one of the beings, but when I try to look closer, I can't make out which god it is. Then things shift, and there is infighting, petty arguments that turn to scheming before a massive betrayal. It's all a jumbled, blurry rush of images, sights, and sounds, and all these feelings don't point to the reason why or how.

I toss and turn as the scenes move from the gods to their creations. I watch as the Una's appear with the orb of power, sharing it amongst the galaxy, and then the mood changes, getting darker. I watch as the Aaz'axian leadership discovers they can harness that power into a weapon. The Una's heartbreak is like a stab in the chest, and I watch on as they retrieve the power they shared, locking it into the orb once more. The Aaz'axians' fury thrums in my soul like it's my own, and I flinch in my sleep.

The scene changes again, and this time I feel my cheeks grow damp as tears trickle down my face. I watch on, helpless to do anything but be a captive audience to the war amongst the galaxy, unable to wake myself from this nightmare, as the Aaz'axian leadership forces their people to decimate the Una's and anyone who gets in their way. Bodies lie broken and unmoving in the wake of the Aaz'axian forces. I observe in horror as the Aaz'axians try to refuse the command chip, and they end up dying along with the people they are trying to subjugate. The Aaz'axian women get sick and start dying, and the Una's are reduced to mere hundreds. Reel after reel of death, destruction, and devastation play out.

Finally, I see the Una's on Skar, meeting with an Adams ancestor, and I watch as the remaining Una's are absorbed into the orb, sacrificing themselves to smother the power signature of the orb so there is no way of it being found. Then, I hear the whispered words, "You are the key, Lila Adams."

I sit bolt upright, my breath heaving from my chest, and my body damp with sweat. I wipe at my tear-stained cheeks as I replay everything in my mind, getting stuck on those final murmured words. The key? How am I the key? Surely my dreams were just a product of my overactive imagination after the conversation with Brannock and Xavier. Who knows if that's what happened? My mind is trying to make sense of it all and is creating its own scenarios. I get up and go to the sink in the small, attached bathroom, getting myself a glass of water. I drink the whole thing down, trying to soothe my overheated body and scratchy throat. Note to self—no heavy conversations before bedtime. My overactive imagination extends into my dreams and makes getting a restful night's sleep impossible.

Feeling drained and mentally exhausted, I climb back into bed. I kind of wish Xavier was here. I could use a little distraction, but I know he won't drop his guard while we are on a ship with unknowns, so I close my eyes and hope that when I sleep, my dreams will be filled with sexy times with my mates or spending time with my children instead of gruesome clips of war and destruction.

We have finally arrived in orbit around Husadavia. We are instructed to meet after breakfast in the transporter room where we will be beamed down to the planet. The harvesting equipment has already been sent ahead and will be waiting the moment we touch down.

"There are eight different fields of halla fruit spread across the planet. One of them sits on the very edge of the death forest. We need to make our move then," Brannock explains quietly as we sit at a table, eating our breakfast.

"When do we get to that field?" I ask, knowing they have memorized the schedule.

"It's on the third day in the afternoon," Xavier tells me, taking a sip of his drink. I'm really not hungry, since my nerves are pretty high, but I attempt to eat the meal in front of me. It's a brown gruel-like mixture that is supposed to be hearty and filling for the workers. It doesn't taste too bad, like oatmeal with some brown sugar mixed into it.

Apparently, we will spend eight hours a day harvesting before returning to the ship to rest overnight before starting again. Lunch will be provided down on the planet in the form of sand-wiches and fruit, and dinner will be served when we return.

"We probably have four hours of daylight to find her before it gets dark, and from my experience during the war, we don't want to be on the planet in the dark," Brannock tells us. "Most of the creatures on this planet are nocturnal. During the day, we only have to contend with the aggressive plants and one or two smaller predators. At night, the large predators will create insurmountable odds. It's when we lost most of our regiment when we tried to establish a base here."

That's right, I forgot that was one of the main reasons he was part of the mission—his previous experience.

"But the small daytime predators are in large numbers, which is what makes them dangerous. If there were only one or two, you would have no problem defending yourself against them, but there are so many of them that they can decimate a being in seconds. The plants are just as aggressive. Most of them are triggered by movement, because they survive on consuming the smaller animals. There's also a vine which will wrap you up, paralyze you, and then consume you over a period of time."

"Can the vine be destroyed?" I ask, thinking that would solve the problem of being consumed.

"Yes, fire will work, but the victim was still paralyzed, and we weren't able to cure them. They fell into a coma and the poison killed them."

"Fuck." Xavier scrubs a hand across his head, but he has no hair to yank on in his glamour.

"Hang on, don't forget I have my Celestian form. I should be able to heal anything if we need it," I remind them, and they both look a little less frustrated.

"Yes, but it means changing forms. We'll save it as a last resort," Xavier replies, reminding me that I need sex to fuel my mimic power, which really wouldn't be a problem if I would stop being so sensitive and fuck Brannock. I want it to be for better reasons then I need a power boost though.

"Okay, I suggest we stay in the middle of the pack of harvesters. The ones on the outer rim will get picked off first if they don't keep up with the being who repels everything," Brannock says. "We'll harvest, and Lila will try to mimic the being, and then we will be able to form a better plan after we do that."

"And we still haven't seen any sign of this being?" I ask, yawning, my eyes heavy with exhaustion. I'm back in my earth elemental form now, and it's a struggle. Seriously, we can't get down to the planet fast enough.

Before either of them can reply, a hush falls over the room, and the three of us look up.

Standing in the entrance to the cafeteria are Oak and Elm, the two tree dudes in charge of the harvesters, and behind them in the shadows is a hooded creature. The harvesters murmur quietly, one or two standing up to see if they can get a better look.

I try to subtly do the same, but all I can see is a long, dark hooded cape, and inside that hooded recess is nothing. Is the creature like the dementors out of *Harry Potter*? I look down to see if he's floating, but the cape is so long it drags along the ground, and I can't tell.

Xavier narrows his eyes, and I feel him stretch out with his powers, trying to get a read on the creature. He suddenly cries out and grabs his head, cursing quietly under his breath.

"Are you okay?" I ask him.

"Yeah. I don't know what he is, but he's powerful enough to keep me out of his brain. Maybe if I could see his eyes, it would be easier, but I have a feeling it won't work."

The being is looking directly at us, and I feel like maybe we've made a grave error by drawing his attention to us. We're on his radar now, and that may be a bad thing.

"Shit, let it go for now. We can try again on the planet. I'm sure he will be distracted while keeping the flora and fauna at bay," I suggest, and Xavier agrees.

"Are your mimic powers active? Could you mimic him like this?" Brannock whispers, and I shake my head.

I look inward, and I'm shocked to find that the usual insistent presence has disappeared. I shake my head. "Nope, there's nothing. In fact, they are the quietest they've been since I became aware of them. It's almost like they've become dormant."

Xavier and Brannock exchange another worried glance.

"Don't worry, I feel okay, apart from the elemental's weakness. Come on, we've got this." I try to be positive, but the whole time, I feel the hooded figure's gaze on us, even though Elm is talking to the rest of the harvesters now.

"We have ten minutes before we start sending you down to the surface in groups. Master Z will project a circle of green energy. This is what keeps the creatures at bay," Elm announces.

"Make sure you are aware of it at all times and stay within it as we move. If you lose track or don't pay attention and move outside the range of the circle, you will die. We won't put ourselves at risk to save you. You are responsible for your own safety," Oak adds, and there are a few worried looks amongst the harvesters, but they are here now, so I doubt they are going to be allowed to change their minds.

"You have a quota of three baskets per harvester a day. If you don't meet this quota, you will be punished. Do not make us punish you." Elm smacks a baton against his hand, and it pulses with electricity.

"Holy fuck, is that a cattle prod?" I feel a little ill. I hope the baskets aren't huge. This form is small, and I doubt I can manage as much as the rest of the harvesters.

"Yes, it looks like it," Brannock murmurs.

We watch as the hooded figure leans in and speaks to Elm and Oak, and all three of them turn to look at me.

"You, Elementi. You will be permitted to work with someone because you will not be able to manage the size of the basket, but the two of you must fill five baskets between you."

Fuck, I'm not sure that's as generous as they think it is. Am I being set up? My elemental powers should help. I can coax the tree to give up the fruit all at once instead of picking each individual piece, so maybe we will be okay.

"I'll work with Lila so you can concentrate on getting into Master Z's mind," Brannock offers, and Xavier bites his lip with worry but agrees.

"Okay, and tomorrow we can swap if I don't get anywhere."

The three boss beings disappear—I'm assuming to transport to the planet before us. We finish our meal and follow the crowd to transport down.

CHAPTER THIRTEEN

Lila

We beam down with the fourth group, and as soon as I hit the planet's surface, I shove my hands into the dirt, soaking up all the energy around me. As I absorb the energy from the ground, I take in the scenery. A large field of bushes stretches out in front of us, but there's an eerie sort of atmosphere and no sound—no leaves rustle in the breeze, and no insects or birds chirp. Surrounding us in a large circle is a green haze of magic that must be the protective dome we need to stay within.

"Ah, Lila. Better stop that," Xavier hisses out of the side of his mouth, and when I look around, I discover the plants next to me—big, dark green bushes that probably stand at normal head height for me, with bright orange strawberry-sized fruit on them—are drooping, and the fruit looks a little desiccated.

"Shit!" I yank my hands out of the soil, and the earth closes back up. I look around to see if anyone noticed. Oak and Elm are distracted handing out baskets, but the hooded being is looking directly at me.

I brush the dirt off my hands and move into the crowd as Brannock and Xavier get their baskets. I gaze at the field. It's more of an orchard than a field, the bushes almost tall enough to classify as trees. People are spread out, collecting the fruit, but on the edge of the field, I see a bunch of small creatures watching us. I walk closer, eyeing the hazy green circle we are encased by. I'm assuming that's the limit of the being's magic. Out of the corner of my eye, I see him tracking me just like I'm keeping an eye on where he is at all times.

My attention turns to the creatures, and a small smile crosses my lips. They are tiny balls of fluff, a little like a Furby toy I had when I was smaller crossed with a Pomeranian, and I have no idea how they protect themselves, because they are bright yellow, blue, and pink. I squat down to take a closer look, and one of them lunges at me, their teeth bared, followed by five more. I scream and scramble backward as they hit the magic barrier and disintegrate. Holy fuck, they had teeth like a piranha, and I have no doubt they would have eaten my face off.

I gasp for air as I try to settle my heart rate. The rest of the creatures move with agitation, like they really want to have a go at me.

"You shouldn't stir up the creatures," a quiet voice says from behind me, and when I look up from the ground, I freeze. The hooded being is standing over me. He's so close, I feel him brush against my wings, and a little shiver flows over me. He isn't looking at me, but at the swarming creatures, yet I still can't see within the darkness of his hood. Instead, my gaze drifts down his form, and I notice that the cape bulges in the back like he has a giant hump. Maybe he's deformed, and that's why he keeps himself covered. I feel a pang of sympathy for the creature. Suddenly, the bulge wiggles like he has a bunch of ferrets under the cloak, and they are excited to see me. I gasp in surprise, but slap my hand over my mouth, hoping he didn't hear it.

"Shoo." He waves a hand at the creatures, and I almost snort with amusement.

"Pretty sure that's not going to work, dude," I tell him, but as my gaze returns to the swarm of terrifyingly cute creatures, my mouth drops open. They turn around and disappear into the jungle that surrounds the field of halla bushes. Whoa, he really does have a way with the creatures here. Maybe he's a whisperer of some sort like me. I guess that wouldn't be too far-fetched.

"I am not deformed."

"Huh?" I shake my head and turn my attention to his words. Oh fuck, did I say that out loud?

"No, you didn't, young Elementi, but I heard it anyway. Come along, you do not want to get caught outside of my magic barrier. I do not make exceptions, even for one such as yourself." His words are a gentle reminder of the danger I just witnessed, but I feel safe and secure in the knowledge that he is protecting us. It's a weird kind of sensation, and I don't know how I feel about it or why I'm feeling that way. I thought I would be scared of him, but he radiates an aura that feels like an old friend.

He moves away, and I catch sight of a foot underneath the robe. It looked like a pale humanoid foot, but with claws for nails. I try to peer into the robes, but they sweep together before I can see anything else. Damn it, if he doesn't reveal himself, then how am I going to mimic him?

I think about what he just said and slam up barriers inside my brain. Holy fuck, he can read my mind. I'm still panicking when Brannock and Xavier find me, both carrying baskets bigger than my current form.

"Are you okay?" Xavier asks, holding out a hand to help me to my feet. I take it but use my wings to launch myself into the air.

"He can read minds," I hiss at him, and he looks around.

"Who?" he asks, and when I look around, I discover the being is now on the other side of the magic barrier. I don't know how he got there so quickly.

"Him." I nod in his direction, and both men turn to look.

"How do you know?" Brannock asks.

"He basically told me when he was over here."

"You spoke to him?" Xavier gapes at me in shock. "I was just having a conversation with one of the other harvesters Dopnoo is friendly with, and apparently, he never talks or interacts with anyone, and he's done three harvests."

Brannock nods. "Yes, I asked a few of the others as well, and they all said the same thing. He doesn't talk, and he never removes his cape."

"Well, we are going to have to come up with a plan, because I can't mimic what I can't see," I tell them, not to mention not knowing is driving me crazy. I just need to see what's under the hood now.

"Okay, but for now, we're starting to draw attention, so let's do the job while we try to come up with a plan." Brannock points at the basket in his hand. "We have to fill five of these today, or we'll be punished. The punishment will be bad. The beings I talked to were terrified of not getting their quota."

"Well, that fucking cattle prod didn't look like my idea of a good time either, so let's go." I bounce up and down in the air in agitation, not wanting to know whether this tiny form can take a hit from the stick or fry me like a lightning bug in a bug zapper.

"Okay, let's split up and try and gather as much

info as we can while we work," Xavier suggests, and with a wave, he wobbles off toward another group of harvesters and starts picking the fruit bushes. I follow Brannock in the opposite direction, and we find a tree that hasn't been harvested yet and get started. The fruit is almost as big as my hand in this form, and it's quite easy for me to pick, but it means I can only do two at a time before having to place them in the basket. I fly down, but I underestimate how delicate the fruit is, and I squish one of them in my grip. The fruit bursts, sending a spray of orange juice all over me. I freeze, hovering in the air, my body dripping. Holy crap, that was a lot of juice in a relatively small fruit. I hear a snort of amusement, and when I look up, I discover it isn't Brannock. He hasn't even noticed what happened, busy yanking the fruit from the bushes and filling our basket. He doesn't seem to have any trouble handling it.

I look around to see who is laughing at me and discover that once again, the hooded being's attention is on me. This isn't good.

"Handle them with care, little one. The juice will become uncomfortable if you end up wearing too much of it, and you will be that much more attractive to the flupkups." His warning is soft and caresses me like a hug, and I feel his concern for my safety.

Although I'm a little worried I have this being's attention, I'm also curious and can't help myself. "Flupkups?"

"The creatures from before. They are addicted to the halla fruit. It's what makes them so aggressive. You just became an even more tasty snack for them… and me." He mutters the last bit, but I must have heard wrong. He can't have said what I think he said.

I look down at myself. I'm starting to get sticky as the juice dries in the warm sun that shines down on us. When I look back up to respond, he's gone again, back on the other side of the magic barrier and standing over another group of harvesters. Did I imagine that?

"Uh, did you see that?" I fly down and around the bush to Brannock and the basket, dropping the fruit that survived in. He's moving quickly and already has a good layer covering the bottom of the basket.

He stops what he's doing and scans my tiny form. "Why are you wet?" he asks, reaching out and swiping his thumb across my lip, catching a stray drip. "And sticky?" He brings his thumb up to his mouth. "You're supposed to pick it, not play in it." His eyes sparkle with humor as I watch him suck the juice off his stubby digit, and I think about what other kinds of juices he could be sucking off.

Gah, focus, Lila, I scold myself internally. *Rescue Grandma then ride the Aaz'axian to celebrate.*

"Ah, the fruit is a little more delicate than I thought. I assumed they would be like an Earth citrus and thick-skinned, but they are more like a grape, with a thin membrane then full of juice on the inside with the smallest amount of pulp to hold it all together, and I just squeezed too hard."

He chuckles and keeps picking. "Did I see what?" he asks, reminding me of my question.

"That being was talking to me again," I tell him, and he stops picking and looks around.

"He's all the way over there. Are you sure it wasn't one of the other harvesters?" We both look at the bush next to us and the two beings who are working it. They are unusual, and I haven't seen their species before. Both of them have two heads and four arms on a black-skinned body. Each head has only one eye, but both have a nose and a mouth, with a long mane of pure, snow-white hair mohawked down the middle. Their bodies are large and brawny and seem to move with unnatural speed as they focus on the task of picking the fruit from the bushes.

"Nope, definitely not them."

"Hmmm, well, let's try not to draw his attention too much. I'm sure if we just do the job, he will lose interest in us."

"Okay," I agree, and then I groan as I look at how much we still have to put in the basket. "This is going to take us forever, and even longer if I keep squishing them." Manual labor and I do not play well together. I look around to make sure nobody is watching us, and then I hold my hands up. Ever since I came to this planet, I've felt power running through me—a connection to the plants. They seem to call to me. It's this low-key humming in the back of my mind. Focusing on the fruit, I coax it towards me, asking the bush to release its hold on its precious bounty.

I feel the bush's reluctance to give up its produce, but I continue to encourage it, and one by one, each individual fruit pops off and floats in the air. Once I feel like the bush has given me everything it has, I carefully direct the fruit to the basket, controlling its movement through a form of telekinesis, something I hadn't managed to produce at all in my Skarrian form.

The fruit lands gently in the basket, and I drop my hands, breathing a little heavily, my power drained, and then I drift down to the ground, my wings too tired to hold me up.

"Phew, that was hard work," I mutter to Brannock as we both look at the three-quarters full basket.

"Are you okay?" he asks, stepping toward me with a hand held out like he wants to support me.

I nod, leaning against the bush slightly to get my balance. A shadow passes over us, and when I look up to find what's causing it, I have to shade my eyes. The sun directly above is stopping me from seeing. I'm going to guess it was Tirrian, but I don't know for sure. I'm hoping it's not another unknown predator waiting to devour us.

I wave him off. "Yeah, I'm fine. It just took a lot out of me. My form isn't in full working order."

"That's because you spent too much time in space, little one." The chatty being is back, and Brannock hisses slightly before moving in front of me like he wants to protect me.

"Elementals are not supposed to be without their element for long periods of time. It can damage them permanently. You need to spend a few days here just to absorb what you need to from the surrounding environment. If you take too much at one time, that's when you suck the life out of things. I will arrange with Elm and Oak for you to stay on the planet overnight so you can heal."

"But don't all the predators come out at night? She won't survive even a few hours on her own," Brannock argues, and the being turns his attention to him—or I think he does, since we still can't see any features.

"You may as well drop that glamour, Aaz'axian. I can see right through it. You can tell the warlock the same thing. These creatures are slow and cumbersome, and they will not be a benefit to your harvesting job."

My mouth drops open in shock, and Brannock and I exchange a glance before he sighs. His glamour shimmers and fades away, leaving the pretty form I've grown attached to.

"As for her protection, I will ensure she is

unharmed," the being continues, but Brannock shakes his head, stubbornly crossing his arms.

"No way, for all I know, you will feed her to one of the predators the moment we return to the ship. We don't even know what you are, so how do you expect us to trust you with our friend?"

"That goes both ways, Aaz'axian. I am not the one who was pretending to be something I'm not."

Oh snap. I guess he has a point. I wonder if he knows that I am not really an Elementi either, but then again, I guess I am. He hasn't said anything, so I am not going to bring it up. Maybe this is the chance we need. Maybe if I spend time with him, I can convince him to help us rescue my grandma.

"Okay, I'll do it," I blurt out, and Brannock glares at me.

"No, you will not. It isn't safe. Remember what I told you about nighttime?" I roll my eyes, and Brannock's glare gets narrower.

"I assure you she will be perfectly protected by me."

Brannock growls at him. "I don't care, she's not staying."

"If she does not, she will die. This form cannot return to space as it is. It needs complete immersion within its element to begin healing. If she returns to space, she might not make it through the night."

Brannock's glare drops, and his expression turns to one of concern. He bites his lip and sighs.

"Your mates are going to kill me," he mutters

but nods his head. "Fine, but the warlock and I will stay as well."

"No, you will not. I cannot protect her to the best of my ability if I am protecting you two as well." Damn, this creature knows exactly the right things to say. "Now finish up your job. Trust me, you do not want to know what the punishment is for not achieving your quota." The being disappears, only to reappear across the field next to Xavier. We watch as he leans in and speaks to my warlock, who startles before looking at us. His eyes widen as he sees Brannock in his real form, and he heaves out a sigh of acceptance before his body returns to his normal warlock form, then his mist expands outwards, covering him from head to toe.

The harvesters who were sharing the same bush as him quickly back away, hurrying to find a space that is far from my husband. We watch as the two of them talk for a moment before the being returns to watching over the rest of the crew.

Lila, why is Master Z telling me that you will be staying on the planet overnight? Xavier growls into my head.

According to him, I will die if I return to the ship tonight. This Elementi needs complete immersion into the element to survive. They overdid it in space.

Just change forms, he snaps at me, but I shake my head.

No, this might be the chance we need. He might lose his hood and give me a chance to mimic him, or I might be able to convince him to help us with Grandma Liliana.

I will not leave you alone. You can't ask this of us. He sounds desperate and angry.

I know I shouldn't be asking you, but I am. Remember, I have the communicator to our ship, so I can signal to them if I need help, and they will send down Saxon, Silac, and Tirrian. I have backup, I remind him. I can feel his frustration, despair, and reluctant acceptance. *And I still have all the other forms at my fingertips if I need them.*

Fine, but if you die, Lila, I will find a necro to call your ghost, and I will lecture you for the rest of your undead life, he threatens, and I can feel how worried he is, so I let him be, sending waves of love and gratitude.

I know this could possibly be a too stupid to live moment, but I need to take the chance. I am confident in my abilities. Xavier trained me to the best of his knowledge, and I am secure with the fact that backup is just a teleporter away. There's also that feeling of familiarity I have for the being. There's just something about him that makes me feel safe, and if he can help me with the death forest, then I'm going to take any chance I can.

CHAPTER FOURTEEN

Lila

I'm unable to repeat the same trick that I did previously by using my magic to harvest the fruit, my energy being at an all-time low, so Brannock and I have to fill the baskets the old-fashioned way. Xavier has no limits anymore now that they are aware he is a warlock, and he completes his quota within the first hour. It took him a little bit to figure out how to magic the fruit off the bushes without them exploding, but he finally figured it out. We all had a laugh as he exploded a whole bunch, covering him and a few closer harvesters with the juices, but he was growled at by Oak and Elm. Neither of them is nervous around him because they don't know who he really is, and they threatened him with punishment if he did it again.

I kind of would have liked to have seen that, to be honest, but he got his magic under control, so I guess we won't.

When Elm and Oak discovered what he could do, though, they made him fill an extra ten baskets. I thought he was going to have a tantrum and announce that the crown prince of the warlocks did not do manual labor, but he surprised me by staying quiet. He is going by the name Xane, and when people asked why a warlock was harvesting fruit, he explained he was looking for a little adventure, telling everyone that Brannock and I are his harem when they ask.

By the end of the day, Brannock and I managed our quota, but I'm exhausted. I'm so tired, I can't even fly, so I walk alongside my Aaz'axian friend as he carries our final basket to be placed with the others that have been harvested. These are beamed aboard as the crew sits around, waiting for their turn to return to the ship. We are a sweaty, sticky group, but we had no casualties today, everyone staying within the green barrier as we moved across the field. There are quiet conversations happening all around us as Xavier approaches us in his mist form, taking a seat next to us. The people close by shuffle back, not wanting to get too close to the warlock. We overheard mutters of disapproval from our fellow crew members when he used his magic to make the job easier. Discontent isn't a favorable option in a crew like this. It breeds jealousy and aggression.

"You better watch your backs tonight. A few of these people are gunning for you," I tell him quietly, and Brannock nods, having also heard the rumbles.

Xavier scoffs. "We'll be fine. They'd have to be lucky to get the jump on either of us, though I'm kind of glad you are staying on the surface now. You would be the obvious target, since you're small and a part of my harem. That's one way to cut me down—remove my power source."

"I didn't think about that," I reply, my worry for them making me feel worse. My head is throbbing, and my stomach rolls with nausea. I'm not sure if that's because I'm hungry, worried, or my lack of energy.

"Okay, everyone, gather in the same groups you traveled down in, and let's get moving," Elm shouts. There are grumbles and groans, others obviously feeling the pain of hard work today. The clearing that was full of baskets is now empty, and it quickly fills up with the first group. We watch as they disappear, and the space is quickly filled with the next group, everyone eager to return to the ship for food, showers, and a rest.

I look around to find Master Z, unsure if I'm still supposed to remain on the planet or not. Maybe he was exaggerating about me dying if I didn't stay behind. I can't see him anywhere, so I decide to travel back to the ship. I'll head straight to my room and change into my Lila form, which should keep me from succumbing to the weakness of the earth elemental form, but I couldn't very well tell him that.

The third group disappears, and it's our turn. Just as I'm about to approach the clearing with Xavier and Brannock on either side of me, protecting me from our fellow crew, a hand lands on my shoulder, stopping me. I watch the people already in the clearing stumble backwards at Master Z's sudden appearance. I know it's him without even looking because that same wave of comforting warmth I've been feeling all day washes over me. It's like stepping into a warm bath on a cold winter night. The first bit stings a little before you practically melt into it.

"Come with me. She will be safe with me, I promise," he says to Brannock and Xavier. Xavier's mist slides inward, exposing his form to everyone. It's not his *true* form, but a slightly different version. He's pinker than his normal lavender hue, and his hair is not the deep indigo it normally is, but a pale lavender. He's still wearing all of my marks, but I can tell I'm the only one who can see them. He's making everyone else see a lot less of them to make light of how powerful he is.

I see the shock in Xavier's eyes, and he stutters slightly. I feel an instant rush of anxiety and try to step away from the being whose hand is on me. I have never seen my warlock at a loss for words, and my heartbeat starts to race, but he gives a resigned nod and puts his hand on Brannock to stop him just as they disappear.

My mouth drops open in shock once more. What the actual fuck? My husband just left with no arguments after one assurance from this creature. How did he get him to give in so easily? And what was the shock in his eyes? Why didn't he talk to me inside my head? Did he manage to get inside this being's brain? The warmth and comfort I was feeling seeps away, replaced with anxiety once more.

"No, I showed him who and what I am," Master Z mutters to me as the rest of the group gives us a wide berth as they continue to return to the ship until only Elm and Oak remain.

They approach us. Elm looks confused, glancing from me to the being behind me, but Oak looks pissed.

"What the fuck are you doing?" he snaps at the male behind me.

Elm stiffens and elbows his partner in the trunk, but Oak ignores him.

"If you want to use this little one as a fuck toy, I firmly applaud you. Maybe I'll have a turn once you're done. I'm sure the warlock won't mind. I've heard they like to share their harem and feed off the lust it creates, but you can do it back at the ship. I don't want anything to happen to her if you get bored. She is an asset to this operation, and when she's back to full power between her and the warlock, we should be able to harvest well above our quota for the season."

The being's hand tightens on my shoulder, and I feel the air around us chill significantly. Goosebumps break out over my skin, and a shiver of terror runs down my spine.

"Oh fuck." Elm backs away, holding his hands up. "I have nothing to do with this. You can do as you please. I have no quarrel with you." He makes a very smart choice. Too bad the same can't be said about Oak.

Oak still hasn't caught on to the danger right in front of him, but Elm backs far enough away so he's now in the clearing.

"Go," the being behind me intones, and Elm disappears in a wave of light, transporting to the safety of the ship.

Oak just crosses his arms and raises an impatient eyebrow. "Well, come on then."

Now it's just the three of us in the clearing, and I watch with horrified fascination as the green barrier that had been keeping us protected throughout the day starts to shrink, but Oak doesn't even notice.

He just taps an impatient foot, like he's dealing with two unruly toddlers. Fuck, can't he feel that ominous chill that resonates from the male behind me? I'm practically paralyzed with terror, even though I know I am not the focus of his anger.

The green barrier shrinks farther, and the sounds of nature that have been missing all day finally start to reach my ears. Terrifying yips and howls punch the air as the wind kicks up and starts to rustle the halla bushes, causing a few missed fruits to fall off here and there, littering the ground beneath them with orange blobs, because they split on impact.

Oak finally seems to catch on to the fact that he is in danger. He drops his arms and looks around as the barrier continues to shrink. It's only just surrounding the three of us now, and I can see the flupkups. They are worked up into a frenzy, a mass of writhing, energetic fur with overactive salivary glands and snapping teeth. They sound even scarier than the howls and yips, because they are kind of purring—a sound you expect to come from an overindulged, relaxed house cat. I have no doubt that if the barrier shrinks more, we will be devoured. I step back, feeling the being's body behind me, but I'm too scared of the furious Furbies to worry about who or what the creature behind me is. He made it pretty obvious that he means me no harm.

Unable to look away, I watch the green barrier shrink. Oak yelps and takes a step toward us. Master Z wraps his arms around my waist, yanking me against him, and takes another step back, shrinking the magic barrier even more. The scents of orange blossom and cedar reach my nose, and I relax again. The fragrance is comforting and slightly arousing, but I'm still alert to the danger occurring directly in front of me.

Oak shrieks as a bright blue flupkup latches onto his wooden arm. He shakes it hard and steps back into the circle of the magic barrier, the flupkup disintegrates on contact. His arm drips with a sappy-looking substance, which I'm assuming is his blood.

"Please don't," Oak begs, but I can see in his eyes, he's resigned to his fate. He shouldn't have spoken to a more powerful being, one who controls his safety like that. Even the naive Earth girl recognizes the truth in that.

The being gathers me closer to him, his touch gentle in a way I hadn't expected. I'm still unable to make out any of his features, his arms draped in that blasted cloak, but I feel safe and comfortable, so I don't struggle.

The barrier winks out of existence in a flash, and the flupkups pounce, Oak disappearing in a swarm of brightly colored fur. His screams are piercing and horrifying, and I feel a tear leak down my cheek as they cut off. I'm not sure he deserved that punishment, but I have come to understand the galaxy doesn't work like Earth does, and these kinds of reactions and punishments are normal and expected to keep your reputation and power base. I stay quiet and watch until the swarm finishes devouring their meal before disappearing throughout the halla bushes, not paying one lick of attention to either of us.

"I'm sorry you had to witness that," Master Z murmurs behind me, not really sounding sorry at all.

"I'm sorry he was an idiot who overestimated his worth," I reply, and I hear him chuckle.

"Come on, let's get you somewhere more comfortable, and then we can talk." We dissolve into particles as he teleports us away from the halla field, and I can't help feeling excited that I might finally get some answers.

CHAPTER FIFTEEN

Lila

When our bodies reform, we are inside a rustic but stylish log cabin, with stone and timber walls, and a vaulted roof with timber beams. There are a couple of skylights that allow the remaining twilight inside, but the sun is slowly disappearing, and I know night is creeping up on us.

The arm around me drops as I take in the rest of the space. Stretched out in front of me is a large, open room full of plants on just about every surface, including the walls. Down the far end, I see a low to the ground mattress, surrounded by thick curtains that are currently tied back. There are two doors on the right side of the bed, so I'm guessing a bathroom and closet. Off to the right of the room is a small kitchen with a wood stove for cooking and a hand pump for water. I guess there is no power here on this planet. In the middle of the room is another large, sunken area, and this one is filled with plants and a full-sized tree, where one of the branches has grown to be a chair. The ground surrounding it is dark dirt. There's a small bookcase, also made from one of the branches of the tree with a few books as well as a lantern with a fat candle inside it. To the left is nothing but panels of glass, providing an unobstructed view of the forest I can see outside.

"Are you hungry?" he asks quietly as he steps away from me. I whirl around to face him, but he's still covered by the cloak. He claims he isn't deformed, but I'll believe it when I see it.

"I'm starving actually," I reply, my stomach making an embarrassingly loud rumble. I slap a hand over it and blush.

"Well, why don't you show me your real form, little mimic, and maybe I'll show you mine?"

There's a stunned silence between us as I process what he just said. Crap, he knows I'm a mimic.

He chuckles. "There is very little I don't know," he tells me immodestly. "You are welcome to stay in this form, but you need to submerse yourself in the soil while I find us something to eat."

He waves a hand, and the soil in the sunken area flows back, revealing a body-sized space, kind of like a shallow grave. My nose wrinkles up.

"If you are worried about your need for sex if you change your mimic form too often, then we can get your mates back here to help you," he says matter-of-factly.

"Only one of them is my mate," I mutter, weighing my options.

"Hmm." He sounds skeptical. "That may only be a technicality. The threads of your soul are already melding with the Aaz'axian. It isn't as strong as the ones with your warlock. They are unbreakable."

"Will I really die if I use this form without being in contact with the earth element?"

"It is very weak. You could recharge that form so that if you need it again, you won't feel sick," he offers.

Making the only logical choice, I heave out a sigh before I walk down the stone steps and into the sunken dirt pit, lying down in the space. He waves a hand, and the soil flows back over me. "Rest well, little one. We can talk when you are feeling better."

He disappears. I should be worried that he left me here alone, buried in dirt, but I don't. In fact, I feel warm and comfortable, and my eyes start to droop. Embracing the need to rest, I allow sleep to wash over me, confident in the fact that I am safe despite the sounds of animals I can hear outside and a bunch of vines tapping on the glass like psycho stalkers trying to get in. I very much doubt he brought me to his home just to let me be devoured by the plants. Why did he bring me here? I know it's not just for my elemental form now. When he returns, I have many questions, but I also plan on reverting to my real form so maybe I can see his.

I'm not sure how long I sleep, but when I wake, I feel a hundred times better. My body no longer aches, and the headache and nausea are gone. All that remains is a burning hunger. I try to look around the room to see if Master Z returned, but it isn't easy from the sunken pit.

I look up at the skylights and see twinkling stars, but no moon, and it's not enough light to illuminate anything around me. I see the outline of the tree and other plants that are down here, but from this angle, the rest of the room is blocked off. Someone might be up there, but I don't hear any movement. I can still hear the vines tapping at the windows. Does that mean he hasn't returned? Did something happen to him while he was out getting us food?

A wonderful smell reaches my nose, and my stomach rumbles with hunger once more. I use my own powers to open up the dirt this time. It's almost as easy as breathing. All I had to do was think about it, and it happened. I stand up and wave a hand over my body, and all the dirt covering me flows back into the pit, then I close it up. I could really use a shower, but I think food is the bigger priority.

"Ah, you're awake and fully healed." The quiet voice from above has me looking up. I can only see a shadow of him, but I can tell he's still wearing that cloak. He chuckles quietly.

"Come eat something, and we will talk." The stone steps light up, illuminated by what looks like little bioluminescent mushrooms that popped up out of the ground. I follow the mushrooms, and when I climb the stairs, I discover the rest of the living space is lit by the same bioluminescence. All the plants dotted through the room seem to pulse with it, giving the space an eerie sort of romance. I gape at it in wonder. It really is beautiful.

Master Z leads me over to the kitchen, where there is a cauldron-like pot over the burning fire pit. He grabs an earthenware bowl and ladles something into it from the pot before passing it to me. Steam drifts off it as he turns to get one of his own, the smell making my mouth water. He grabs what looks like a plate of fresh bread he had sitting on the side, keeping warm, and leads me to a seating area in front of the glass panels. There are two large, soft-looking chairs sitting there that weren't there previously. Master Z gestures for me to sit, placing the bread plate on the little coffee table between us. He passes me a spoon, which I take, before he starts eating, but then he pauses.

"Drinks. We need drinks, right?" he mutters almost to himself. He waves a hand, and a bottle of what looks like wine and two rustic goblets appear next to the plate of bread. "Sorry, it has been a while since I had guests." He sounds slightly embarrassed, but I still can't see him, which is driving me mad.

He puts his bowl down and uncorks the bottle. "Have you had Husad Mead before?" he asks, pouring some into each of the glasses. I shake my head. "Well, you should know what you are risking life and limb for then." He passes me one of the goblets, and I place my bowl on my lap and take it from him. "Though I have my doubts that such a powerful group is here just because they wanted to earn some extra money, especially since that group contains the crown prince of the warlocks. Did he decide he wanted to slum it with the general population for a while?" I'm mid sip when he says this, and I almost choke on the potent yet tasty liquid. It has a smoky quality to it, almost like bourbon, but there are fresh citrus notes as well. It's delicious, but I can tell it's strong.

Sip slowly, Lila.

I try to come up with some kind of plausible excuse, but he places the bottle down and waves a hand. "Let us eat first. That might give you enough time to come up with some kind of reason." I hear the amusement in his voice, and I know I'm going to have to tell him the truth. He's looking after me, so it's the least I can do.

I put my own goblet down on the little table and concentrate on my stew. The first mouthful has me groaning out loud. "This is delicious," I tell him, shoveling more in quickly. I'm starving and can't get enough.

"Here, have some bread, use it to soak up some of the broth. That's what I do." He holds out the plate, sounding pleased that I'm enjoying the meal. It has some kind of meat and vegetables with a rich gravy-like broth that tastes like it might have some of the mead in it as well.

"Where did you get all of this? Is there a society on this planet? All of our research showed it was uninhabitable, which obviously isn't the case." I wave my spoon around at the dwelling we're in.

"I made it all. I do supply runs when we pick up new harvesters, and everything I have stores well underground. I grow the vegetables in my garden and hunt the meat. Flupkups are fairly stupid creatures and easy to trap."

I pause with my spoon midway to my mouth and look down at my food. Flupkup stew. Oh well, it tastes like beef, and I don't think there are any other options, so I keep eating. If I can eat raw fish while pregnant with my babies, then I can eat this.

"You have babies?" Master Z sounds curious. "Tell me about yourself, little one. I want to know everything. I haven't seen a mimic since the Aaz'axian-Una's war."

I was warned that I shouldn't be telling everyone my story, but there's something about this creature that makes me feel safe, and since he already knows, what's there to lose? I don't know if he's lulling me into a false sense of security and then going to kill me, or if my instincts are correct, but I'm going to go with my gut this time, so I tell him everything. Our meals are well and truly finished, and two bottles of Husad Mead have been consumed when I finally get to the reason we are on Husadavia to begin with.

My mind is a little foggy, and I must be rambling by now, the mead having done a great job of relaxing me.

Master Z has listened quietly, asking a question here and there when he needed clarification, but at hearing that my grandma has been placed in a stasis box in the middle of the death forest, I see his body grow tense, and the air around me seems to prickle with tension.

"Someone placed your grandma in the middle of my forest?" he asks, his voice eerily calm despite the tension now circling us.

"Yes, a faction known as the Syndicate. We still don't know who their members are. That's on the to-do list after we rescue Grandma Liliana."

"And your plan was that you hoped you could mimic me and use my powers to control the plants and animals to get to her?" Thankfully, the tension drops. He doesn't seem annoyed, just curious.

"Yes, that was the plan, but to mimic you, I have to be able to see you, and since you keep yourself covered, we were waiting until we got closer to the forest to follow through."

"And what were you going to do to get me to reveal myself?" This time, he definitely sounds amused.

"Well, the only plan I had was tripping and falling and taking your cape with me," I admit sheepishly, and he's silent for a moment before he starts to laugh loudly. It's a raspy kind of sound, like it's been a long time since he laughed, but I like it, and I find myself giggling as well.

"I didn't say it was a good plan," I tell him between giggles.

"Well, little one, you trusted me with your tale, so it is only fair that I give you mine. What do you know about the creation of the galaxy?"

"Not a lot, to be honest. Earth, the planet I'm from, is cut off from knowing what's really out here. I've had a crash course on everything galaxy related, but I was recently told of the gods of creation—life and death and four elemental gods who created the different races to worship them, which gave them power, but they disappeared shortly before or around the time of the Aaz'axian-Una's war, and knowledge of them was phased out by the newly formed Galactic Council after the end of the war."

Master Z growls at the mention of the Galactic Council. "Yes, what you know is true, but the gods didn't get their powers from their worshipers. They already had all the power they needed. Creating races was just a way of passing the time for them because they were bored. It gave them a purpose, one which they thrived at. As close as any blood brother or sister, though not related, they were a family—a family that celebrated their wins and commiserated with each other's losses, but like all creatures, the gods were not inherently bad or good, and they were subject to the whims of their emotions and thoughts and feelings just like any other being. Jealousy started to drift in. The nature of each god's power dictated the kinds of creatures they created, and while death created a number of races that thrived, many of them had powers that were intimidating to the rest of the galaxy, and because of those powers, they were shunned. For example, while necromancy is an impressive power, if you don't understand it, it's easy to assume the power is inherently evil. This fostered resentment, which, when left to fester, grows until it's an entity of its own, much like my beautiful plants." He points the goblet in his hand to the surrounding foliage.

"So what happened?" I'm fully invested in this story now, even though in the back of mind, there's something shouting at me to think about everything he's been telling me and how he knows all of this.

"Betrayal is what happened, but how or why is unknown, still to this day. The four elemental gods found that their power had been diminished, reduced to less than half of what it had been, and then death and life disappeared altogether."

"Who was responsible?" I ask, and he shrugs, his whole cloak jolting with the movement.

"The four elemental gods swore up and down none of them were responsible, which left life or death, but with no sign of them, nothing could be answered."

I'm quiet as I mull over what he says. "What happened to the elemental gods?" I ask, almost certain I know exactly what happened to one of them, all of the pieces coming together at once. Master Z stands, and the roof of the building lights up with the same bioluminescence the rest of the plants are producing. I look up, and I see a creeper vine has slithered its way around all the exposed wooden beams while we were eating, the plants now making the room as bright as any fluorescent bulb lit space.

I hold my breath as Master Z's hands come up and grab the two sides of his cloak, and he peels them back, revealing his true form.

CHAPTER SIXTEEN

Caspian

The trip from station Z68 seems to take forever, and we are all on high alert and anxious. The plan is flimsy at best, even though Lila and Xavier were both confident they could pull it off. I'm just pleased that Brannock is with them. He seems to have a level head and is motivated to regain our trust, so he will ensure our mates are careful. Now that I have my own children, I know what lengths I would go through so I could keep them safe. It would be worse if they were being used against me, so while I am upset he didn't tell us immediately, I understand. He didn't know us, so for all he knew, we were terrible people. I forgive him and will do whatever I can to help him get his child back.

He must be frustrated to be so far away from Earth. Once we find Liliana Adams and then sort out Silac's family issues, I have no doubt that Earth will be our next destination. Agent Smith really made a mistake by fucking with us. I think he underestimates the fallout, and he's going to wish he had never been born. The Syndicate is going down, and Xavier will crack Agent Smith's fragile little human brain to get all the information we need regarding it. I can't wait to watch. His screams of pain will be like music to my ears.

"Swim, Daddy?"

"Huh?" I had been staring out the window of our residence as the ship follows the halla harvesters' vessel, cloaked from view.

"Cally would like to go for a swim in the big pool," Saxon tells me, his eyebrows pulled into a frown as he bounces said child on his lap. She squeals with delight and claps her hands together. Jack and Cordy are on the floor, building a city of blocks with Link. "Are you okay?"

"Ah, yeah." I scrub my hand through my hair. "Just worried about the others."

"Why don't we take the kids down for a swim, and I can check on Nikos? He hasn't met them yet, and he's been dying to. He keeps asking when you'll bring them to swim with him, and now that he's healthier, I think it's a good idea. They need to meet their new daddy, and I'm sure he'd like to try his hand at parenting before his own arrive." Link stands up and stretches his arms high. His shirt rises, exposing the smooth expanse of his shimmery abs, and my kraken cracks open an eye, perking right up. He's been sulking since Lila left the ship without us, and this is the first sign of interest he's shown since.

Easy, I caution him.

He nudges me, liking the idea of shifting and going for a swim if he can't stick a tentacle into Link. I roll my eyes at my horny inner beast. He is as bad as Lila's now. If they had their way, the day would start and finish with an orgy, with a little afternoon delight as a midday snack.

"Yeah, that sounds like a good idea. I could use something to take my mind off everything. Where are the cats? Do you think Echo would like to visit Nikos?"

"He and Maxsim are sleeping. Apparently, pregnant lightning cats need a lot more sleep than normal, and he was worried about Lila, which wasn't good for his blood pressure, so I told him he should lie down. He wouldn't, though, because he didn't want to miss anything that might happen, so Maxsim threw him over his shoulder and took him to their den."

"Probably fucked him into submission. That's what I would do to Lila," Saxon mutters quietly enough so Cally doesn't hear it, but Link and I do.

"And she loves it. Echo probably does too," I point out, looking at the mess our living room is in and grimacing. You would think with so many of us in this relationship, it would be easy enough to keep clean, but it really isn't. We're going to have to look at hiring a cleaner when the crew returns. Each person is usually responsible for their own quarters, but we are a busy family, and it's about to get bigger. I will talk to the Adams brothers. They and the captains have one, so maybe they can share them with us.

"It's all those pregnancy hormones," Link adds as he starts to pick up the blocks. The children begin to complain, so I jump in to distract them.

"Do you two want to go for a swim with Cally and me?" I ask them. "We can meet the pretty mermaid in the pool."

"Mermaid?" That gets Cordy's attention. Lila has had them watching a kid cartoon with an unusual group of friends—a mermaid, a fish, and a crustacean. There was singing, and it had an evil octo-lady that I told the kids was their grandma Mira. Lila was horrified and told me my mother will kill me. She's not wrong, but it was funny, and I can't wait to tell my brothers.

"Yup, help Daddy Link clean up, and then we'll go meet Daddy Can of Tuna."

"Caspian," Link scolds me, but Saxon bursts out laughing. He's so serious all the time that when he laughs and his face lights up like that, he's kind of stunning, and I find myself staring a little too long. He catches me and winks.

"I won't come. I need to feed, and there's a bag of Lila's blood in the fridge. I'll also prepare some bottles with blood for these three for when you return." He stands up and comes over to me, handing me our daughter. I take her, and he leans in to give her a kiss on the cheek, but she ducks, and he gets me. We both kind of freeze, stunned by what happened. Cally just cheers and uses her hands to hold our heads together.

"Kiss, kiss, kiss," she chants.

Saxon's tongue flicks out, and he licks my lip before giving it a little nip and pulling away. I blink in shock. When we played before, I was always with Link, and he was with Xavier, but that was nice, and I wouldn't mind repeating it. He smirks at my stunned expression and gives me a wink. Playful Saxon is hot, and my inner beast is here for this. He suggests we stick a tentacle in him since I won't let him stick one in Link.

We won't be sticking our tentacles anywhere, I scold him, and he goes back to sulking.

"I want kisses." Cally smacks her hands against my cheeks, startling me, and then pushes them together, making my lips pucker before she lays a sloppy baby kiss on them. My heart swells, and I make kissy sounds, and her laughter is music to my ears. God, I love my babies. My life is pretty fucking amazing. How did I ever get so lucky?

Half an hour later, we are leaving the elevator on the Aquilian level. It takes an unusually long time to wrangle three kraken babies and get them where we want them to be. It's hard work, but I wouldn't have it any other way. It didn't help that their great-grandpas were walking by on their way to the flight deck, and all three needed cuddles from all the babies. You can practically feel the anxiety dripping off them. I have no idea what it would be like to be without your wife for close to twenty years and know she was out there somewhere. At least it must be a relief to know it wasn't voluntary. I do not envy the person who took her when the Adams men discover who it was.

"Swim with us, Daddy Link." Cordy drags the cyborg to the side of the pool and strips, unconcerned about being naked before shifting into her kraken form and sliding into the pool. They don't have a half form yet, but I'm assuming it's coming. I can't remember a time where I didn't have one, so it must be soon—maybe once they have Aquilian siblings to swim with and can't communicate with them underwater in beast form.

"I want to see how Nikos is doing. How about I meet you in the cave underneath his home?" Link suggests to me, since Cordy has disappeared and Jack and Cally are already naked and shifting. There are no predators to worry about in the pool, but I'm not sure what kind of protective instinct Nikos has now that he's expecting. I don't want the children to sneak up on him and scare him.

"We'll meet you there. If I see him, I'll let him know you're here." I strip off my own clothes and hurry after my children. I find them swimming amongst the coral reef, a game of tag already in play. It looks like Jack is it. I watch them with pure joy in my heart for a few minutes before I call out to them. *Come along now. Daddy Link is waiting for Daddy Can of Tuna, and it's our job to find him.*

The kids zip in and out of my tentacles. Their beasts have taken control, but they know I need them to come with me.

Lila told me that Nikos was in the jimble gem cave last time she was in here, so I have a feeling that's where I'll find him. I haven't shown the kids the cave yet, so now is as good a time as any. I dive down deep, using my tentacles to propel me along. I don't go as fast as I normally do because I want the children to keep up. They dart in and out of small crevices, weaving their way through the reef in a completely different way than me, but I can feel them nearby, so I don't worry.

Eventually, we make it to the bottom of the

deep pool and the pretty, sparkling cave that Lila likes so much. At the entrance, I hear a low, haunting melody being sung, and I frown. That sounds so sad. Now I'm worried about our silly can of tuna. *Nikos?* I call out, and the music cuts off. My children gather under my tentacles, wary of the dark entrance. They have good instincts, but I pulse my tentacles to let them know there is nothing to be scared of.

Caspian? Nikos replies, and I move into the cave with the children sticking close to me. *Is Lila with you?* he asks hopefully.

I move into the opening and see him sitting in the anemone, his stomach even larger than it was when I saw him last.

No, I'm sorry, she isn't. She's still searching for her grandma. His hopeful look dims. *But I brought our babies to meet you,* I tell him, gesturing for the kids to move forward.

His eyes light up, and he grins, waving the children forward. *Come let Daddy look at you,* he calls out, making grabby hands, and I roll my eyes. The kids can't understand him in beast form, but the gestures say everything. Lila told me the silliness is an act, but I won't call him out because I can feel the kids' excitement. They all zip toward him and splat against him like leeches, their little tentacles wrapping around his body. Jack spreads out across his belly, and Nikos looks like he's wearing a Jack apron. Nikos is knocked over, but he's laughing madly.

Oh my goodness, they are adorable. He giggles.

Careful, I warn my children. *Daddy Nik is going to be having your brothers or sisters soon, so don't be too rough with him.*

He strokes his hands over the babies, his eyes wide with awe when he looks at me. *They are beautiful, Caspian.*

I puff my chest up just a little. *Yes, they are. Jack is the one who is currently giving kisses to your belly, Cordelia is the one whose tentacles are tangled in your hair, and Calypso is the one who's trying to strangle you.* I point to each child as I introduce them.

They have lovely names. How did you decide on them? he asks. *I am having trouble making a decision.*

Lila and I picked Cordelia's name from a book my parents had, and she let the rest of us decide on the other two, and both of them were from an Earth pirate movie.

His eyes light up. *Would you help me pick some names for my babies? Are there Earth mermaid movies?*

Yes, of course we can. The children have a favorite one that they watch at least once a day. I can arrange to have a screen put in the cave under your house, and you can watch it and see if any of the names appeal to you. I will ask Lila if there are any other good mermaid movies.

Thank you. I like the idea of giving our babies Earth names like their mother.

Come on, why don't we go for a gentle swim? Link is waiting to check on you as well.

He nods and flicks his tail, moving much slower than normal. *Okay, but I can't move very fast at the moment,* he warns me, and I call the kids off him to make it easier, but he puts out his hand.

They are okay. They barely weigh a thing. It's the two inside me that are the problem. One of them is pressing on my spine, and it makes it hard for me to flick my tail. He winces and slaps his hand over his lower back and groans.

Shit, do you need some help? I ask him. *How about I tow you through the water so you don't have to move?* I go over to him and shoo the children away. *Daddy Nik is hurting. How about you swim ahead and tell Daddy Link we're coming?* I tell them, and they peel themselves off the poor encumbered merman and disappear. I wrap my arms around him and turn him around so his back is to my front, then I propel myself forward with my tentacles.

Hang on, we'll see if Link has anything to help you. I'm anxious and worried about the can of tuna now. It can't be easy to be so round, and unlike my babies, which were encased in eggs, his are fully formed, and their tails must be pushing on some nerve or something. I look down his body as I maneuver through the reef, wanting to see Link as soon as we can. His stomach is way bigger than Lila's was.

Link told us twins are uncommon for Aquilians, so maybe there are complications we hadn't anticipated. Well. Link probably did, now that I think about it, but he probably didn't say anything because he didn't want to worry any of us, especially Lila, unless it was necessary. I would say it is necessary now, and our wife is on another planet and not where she needs to be, but I'm here, and I'm going to do everything I can to support my mate's mate and our new babies.

CHAPTER SEVENTEEN

Link

Three little krakens break the surface of the pool underneath Nikos and Nixie's place. I smile when I see my children and expect Caspian's head to break the surface quickly after them, but he doesn't. I wave the babies over to me, and they cooperate by swimming over to the edge and using their tentacles to climb out. I grab three towels out of the cabinet and squat down next to them.

"Can you change back so I can speak to you?" I coax them, a little annoyed that I can't mind speak like Xavier or one of the shifters, but I'm not the only one. Saxon can't either, so I'm not completely left out of the loop. One by one, they shimmer before I have three naked toddlers standing before me. I manage to get a towel wrapped around both Cordy and Cally, but I'm not quick enough, and Jack takes off up the stairs of the small house, shouting, "I'm naked! You can't catch me."

Torn between chasing the little naked boy or finding out where Cas is, my concern for Nikos wins out. "Where's Daddy?" I ask the two little girls.

"He's bringing Daddy Nik. He can't swim very well," Cally says before sticking her thumb in her mouth. Swimming always wears them out, and Saxon says he's going to be waiting back at our home with bottles for them before their nap.

I purse my lips and turn my attention back to the pool. "He can't?" That's not ideal. I know twins are unusual for Aquilians, and there can be complications. I hope this is just a case of Nik being a first-time expectant father, and he's more uncomfortable than anything, but I guess I'll find out.

"I'm naked, and you can't catch me!" I hear Jack shout, and when I look, he's halfway up the stairs and shaking his little naked bottom at me. Who the fuck taught him to do that? "I need to pee." He turns around and moves up to the edge of the steps, taking his penis in his hand and pointing it over the side.

"No!" I shout, but it's too late, and a small stream flows into the pool below. "Oh, Jack." I shake my head in exasperation as Cas and Nikos breach the surface, just missing the small golden stream.

"What the hell?" Cas bellows, looking up and finding his son peeing into the pool.

"Jack, no," he growls, and Jack just giggles, finishing with a little shake. He turns and races the rest of the way up the steps.

"Damn it!" Cas shouts and swims over to me with Nikos wrapped in his arms. He leaves him to lie in the shallow beach section on the side of the deck before he climbs out and hurries over to grab a towel, drying his body off before chasing Jack upstairs in his half form. Cordy and Cally stay where they are, their towels hugged around them as they giggle like crazy at Jack's antics.

"Are you okay?" I ask the merman. I look him over, and his belly is way more distended than it was the last time I saw him. He rubs the large bump and grimaces.

"Yes, but since I've been eating everything you gave me and taking all the supplements and medications you prescribed me to get better, the babies have grown quickly."

"Yes, they were slightly undersized at the last scan. That's a good thing," I reassure him, and he smiles wanly.

"But they push on a nerve in my spine that's making it hard for me to swim. I basically don't move anymore. I don't think it will be long before they are here. When will Lila return?" he asks, worry creasing his brow.

We've been in Husadavia air space for twenty-four hours. Lila, Xavier, and Brannock would have had their first day harvesting and should be returning to the ship shortly. They said they would be near the death forest on day three. "Hopefully only two more days," I tell him, worried he may not make it that long, but he nods.

"Good, she will be back in time then. Their birth is not imminent, since my scales have not changed color yet." He nods down the length of his tail, and I toe off my shoes and remove my pants, leaving me in just my boxers as I step onto the small section. I hear a squeal and a bang, followed by a growl, and look up the stairs, wondering if I should go find out what's happening, but I'm sure Cas has it all in hand. Fingers crossed.

"Your scales haven't changed color?" I ask the merman as I run my hand over his belly, following with my eyes. I use all of the scanning tools available to me to check that he is okay. I can see where the second twin is pushing on his spine, so I put both my hands on his belly and massage a little, trying to get them to move into a different position in the hopes that it might relieve his pain. I don't want to give him any pain relief because I'm uncertain of the babies' tolerance. I may have to assess my databases for more information, and if I'm unsuccessful, I'll make a call to Nixie and her mother. That woman is unpleasant and wasn't very nice to Lila, so I will use it as a last resort.

"Yes, the scales around my sexual slit will

become paler, fading to white when it's time to give birth. The only time they ever open on their own in mer form is when we give birth. Any other time, they need to be activated by another participant." He grunts and then groans as his whole belly rolls. The girls are standing on the side, watching us now, their curiosity too great.

"What is that?" Cordy asks, pointing at Nikos's belly.

"That's your brother or sister," I tell her, and her eyes widen.

"Really?" She sounds fascinated. "Can I touch?" she asks while Cally just watches silently, her thumb still in her mouth.

I look at Nik who nods eagerly, his eyes wide with amazement at seeing them in their humanoid form. "They look so much like Lila," he says as Cordy clasps her towel to her little body and climbs down into the pool. Oh well, it will dry. She toddles over to Nikos and reaches out to touch his belly, but it rolls again, and she squeals and snatches it back.

Nikos chuckles and reaches out with his own hand, taking her small one in his and laying it against the baby bump. "They will be here soon, and you will all be able to swim together," he tells her gently, and I watch with deep joy as her eyes widen with amazement.

"Do you want to know what you're having?" I ask him, restarting my scans.

"I do, but I don't want to know without Lila

here," he explains, and I nod as I hear a little splash, and when I turn to look, Cally has joined us and is inching toward us with her hand held out. She places it next to Cordy's, and they both grin when the merbabies wriggle like they can feel their sisters are there.

"Oh, they like you." Nikos smiles despite how uncomfortable it must be. There is less room in there than there would be with a human twin birth because both his babies have tails. "They are going to love their big sisters," he tells them, and I watch them puff up with pride.

"Too bad their big brother is a shit head." Cas's voice carries down the stairs, and then he appears in half form with Jack firmly tucked under his arm, his head facing backward.

"I'm sorry, Nik, but Jack knocked over the sculpture of a phadoll you had in there. I will ask Xavier to fix it for you when he returns, but he's off with Lila at the moment." Cas gets to the bottom of the steps, and I see Jack wiggling like mad, trying to escape, but he's not having any luck.

"What do you say to Daddy Nik?" Caspian growls and flips his son around so he is tucked against his body and looking at us.

"I want to touch," Jack calls, reaching out with his arms when he sees both of his sisters touching Nik's belly, whispering to each other and giggling every time the babies move.

"Not until you apologize for breaking his

precious things and peeing in his pool," Cas says firmly. "We do not pee in pools in human form. We use the bathroom like everyone else does."

Jack pouts and crosses his arms stubbornly but mutters, "Sorry."

"Jack, do you like it when Cordy smashes your block tower when you've worked hard to build it?" I ask him, trying to explain it in terms he might understand. They are intelligent for their age, but sometimes their emotions get in the way.

He shakes his head vigorously. "No, she's mean. Mean, mean, meany bum," he shouts and sticks his tongue out. Cordy ignores him, too enthralled with Nik's belly to pay attention.

"Well, that's how Daddy Nik feels about you breaking his precious things," I tell him, and he stops glaring at his sisters and turns his attention to Nik. He wiggles in Cas's arms to be let down, and Cas lets him. Jack hurries over, still as naked as can be, and jumps into the pool, splashing his sisters with the action. They squeal with annoyance, but he just smiles as he hurries over and wraps his little arms around Nik's neck.

"Sorry, Daddy Nik. I love you." He places a kiss on his cheek, and Nik melts. I roll my eyes and exchange an exasperated glance with Cas. Jack has learned how to work the room. His grandpas are giant pushovers, as are most of his fathers.

"Jack, to make it up to Nik, I think it would be nice if you draw him a picture next time you do crafts with Grandpa John so he can put it in place of his lovely statue until Daddy X can fix it," Cas suggests. It's not much of a punishment as far as they go, probably more of one for Nik than anything else, but both Nik and Jack beam. Another daddy wrapped around a tiny little finger. It's a losing battle. I have high hopes for Tirrian and Silac. They haven't been manipulated by these three yet, so there is still a chance that one of them will be good at disciplining, because the rest of us are failing—except Lila. She's good at it, but she gets upset because she's worried they are going to think she's a bitch. Like I keep telling her, though, there's only one mother in this family, so she's automatically their favorite. I'm not sure it helps.

"How does it feel now?" I ask him, happy with the scans. I know what he's having, but until he and Lila give the okay, I'll keep referring to them neutrally. "The babies have moved slightly. Is it a little better?"

He flicks his tail carefully, and it moves freely, so he sighs with relief. "So much better, thank you," he tells me.

"No problem. I'm happy to help in whatever way I can." Cally is leaning against Nik, her head on his chest and her hand still on his stomach, and she's smiling with her eyes closed. He gives her a little hug, his eyes alight with joy. Cordy and Jack are squabbling over who gets to touch his belly, but he just shushes them and puts both their hands on it just in time for them to kick again. He's going to be a great father.

"Ugh, they must think my belly is a great, wide ocean. They swim constantly," he complains, but the children are thrilled.

"Okay, I think you need to rest, and we need to get these little ones upstairs for some food and sleep." Cas slips into the pool and separates his two quarreling children, because they've started to shove one another. "You two don't get to swim back. Bad behavior does not get rewarded." He has one under each arm, and he starts back up the stairs.

"See you soon, Nik. I'll come back and check on you when I get a chance tomorrow," Cas promises, and Nik looks a little surprised but gives him a wave goodbye.

"You're a part of the family now, Nik," I tell him, and he blinks a couple of times before a large smile stretches across his face.

"Thank you," he says, bowing his head as I bend down and pick up our sleepy baby. She doesn't argue, just presses a kiss to his cheek before wrapping her arms around me as I lift her.

"You have the communicator over there if you need it." We put one on the edge of the pool in case he goes into labor or needs us for any reason. "We can be here in a flash. If the pain returns, let me know and I can try to move the babies again," I tell him. "It might be a good idea just to stay in this pool for now."

"Yes, I was thinking the same thing. I wish I could shift like Echo can, and then I could go upstairs. It's a little lonely here," he tells me.

"Yeah, I know. Lila would be here if she could. I'll tell Echo to come visit. Do you have all the things you need for the babies?"

He nods. "Yes, it should all be waiting for us on Fluxx when we arrive. Echo and I did some shopping when he came to see me last time."

"Okay, well, get some rest." I wave goodbye and follow Cas and his two bundles of grumpy up the stairs. The path across the pool has been left open permanently so both Echo and I can come and go.

The smashed statue is still in pieces on the floor, but I know Cas wants to ask Xavier to use his magic to fix it, so I leave it instead of tidying it up. When Cally and I reach the landing near the elevator, Cas already has the kids redressed and is waiting for us. The wet towels lie in a pile to the side.

"I'll come back and get both of those," he tells me as I toss Cally's wet one in the pile and dry her with a new one before dressing her.

"Can you grab my clothes too?" I ask him, looking down at my mostly naked body. I didn't think to put them back on after I finished examining Nikos.

Caspian chuckles and winks. "You're as bad as Jack, wandering around mostly naked."

I shake my head as the two babies in his arms

giggle. Cally is basically still asleep despite all the commotion and me redressing her.

"Don't encourage them," I scold half-heartedly.

"Nothing wrong with being naked. It's a shifter thing," he explains, and I just roll my eyes. Of course it is.

When we get back to our suite, I find the cats sitting at the counter, having a drink.

"Oh, you're back!" Echo leaps to his feet and hurries over, taking Cordy from Caspian. "Saxon left bottles for them in the warmer. He said he added blood." He hurries back to the counter and pulls the three bottles out of the special warmer we use. He gives them a shake to mix the blood into the milk before handing one to Jack and one to me. Cally is still resting her head on my shoulder, so I sit down on the couch and feed it to her. She drinks it down with her eyes still closed. Jack and Cordy both take their own bottles but stay in Cas's and Echo's arms.

"Saxon went to talk to Broderick on the flight deck. He was restless and wanted to make sure everything was okay," Maxsim says, patting the seat next to him so his mate will sit down.

"How are you feeling, Echo?" I ask him, noticing his belly is a little more round today than yesterday.

He smiles brightly. "I feel good, strong, and I have quite an appetite. The babies must be growing."

"That's good. Would you pop down and visit with Nik? I think he's lonely, and he can't move a lot anymore, which makes swimming difficult." His bright look fades, and a crease appears between his brows with his worry.

"Of course I can. He must miss Lila a lot," he agrees.

"Take this with you." Cas puts Jack on the sofa next to me and Cally and holds up a tablet. "Link told him about the mermaid movie, and he wants to watch it."

Maxsim groans. The kids have made both cats watch it over and over again with them.

"He wants to pick Earth names for his babies as well," I explain, and his disgruntled look disappears as Echo nods.

"It is a good idea. Maybe Lila can suggest some for us too. I like the tradition of naming our babies Earth names." He rubs his own belly with the hand not holding Cordelia.

The babies don't take long to finish their bottles, and the three of us lay them down in their beds to rest, all of them out before we leave the room.

"I need to find some clothes," I tell the two of them, leaving them to return to the kitchen while I head to my room. My eyes drift to the clock on my bedroom wall. Lila and the guys should be returning to the harvesting ship soon. They were planning on contacting us to give us an update.

Maybe I'll go to the bridge so I can be there when it comes in.

CHAPTER EIGHTEEN

Maxsim

Once Echo helps put the babies to bed, he leaves me and hurries off to check on Lila's can of tuna. I can see his worry for the merman, which makes me anxious because I don't want anything going wrong with Echo's pregnancy, but I can't be selfish and demand that he doesn't go. It's a fine line I have to walk to keep my mate and my alpha tendencies happy.

Maybe it will be a good distraction. He was worrying something fierce about Lila, and Link said his blood pressure got too high and he needed to rest. He refused, not wanting to miss out if something went wrong with the mission, so I fucked some submission into him, and he quickly became pliable and had a nap once he was full of my cum.

He looked so pretty on the end of my dick, but it did feel like something vital was missing without Lila. I'll have to fuck her into submission when she returns too. I'm sure she will give me a reason to need to, since she's very feisty.

I smile and reach down, adjusting my cock, which has decided to make itself known with my dirty thoughts.

Instead of worrying about Echo, who is perfectly safe, I switch my worry to the mate that is not perfectly safe.

"I'm going to the bridge to see if there's any word from Xavier or Lila," Link announces when he returns from putting the kids to sleep. He returned from the pool wearing nothing but a pair of tight boxer briefs, but now he's covered in another one of his uniforms. The cyborg is a very handsome man, and Echo suggested that maybe once our babies are born and Lila or he go into heat again that Link can help us. He explained that he can create a bulge like a knot with his nanobots. It's how he helped Lila the first time. I can't say I wasn't intrigued, but I'm not sure I could control my jealous tendencies and not maul him if he did. Maybe due to the fact that he doesn't smell like a cat, my jealousy wouldn't be too bad. After all, the omega controls who they have in the streak, and if both of mine want him to join us, then who am I to complain?

"Can I come?" I push away from the counter,

abandoning my drink now that there's finally something for me to do.

"Sure, what about you, Cas?" Link asks the kraken who shakes his head.

"No, Echo went to spend time with Nikos, and I don't want to leave the children unattended. Let me know what happens, will you?"

I can see the worry for our wife in his eyes, and we both quickly assure him we will keep him updated.

"Maybe it's time we started looking for a nanny," Link muses.

"Or two," I add, thinking about the coming four additions.

He grimaces. "You're not wrong. We're going to have to return to running the circus soon, which will keep us all busy. It won't hurt to have some help with the children."

We make our way along the corridors, walking instead of taking the sideslip. "Are you worried about the mission?" I ask the cyborg after a moment. I can practically feel the tension dripping off him.

"Kind of. I just want to be done. Waiting drives me nuts. I know I wouldn't have been much help, but I wish I could have gone with them. This separation is hard."

I nod my head, my tail twitching behind me with agitation. "I know exactly how you feel. I've never felt so disadvantaged by my species as I have since I've been Lila's mate. Before, I was happy keeping to our own den and environment, but now, I wish that I had high temperature tolerance as well." It's been playing on my mind since they had the mission to Rilu. Both Echo and I have discussed asking the warlock for a more permanent weather charm, which he spelled Echo with so he could sit underneath the sun lights in the Aquilian living space with Nikos. That way we aren't a liability to our wife and the rest of her mates, and we can participate in missions. Well, I can anyway. I wouldn't risk Echo's safety, even though he is a formidable fighter, but it's the alpha in me needing to protect his omega. The only reason I'm slightly more relaxed about Lila going is because I'm confident in her mimic ability making her damn near invincible.

"That's easy to fix. My lack of power is not," Link grumbles, and I slap him on the shoulder.

"If we were all running into danger, there would be no one to look after our young. You are just as important if not more so because you protect our offspring. Lila would be inconsolable if anything happened to them. Don't doubt yourself, my friend," I say gruffly, not great with emotional stuff but wanting him to know he is a valued and important member of our streak.

We reach the flight deck and find Saxon with Broderick, but both Silac, Tirrian, and Ghosie are here too. I guess the three of them are just as anxious as we are, since their affections for Lila are well-known, but they don't have the added distraction of our family to keep them busy—not yet anyway, though I doubt it will be long before they are full members of our rapidly expanding streak.

"Have we heard from the away team yet, Rick?" Link asks as I take a seat at one of the empty consoles, nodding a greeting to the four men.

"Not yet," Broderick Potter replies, his eyes on the big green planet visible through the flight deck viewing window. We are still cloaked from the harvesters' ship, but it is sitting close enough that Xavier can teleport to us if he needs to escape quickly.

Link's face falls, echoing my own disappointment.

"Ghosie and Tirrian just returned from the abandoned carevasta bear ship that's floating on the other side of the planet," Saxon tells us. "They were just about to tell us what they found."

"Which was nothing," Ghosie grumbles, putting his feet up on the console in front of his seat and leaning back with his arms crossed. "I couldn't get into the ship logs. They were password protected, which isn't uncommon for carevasta bears. We aren't a trusting lot."

"They definitely planned to return. We found two dead females chained up in the bedrooms," Tirrian says soberly. "They had no identification, nor were we able to tell what species they were. The bodies were fairly decayed. We're only assuming they were women because they were chained."

"Would I be able to offer some assistance?" Link is frowning at the news. "I can try to access their records. It isn't hard to bypass passcodes with direct access and take DNA samples of the dead females in the hopes they are in a missing database somewhere." He holds up a finger, which changes to a port that will plug directly into the ship.

"We were just talking about Silac returning and trying to hack his way in, but that's a better idea," Saxon says, and Broderick agrees with him.

"Come on, I'll send you both back to the ship. Tirrian can stay this time since you didn't encounter anyone alive."

Ghosie drops his furry paws from the console and stands up and stretches. "Hopefully you can find something helpful. There should be a record on who at least financed the mission. Bears don't like to be cheated, and they would have had to pay a fifty percent deposit up front. Even if they never paid the remainder, there should be some sort of trail to follow."

"Something that hopefully points to the Syndicate if Zamala is correct," Link agrees, and the three of them head to the teleporter room.

I'm feeling agitated and restless, so I stalk back and forth across the viewing window. My gaze remains on the large green planet, even though it's way too far away for any of us to make out any detail.

"They should have contacted us by now, right?" I ask the room as I try to work out in my head how long they've been on the planet.

"We registered a teleportation signature about twenty minutes ago. It went back and forth a number of times and just went quiet." Silac's finger runs over the screen in front of him. He is tech savvy as well and has been helping to keep his mind off the fact that his father has been turned to stone by the head of the Bravlana basilisks.

A low rumble escapes my chest before I can stop it, and I feel my lightning spark unbidden.

"Easy, Alpha. I know it's hard to have your mate away for so long. It should be any moment," Tirrian cautions, holding his hands up in a placating gesture. I snarl at the alpha dragon, and smoke starts to drift out of his nose. "We are all worried too. At least you can feel her since you're mated to her. Some of us don't have that."

"You would if you hadn't been such an asshole to her," I snap at him. I'm not ready to forgive him as quickly as everyone else—probably because I still feel residual guilt from my treatment of her. Both of us were horrible to her, and I want to shake him and tell him to get his shit together so he doesn't regret it like I do.

"I know, my friend, and I promise I'm trying. I will grovel if she will forgive me. I have a lot to make up for," he says calmly, and I feel my anger ease at his promise, but my agitation doesn't.

"Make sure you do. It makes Echo anxious when Lila is upset," I growl at the dragon before turning my attention to the snake.

"You too." I know why he's been holding back, but again, his rejection hurts her even though she understands why. She is an emotional creature, and her feelings need to be protected. I can help with that, even though I made my own mistakes.

"Yes, Alpha." Silac bows his head, wisely knowing not to argue with an agitated mate, but then his whole face changes, and he goes on high alert. His hood flares, and his eyes flash to the black of his beast. I unsheathe my claws just as Xavier and Brannock appear on the flight deck.

"Where's Lila?" I demand as the two finish forming, my lightning sparking more violently around my body. Saxon is on his feet, and both Silac's and Tirrian's eyes keep flashing back and forth, both of them having trouble controlling their beasts.

"Easy, alphas." Xavier sends a wave of reassurance my way, and I feel my body relax under his power, the sparks dying away. The other three men seem to relax as well. "She is fine, but we have some news, and we thought it would be better to share it personally so you and some of the others don't lose your shit," Xavier explains.

Neither of them look particularly worried, so I wait patiently.

"Where is everyone else? They should probably be here so we don't have to explain it twice," Brannock asks, making a smart suggestion.

"Link and Ghosie are on the carevasta ship that brought Lila's grandma to the planet, but they never left. There are a couple of dead bodies, and they are trying to access the mainframe since everything was password protected," Saxon answers calmly.

"Caspian is watching the babies, and my omega is visiting with the can of tuna," I tell them. "I'm not sure where the Adams brothers are, and Broderick is manning the teleporter for Link and Ghosie."

"Let's head back to our suite and gather everyone so I only have to tell the story once," Xavier suggests. "The flight deck will be fine unmanned for a little while."

"Is this going to be upsetting information?" I ask as we use the sideslip elevator to return to our suite. We step out in front of it, and Xavier shrugs casually.

"I can't predict how any of you are going to react, but it is surprising," he admits, and Brannock snorts.

"Surprising is an understatement. The warlock lost control of his mist when he found out."

"Maybe we should leave Echo and Nikos out of

this for now. They are both in delicate conditions, and I don't want to alarm them," I suggest, and both Silac and Tirrian nod their heads, agreeing with me, but Saxon just raises an eyebrow.

"Fine, but we are telling them it was your idea when they are upset about being kept in the dark."

I wince and run a hand through my mane in agitation, but I finally nod my head, willing to take the fallout he is most likely correct is coming.

When we get to the suite, Caspian has the same reaction Tirrian and Silac did, jumping to his feet, his beast surging into his eyes.

"Where's Lila?" he demands with a growl that's almost worthy of a lightning cat.

"Hey, easy, my friend." Xavier releases another wave of reassurance, and Cas's body shudders before he relaxes back into his seat. "She's fine. We'll explain what's happening when everyone arrives."

While he says this, Saxon uses the communicator on the wall to establish the whereabouts of the Adams brothers, asking them to join us in the suite.

"I'll just go retrieve Link and Ghosie." Xavier doesn't wait for an answer before he disappears. Saxon shakes his head and makes another call to Broderick, also requesting his presence in our suite.

The living area is much larger now due to the expansion, and there is enough seating for us all, but I'm too wound up to get comfortable. Instead, I pace back and forth, waiting for everyone so we can hear the news.

I'm so caught up in my worry, I don't notice Brannock approach me, and I almost fry him with my lightning when he puts a hand on my shoulder.

"Easy, Alpha. Your omega is fine." Brannock's voice holds a hint of power. The Aaz'axians can mesmerize, but I don't feel like my mind is being taken over, just that he made me feel a little calmer. "Trust us. If we were worried, we would have launched an attack on the being who has our Lila."

"Someone has her?" Tirrian's voice is deep and rumbly, his dragon merging with the male, driving his aggression higher.

"Yes, but if you take a moment to breathe and let us explain, you will understand she is perfectly safe… I think."

"You think?" Tirrian bellows, and I start to growl, all the tension returning to the room.

"Yes, Xavier believes she is, and I trust the warlock. If he is comfortable leaving his mate behind, then I have to be."

The room to the suite opens, and the Adams brothers hurry in, looking heart broken and worried. They see Brannock, and panic enters their eyes.

"Where are Lila and Xavier?" William demands as John collapses onto one of the sofas, Eric taking his hand and giving it a squeeze.

Brannock tries to calm the room again. "She's

fine. That warlock better hurry up, because this is ridiculous," he mutters, rolling his eyes at the dramatics.

Thankfully, the warlock appears with Link, Ghosie, and Broderick, and everyone turns to him.

"We have information on the being who controls the planet's occupants."

"Was Lila able to mimic him?" Link asks, remaining calm as he and the bear find seats. I'm not sure why the bear is actually needed for this conversation. Sure, he and Lila are wearing each other's attraction marks, but they have barely spent any time together. I growl quietly under my breath when I think about what his shipmates wanted to do to her. He gives me the side-eye but says nothing.

"I'm not sure, to be honest," Xavier says, wincing slightly, "but I do know who he is."

"Well?" Eric prompts before anyone else can. "For fuck's sake, Xavier, spit it out, and where is Lila?"

"The being is the forgotten earth elemental god, Zeydan, and Lila is with him. He claims she is his mate and requested she stay on planet. Her Elementi form is sick, and she would have perished had she returned to space in that form."

"Why didn't she just change?" Caspian asks.

"Because it still won't help that form in the long run, and she knows that." Xavier sighs. "Zeydan promised that he would protect her with his life."

"Does he know she is a mimic and not an actual

Elementi?" Saxon asks, rubbing a hand over his chin. He is just as calm as the cyborg. I guess the lack of a beast inside makes it easier to stay level-headed despite the situation.

I grit my teeth and retract my claws as I try to do the same.

Xavier shrugs. "I'm not sure. He didn't say anything, but he did say that the dragon was welcome to return tonight if we were worried." Xavier's gaze locks onto Tirrian. "You weren't exactly stealthy," he scolds.

"What did you expect? I'm a giant dragon. It's kind of hard to stay hidden when there is no cloud cover." He doesn't sound apologetic. "Send me down now. I will protect our mate. It's the least I can do to make up for my behavior."

I nod my head in agreement. It is the least he can do, and having a big, fire-breathing dragon around will make everything think twice about attacking Lila.

"Come on, I'll send you down now." Broderick pushes off the wall. "Where should I send him?" he asks the warlock who winces.

"I'm not sure."

"I'll find her. My dragon will be able to smell her. We'll keep searching until we do," he assures us.

"Please contact us when you get a chance and keep us updated," John asks the dragon.

"I'll lose any communicator I might wear when

I shift," he tells us, "but I will use the one Lila has on her once I find her."

With that, he and Broderick hurry to the transporter. The room is filled with tension, even though Xavier keeps trying to reassure us Lila is fine. He and Brannock don't seem as agitated as we are, but I still get the distinct feeling he's trying to convince himself as much as he's trying to convince us. My fur bristles, and I stare out the window of our home, the feeling that something is coming strong.

"I want a charm to protect myself from the elements," I announce suddenly, interrupting the conversations going on around us. "Please," I tack on, realizing I was a little abrupt. "I want to be able to go on missions too." I love helping with the little ones, but I would much prefer to rip the entrails from Lila's enemies if I can.

"Yes, I'm sorry I hadn't thought to offer it to you before now. That was inconsiderate of me." Xavier bows his head in apology.

"No, it's okay. I haven't wanted to be involved previously. I've been happy staying behind, protecting the children and my omega, but I feel like they are perfectly safe here, and I have battle abilities if needed."

A charm appears in Xavier's hand, and he comes over and slips it over my head. "This is spelled to change with you. It will keep your body cooled to the ideal temperature for a lightning cat, even if it's hot as hell outside."

I feel a wave of cold wash over me. Although I can deal with the temperatures of our living area, it isn't the most ideal, but this makes me feel like I'm in our den. Another charm appears in his hand.

"This is for Echo."

I take it, pleased that he thought to provide one for him too, even though he won't join us on missions.

"I think you should all get some rest," Brannock says. "Xavier and I need to return to the ship so we can head back to the planet tomorrow. Keep us updated on any news from Tirrian, and be ready to go if you are needed."

They return to the harvester ship, and the others take their advice and disperse to rest. I head to our den to wait for Echo. I'm going to have to tell him what's happening, and I hope he isn't going to be too upset.

CHAPTER NINETEEN

Echo

"Ariel is a lovely name for a girl, but I'm not sure Flounder is the best idea for a boy," I say diplomatically to the very pregnant merman as we watch the babies' favorite movie. I think I probably enjoy it as much as they do, but I know the rest of the dads are a little sick of it. I like to sing along with the characters.

When I look at the merman, though, there's a sparkle in his eye, and he starts to chuckle. "I was just seeing if you were paying attention. I would not name my children after a guppy. What about Triton? He was a supreme specimen of a merman, though mers do not have facial hair. That was just weird," he says, shaking his head, and I breathe a sigh of relief. Thank goodness. I'm not sure Lila would have forgiven us if we encouraged the use of the name Flounder.

Nikos winces and puts a hand on his belly as it moves like crazy. My eyes widen. I've never seen it move like that before. "Can I?" I ask him, reaching for his stomach.

"Of course. This is what you have to look forward to," he tells me, grabbing my hand and placing it on his belly. My mouth drops open at how vigorous the babies move.

"Does it hurt?" I ask him, because it sure looks like it does.

"Sometimes, but I don't care. It's all worth it. I can't wait to hold them in my arms. I hope I have two pretty little mermaids who look exactly like their mama." Gone is the ridiculous, silly can of tuna, and in his place is a proud, intelligent man. I've come to know a side of Nikos different than the one he presents to the world. He has a wicked sense of humor and is highly intelligent. I've really enjoyed our shared time and hope that once he has given birth, he will still spend time with me during my pregnancy.

"Would you like me to rub your back?" I ask him.

His eyes widen in surprise. "Would you?" he asks a little hesitantly. "You'll have to get into the pool with me.

"Sure, I don't mind getting wet. Max is the one who hates water," I tell him with a smile, climbing off the bean bag I was sitting on while we watched the movie and stepping down into the shallow section he is lounging in. "Roll to the side," I instruct, knowing there is no way he can roll onto his stomach. He does as I asked, and I kneel down and rub his lower back on one side of his body.

He groans loudly as my hands caress his stiff muscles, careful not to rub too hard and hurt him. I massage in slow, circular motions to ease some of the pain before kneading a little without using my claws, and his breathing evens out.

"That feels magical. Thank you, Echo. You have very nice hands. I like the way they feel on my body," he mutters, way more relaxed than he was. "I bet they would feel magical gripping my cock."

I stop suddenly, surprised by what he said, but when I look down, his eyes are closed, and I think maybe he doesn't know he said that out loud.

"Roll to the other side," I say, moving so he can. I repeat the motions on the opposite side, and he moans, reaching down to adjust himself under his scales.

"Wish I could ask you to ease the ache in my dick," he slurs before he snores slightly.

I smirk at those last muttered words. I'm pretty sure he would be mortified if he knew I heard that inner thought. I'm happy that I can do something to help him. I've grown very attached to the merman, and I don't like seeing him in pain. It calls to my omega side to soothe him. I don't want to look at that too closely, because that is an attachment reserved for streak members, which I guess that's what he is now. They all are, Lila's mates, but what I feel for the others feels more like companionship, except for the good doctor. What I feel for him is something different, and I think I am starting to feel that way about the merman too. I want to pet him and tell him he's pretty and snuggle into his belly and purr for him.

I ache deep inside, even though Maxsim fucked me into submission not that long ago. Maybe if I rile him up by telling him about how I'm starting to feel about the merman, he will fuck me into submission again.

I whisper goodbye to Nikos, not wanting to wake him. He said he hasn't been getting much sleep because he can't get comfortable. Link wants him to stay close to the communicator, and the anemone where he usually rests is at the bottom of the pool.

I grab a towel, drying my fur as I hurry back to our room. Max will grumble if I come back wet, and the cold air in our den isn't fun when you're soaked through.

The suite is quiet when I arrive, and I frown. Where is everyone? It isn't too late, and usually, someone would still be up watching something on the television, reading a book, or talking about their day, but the living area is empty, and the lights are dimmed, leaving only one lamp lit in case anyone gets up in the middle of the night.

I make my way to Max's and my shared room. Lila offered me one of my own, but Max and I have been sharing for so long it makes sense. Plus, there is room for her when she wants to visit us and the babies when they arrive. I caress my stomach, which has started to show a little.

Our babies will need to stay in our room to start with. Their ability to withstand higher temperatures are limited when they are small. They won't be able to co-exist with our other children until they are older. It's something I worry about all the time. I know it also bothers Maxsim that he can't go on away missions with the others because we have low tolerance to high heat. I've been meaning to ask Xavier if he can create a more permanent spell or charm like the one he gave me to spend time with Nikos under the sun lamps.

The door to our room slides back when I press my hand to the sensor, and I step into the space, discarding my wet loincloth in the dirty clothes basket before heading to our sunken nest. I hear Maxsim's rumbling purr, and when I jump down, I'm surprised to find him already asleep. I can't remember the last time we didn't go to bed together, but it is a lot later than I thought it was. His eyes open the minute he scents me, and his rumbling purr becomes louder.

"Omega, why do you smell needy?" he growls at me, sitting up.

I blush, not willing to meet his eyes. "Pregnancy hormones," I tell him, not ready to talk about my small, growing attraction to the merman, but then I notice he has something new around his neck.

"What is that? Did someone give you a gift?" A surge of jealousy whips through me. I know it wasn't Lila, so who is gifting my alpha jewelry? My lightning sparks and lights up the dark nest.

Maxsim reaches up and drags me down into the nest, nuzzling into my neck and nipping his mate mark on my shoulder. I can smell the warlock on him. It's strong, like he was in his presence recently.

"Is Lila back?" I ask him as he pulls away.

"No, she is still on the planet." He sighs and tells me about her new mate, which I find a little tricky to comprehend.

"A god?" I ask, unable to hide my awe.

"Yeah, trust Lila to be mated to a god." Maxsim chuckles, shaking his head. He leans over and grabs something from the edge of the nest and puts it over my head. I can scent the warlock magic now and realize that's what I could smell on my alpha. "Xavier gave us these charms so we aren't disadvantaged by our temperature intolerance."

I look down, picking up the charm that's around my neck. It's a pretty carved stone that I can feel pulsing with the warlock's magic.

"He said it will shift with us." This is exactly

what I was hoping he could create for our babies so they can be with their siblings and not stuck because of the disadvantages of our species.

"Do you think he would create two for the babies?" I ask him, and he smiles gently.

"I think Xavier would do anything you asked him to for our babies."

I heave out a sigh of relief. I've been so worried about them missing out on so much. I want them to be able to sleep and play with our other children.

"We will ask him when he returns from Husadavia," Maxsim tells me, rubbing a hand over my back.

"How did you get these if he isn't back?" I ask, biting my lip as his touch turns from comforting to something a little more erotic.

"He popped back to give us an update," he explains. "That's how I know about Lila's new mate." Maxsim tips his head to the side in a very feline gesture. "It's the being who controlled the plants and creatures on Husadavia for the harvesters. Turns out, he's one of the old gods."

I try to make sense of what my alpha is telling me. "Which one?"

"Zeydan, the earth elemental god. Xavier didn't know a lot, but Lila stayed behind so she could find out more. Before you get upset, the dragon has gone down to make sure she is safe, even though the god assured Xavier she would be unharmed. He must have known her shifter mates would not have been okay with that."

"Why the dragon?" I think about how horrible he has been to Lila, and a growl escapes me.

"The dragon is trying to make up for his mistakes. Don't be so harsh on him. I was just as bad to start with, and thankfully, Lila forgave me. The dragon deserves forgiveness too."

"Hmm, I guess you're right."

"The dragon was the only one who would be fairly safe. There are no large, airborne predators."

"I guess that seems reasonable."

"He's going to radio back in the morning and let us know what's going on. But enough about that, why did you smell so needy when you returned from visiting with Nikos?" Maxsim asks, and I drop my eyes, unable to meet his gaze. "Is it really pregnancy hormones or something else?"

I shrug. "I find the merman sexy, just like I find the doctor sexy. It doesn't mean anything."

A rumbly sound comes from Maxsim's chest, and I wince, worried my alpha's jealousy is going to make an appearance, but instead of his scent turning sour with that particular emotion, it strengthens and deepens.

"Would you like to invite them into your nest to play with us?" he asks, and my eyes widen with surprise.

"You would be okay with that?" I ask him, unable to hide my shock.

"It seems that, like Caspian, now that you are pregnant with our kittens, I am not opposed to inviting others into our bed, or for you to anyway. I would do anything to make you happy, and if that's what it takes, then I would allow them to fuck you and Lila while I watch. Are you sure the merman is interested?"

I duck my head in embarrassment. "I don't know. He made a couple of sleepy comments that made it sound like he might be, but you know what he was like before he mated Lila—all suggestive and lewd comments—so maybe he was just reverting to his old ways."

Maxsim shakes his head vigorously. "No, I don't think so. He dropped that act the moment he realized Lila didn't care about who or what he was. Usually, words muttered at our most vulnerable are the truth. We will discuss this later. Why don't you come here so I can take care of that need? I don't like it when my omega is aching with want." He starts to purr, and I feel my cock leak and my slick drip down my thighs. My body is always ready to fuck, even though I'm already pregnant. It's like I'm permanently in heat, ready for my alpha to drive his cock home whenever he wants.

I whine as he drags me toward him, taking my mouth with his. His tongue caresses mine as his hand goes to my cock, stroking up and down, using my precum for lubricant. I moan and thrust into his hand as his lightning pulses in his grip, mixing pleasure and pain. He growls his approval before releasing my cock.

Grabbing my hips, he manhandles me onto my front. "Present for me," he commands as I lift my hips, giving him the access he requires, unable to stop the whine from escaping my mouth.

"Please, Alpha, fill me," I beg as he uses his hands to spread my cheeks before running his tongue over my slick drenched asshole.

"Such a good omega, dripping with slick for his alpha. Ready for my knot? I'm going to fuck you hard and deep and make sure that you never feel needy." He lines himself up before slamming home. My moan echoes through the cave as I sink into the pleasure my alpha wrings from my body.

CHAPTER TWENTY

Zeydan

The little earth elemental in front of me holds her breath as I reach for my cloak to reveal myself to her for the first time. Anticipation vibrates off her, and I feel a pang of worry. I hope she is not disappointed when she sees me. It's been a long time since anyone saw me in my true form. I lost the ability to glamour when my power was depleted and decided that a cloak was a good way to keep myself anonymous, but this little mimic is my soulmate. I felt it the first time I saw her in the bar on Z68, when she was in her true form, meeting with one of the harvesters. I didn't stick around, because I knew it was just a matter of time before I saw her again, and I needed to make arrangements. Previously, this dwelling was nothing but a place to lay my head and rejuvenate my power in the soil, so I had to make sure it was a comfy and cozy abode for my beloved.

I could have been knocked over with a feather when I finally realized what the pull to her was. I originally thought that maybe she was Lilessa, because she has the same kind of resonance that life had once upon a time, but I quickly dismissed it. Lilessa always claimed we had mates out there, and it was only a matter of time until we found them, but after thousands and thousands of years, we had given up hope—the four of us elementals even more so since Lilessa and Vivax disappeared. I haven't seen any of my fellow gods in close to six hundred years. I have no idea where they are, or even if they still exist. Maybe they chose to fade.

For the first time ever, I'm nervous about my appearance. I have been worshiped by millions, yet this little Skarrian's opinion is more important than any who have come before her.

I slowly drag the cloak back, revealing myself to her. The ears on top of my head twitch with agitation, and my tails do the same thing, all nine of them fanning out behind and above me as I allow the cloak to fall. When I finally meet her eyes, I brace for rejection, but what I find isn't the antici-pated shock, but a deep, throbbing burst of lust. My cock hardens beneath my skirt. It has remained unused and dormant for so long, I thought I had become impotent there as well as with my magic, but the mere scent of my mate's arousal has it rising to attention, making it rock hard. I am thankful for my long skirt and its fullness for hiding the attraction. It isn't something I want to force on her until she is ready.

"Wow, you're a kitsune," she says, standing up and walking toward me. "I've read about them in Japanese mythology. You could be a samurai warrior right out of a fiction book." She reaches out like she wants to run her hand over my naked chest but quickly snatches it back when she realizes what she's doing. I feel a wave of triumph flow through me and struggle to contain my smirk at the thought that my mate is as drawn to me as I am to her. A searing sting on my shoulder makes me shout out loud as the Skarrian attraction mark burns itself into my skin. I see her flinch and feel her somewhat disgruntled acknowledgement as the same thing happens to her. My glee fades as I try to get a read on her feelings, but from what I can tell, she's not disappointed, just unsurprised. I can hear her thoughts.

Of course an attraction mark appears. This man is walking sex on legs. You are only human, Lila, or slutty Skarrian.

I drop my gaze so she doesn't see me laughing at her words. It must be hard for someone who grew up without knowledge of her true nature.

"I don't know what you speak of, this kitsune, but I am happy that my form does not repulse you,"

I say quietly as she walks behind me and brushes a hand over one of my tails. My cock throbs and weeps, and it's all I can do to muffle my groan.

"Fuck, I'm sorry. I don't know what came over me. I couldn't stop myself from touching your tails. That was rude." She sounds embarrassed, and her cheeks are a darker green like she's blushing when she steps in front of me. I reach for her tiny little hands, slightly frustrated by the size difference between us. She's so small, I don't want to break her.

"Don't be, they radiate their own animal magnetism. They want you to pet them," I tell her, and a little wrinkle forms between her eyes as she bites her lip.

"They?"

I release my hold on my pets. One by one, they take form and jump to the ground, crowding around her, their own bushy tails wagging with delight as they smother her tiny form in licks.

She collapses to the ground under all nine of them, and I lose her under the pile as they continue to lavish her with love and attention.

She giggles and squeals, the sound bringing a smile to my lips, her joy palatable. "Such adorable murder puppies. Stop, okay, stop, ugh. I'm definitely going to need a bath now," I hear her mutter, but she doesn't sound distressed.

I whistle and encourage them to retreat anyway. All nine of them sit in a line and wait for her to come to them instead. She stands up and gives them all a pat. "What are their names?" she asks, and I shrug.

"They don't have names. They are me, and I am them." I know that sounds like a bunch of mystical crap, but it's true. They are just different aspects of my soul.

"Okay, they are Baby Z One to Nine." She touches each of them, numbering them one through nine as I watch on with amusement. Each of them have slightly different colors, so it isn't hard for her to tell them apart.

"What does the Z stand for?" she asks once she gets to the end. All nine of them find a space on the ground and get comfortable. They will return when I want them to, but they've been cooped up for a long time, so they deserve a break.

"I am Zeydan," I tell her, sitting down on my chair, willing my cock to go down. I see her mouth my name, and I am instantly craving to hear it out loud.

"I'm Lila," she says even though I already know this much.

"Well, now that I've shown you mine, are you going to show me yours?" I wave a hand, and she nods.

"I guess it is only fair, but I will be naked when I change forms, and this dress won't fit me."

I may be a god, and a benevolent one unless crossed, but I am also a male, and I am not going to complain about seeing my mate naked for the first time, nor am I going to do the right thing and offer her my cloak—at least not straight away.

"Your naked form is not going to upset me in the least," I tell her calmly, my rumbling tone betraying that I'm not as calm and composed as I seem. She playfully rolls her eyes at me, and I feel her acceptance.

Her form shimmers, covered with a sparkly purple mist, and I see movement within. Her body starts to grow bigger, as do her proportions as her wings, tail, and horns shrink and disappear. When the pretty mist fades, it's all I can do not to swallow my tongue. Lila is curvy in all the right places, with generous breasts and ample hips built for holding onto when you slide deep into her pussy. Her long, multicolored hair drapes down her back, hiding her pert cheeks from my view, and her pretty pink nipples are peaked. I'm dying to lean forward and take one of the hardened buds into my mouth, but I hold myself back. She is unaware that she is my mate, and despite the attraction mark on her shoulder, I want to earn my place by her side. I will ensure she can rescue her grandma.

I bend down and retrieve my cloak, holding it out for her. She snatches it out of my hand with a relieved, "Thank you."

She pulls it around herself, and I watch her hold it up to her nose and breathe in deeply. I can't stop myself from purring my approval, knowing that when I get it back, it's going to smell like her too.

"How many forms have you mimicked?" I ask her, trying to relieve the small amount of anxiety I still feel coming from her.

"I have Celestian, Barcoa, earth and fire elementals, a necro, Rilaxian, warlock, Aquilian, and Madovian."

"Madovian? They are a repulsive species. That was one of the last ones Vivax created, pouring all of her jealousy and malice into it. They would not be an easy race to assimilate."

She wrinkles her nose and shakes her head. "They aren't, but one of them was being paid by the Syndicate to infiltrate the circus. We are hoping to use that form to return the favor after we rescue Grandma Liliana," she explains, and I run a hand over my smooth chin. I've never grown any facial and body hair, none of us gods do.

"That isn't many forms," I point out, and she shrugs.

"I also have mates, which have given me more options. I have a kraken shifter mate, which allows me to access their form, a Vilaxian mate, and I drank from the blood goblet which changed me into part Vilaxian, and two lightning cat mates. My other Skarrian power is a whisperer, and I can shift into cat form as well. I have assimilated nanotechnology from my cyborg mate also." That's a little better. I would prefer her to have more forms, but we have time to rectify that. Like the Aaz'axian cord I saw joining them, I also saw one linking Lila to the damn dragon who kept circling us today. They think I didn't see him, but it is hard to miss an object that big in the sky.

A whisperer power—another supposed long-lost power. "Have you tried controlling any other kind of shifter?" I ask her, knowing that lightning cats should not be the only animal she is able to control. I was there when Lilessa created her Skarrian race, and we all added our own input into the kind of powers they may contain.

"No, is that a thing?" she asks, her eyebrows rising in question.

"Yes, Lilessa made it so that a whisperer could help any kind of shifter. That's what the power was originally meant for—helping them with their emerging shifting powers. Fluxx and Skarr are so closely linked because both were created by the goddess of life."

"So you're a god?" she asks, changing the subject from her back to me, and I can see she has questions.

"Yes, I am the earth elemental god. Lilessa was the goddess of life, and Vivax was the goddess of death. Then we had Sanshia, who was the goddess of fire, Tito, the god of water, and Markit, the god of air. I have not seen my co-elementals for many years, and we have no idea what happened to Lilessa or Vivax."

"And your powers were stolen?" She's trying to make sense of the story I told her.

"Yes, and one of the two missing goddesses is involved. We're certain. Which one, I do not know, maybe both of them, and I have no idea how they did it. It should not be possible. All four of us were diminished in power." I grit my teeth as the anger and betrayal that had grown numb over time rears its head again. I clench my fists in an effort not to take it out on my mate. "When we get to the bottom of it, the perpetrator will pay. We searched high and low for both of them, but their power signatures disappeared just after the war. It was like they both ceased to exist. That's why I was shocked when I thought I felt a spark of it in you."

"And you were at the bar, hidden in the corner, concealed by your cloak. You've known who I was this whole time?" she asks, sounding dismayed as she comes to that realization.

"Yes, I have, but it was amusing watching and listening to you all scheme." I try to reassure her, but I don't think it works if her glare is anything to go by.

"Are you going to help me?" she asks, cutting to the chase, her eyes narrowing with her anger. I like seeing her like this. It is much preferable to her earth elemental form, which was weak.

"Of course I will. All you had to do was ask. Shall we stop this ridiculous charade of harvesting fruit?" I ask her, and she grimaces.

"You already killed Oak. Poor Elm is going to be down three more harvesters," she argues, and I scoff.

"My powers may be weak, little one, but I assure you, I can have your quota of fruit picked within the blink of an eye."

"So why don't you help them like that normally?" she asks, her anger replaced by curiosity.

"I am paid to protect them, not to provide them with a bounty. They are allowed to harvest, but they must prove they are worthy of my bounty, so they pick, and I protect, and if they are not worthy, they die. It is a way to pass the time. I have been bored for so many years. If they knew that I owned the company they were working for, they would not work as hard as they do."

"You own the halla mead label?" She sounds surprised.

"Like I said, it is a way to pass the time. I own a lot of different businesses all over the galaxy. Most of them are some kind of food or beverage derived from my bountiful planets."

I feel a being teleport down to the planet, and I cock my head to listen as my protective plants and creatures try to attack it. Ah, it is the dragon, returned to seek out his mate. Luckily for him, I have no predator that is at home in the sky. I guess I cannot fault the beast, I would be the same if I didn't know my mate was safe. I told the warlock exactly who I was and who Lila was to me, which was why he was happy to leave her, and I am sure he informed the Aaz'axian.

A shifter at war with his inner beast would not be able to take Xavier for his word though. He would want to see for himself, and I respect that. I use my magic to clear a path for him, using the plants to light the way and lead him toward us. I will allow him to see for himself she is fine, but then he must return to the other large ship that is circling my planet. My mate will spend the night with me, and when the sun reaches its zenith in the sky, we will go in search of her grandmother. I will enjoy the stroll through my creations, because when my mate returns to the ship, I will accompany her. My life is about to change, and I can no longer be happy with just existing.

CHAPTER TWENTY-ONE

Lila

Zeydan stands up and makes his way over to the wall of glass, peering out into the darkness, his cute little fox ears perking to attention. All nine of his tails are also on alert, and they hurry over to the window and stare outside as well. A few of them growl and yip before they flow back into his form, turning from foxlike creatures with four legs to a part of the magnificent god in front of me.

Holy smokes, he's gorgeous, like something out of my anime fantasies. He's tall with miles of pale skin and long white hair that rivals mine in length. His almond-shaped eyes with vertical pupils are red, surrounded by long, dark lashes. Long, lean lines of sculpted muscle cover his naked torso, ending in a slim waist. The rest of him is covered by a floor-length black skirt embroidered with flowers, and it has a plain green sash tied around it, draping down one side. His feet are bare, but his toes have claws. Where the rest of him is pale, with barely any color apart from the dusky pink of his nipples and pouty lips, his tails and ears are an abundance of colors, like the shimmery greens, purples, and golds of a peacock but with an added blast of red, pink, and orange. All of them differ slightly, creating a vibrant rainbow mass of fur. No wonder I couldn't stop myself from reaching out and touching him. He's beautiful.

I watch him closely, not one bit afraid even though I now know he is a god of creation. Instead of being cautious and terrified, I just want to throw myself at him and lick his abs and claim him as mine before any other bitch can get their hands on him. A growl escapes my mouth as my kraken, whisperer, and mimic let it be known that they agree with me wholeheartedly.

"We are about to have a guest, and I don't think he is going to be happy to smell your attraction to me." Zeydan turns from the window to look at me, a smile on his lips.

Crap, he can smell that? Of course he can. When will I learn? Instead of being embarrassed, I decide to embrace it and shrug.

"What? You have to know you're sexy. I'm not going to apologize no matter which mate of mine is bearing down on us. They should all know better than that by now. They are aware that my mimic is a needy bitch." I move over to stand next to him, peering out into the darkness.

It's no longer pitch black out there though. The jungle surrounding the house is also lit up by bioluminescent plants, but not enough so I can make out details of all the animals milling about in the undergrowth. They are large in size, and I can see an occasional tail swipe back and forth, but mostly they are shrouded in shadow.

"Are they going to attack?" I ask, pointing at them, and Zeydan shrugs.

"Maybe." He seems apathetic to the possibility.

"I would prefer that…" I trail off so he can fill in the blank.

"The dragon," he replies.

I feel my eyebrows jump in surprise. Tirrian is the one who returned? I thought for sure it would be Cas or Max, even with the risk to them.

"Despite the fact that the dragon has been a colossal ass, I would prefer that he didn't get mauled by your creations," I say calmly, not wanting him to hear how worried I am. I'm sure he probably knows, but he does the polite thing and doesn't call me out on it.

"He and his beast have been at war." Zeydan narrows his eyes as Tirrian drops down into the clearing directly in front of the house, the ground vibrating on impact, the vines from before having retreated to who knows where. "But they are in harmony now, and they will only wait so long before they will claim you." There's a hint of warning in his tone, like he's cautioning me not to be surprised if this pushes him over the edge, but I know my stubborn dragon. I doubt this is going to force his hand.

Predators creep out of the bushes, stalking the large dragon. Tirrian's dragon roars and breathes fire in their direction. The shadowed predators tuck their tails and slowly retreat, acknowledging the greater predator before them. Zeydan smiles and nods his head.

"See? He did not need my help. He proved he is worthy of you."

I roll my eyes at the macho misogynistic bullshit. Just because he's the biggest bully in the yard doesn't mean he's worthy. He still has some ass kissing to do.

Zeydan waves a hand, and one of the glass panels melts away. "Come, dragon, and have a meal, see that your mate is fine," he calls out, and Tirrian's large ass whirls around, his serpent-like neck snaking out so he's directly in front of me. His forked tongue licks over me, like he's trying to reassure himself I'm fine. All he's doing is adding to the slobber the Baby Zs covered me in.

"I definitely need a bath now," I mutter.

"How fortuitous that your dragon is here to heat the water quickly for you," Zeydan replies as Tirrian's dragon head retreats, his body shimmering as he changes into his human form. I very much doubt Zeydan is unable to heat water for me, but sure, let's just roll with the plan.

"Lila, are you okay?" he asks cautiously, getting to his feet and approaching slowly, wary of the predator standing next to me. Tirrian's dark body almost blends in with the forest behind him, only his shimmery pink wings adding a splash of color to the landscape, and what a lovely landscape it is. He's naked and beautiful. It isn't the first time I've seen him naked, but it's the first time I'm having a long look. I wipe at my mouth to make sure there isn't a little drool in the corner.

"Yes, come in. We just ate. I'll grab you a bowl, and maybe Zeydan can find you something to wear." I look at my new friend who just smirks at me.

"Are you sure? I don't care if you want him to stay naked while he eats," he says quietly, but I think Tirrian still hears him, because one corner of his lips kicks up like he's trying not to smile.

"Clothe the damn dragon," I growl at the ridiculous god. How dare he call me out like that?

I whirl around and head back to the chairs, grabbing our dirty cups and plates off the coffee table and taking them over to the little kitchen. I can hear the two males murmuring behind me, but I don't bother trying to tune in. They need to sort out their own crap.

I put our dirty dishes in the sink. I consider

washing them, but I'll wait until Tirrian is done. I search for another bowl and grumble my annoyance when I can't find one, but one suddenly appears on the counter next to the hanging pot.

"Thank you," I call. I may be annoyed, but that's no excuse to be rude. I ladle some stew into the bowl, giving him a generous portion, knowing how much food shifters consume. When I return to the seating area, another chair has appeared, and Tirrian is wearing a skirt much like Zeydan's, except the embroidery and sash are the same color pink as his wings, but all the naked abdominal flesh makes me pause for a moment. Hmm, maybe I should instate a rule—no shirts!

"Here." I hold out the bowl, but Tirrian doesn't take it. He places his hands over mine, and when I meet his eyes, I can see a little bit of amusement but mostly worry in them.

"Are you okay?" he asks me, and I nod, giving him a smile.

"I'm fine. Zeydan has been very kind and generous, and he offered to help us get Grandma Liliana," I tell him, and he breathes out a sigh of relief before taking the proffered bowl.

"Good, everyone was worried when Xavier came to give us the heads-up. He tried to tell us you were fine, but nobody was happy with that. He tends to be less worried about you than the rest of us."

"That doesn't mean he doesn't care," I argue, a little annoyed that the rest of them didn't trust him.

"No, it just means he is confident in her abilities," Zeydan chimes in. "As you should all be. She is more powerful than all of you. Look at how you handled my creatures. She could have done the same if she had a dragon form of her own." None of us miss the dig, and Tirrian winces and nods.

"Yes, I've been stubborn, I admit that, but I will do my best to make up for it now. It was one of the reasons I returned. I want Lila to have my form, but it would be best for me to give her a mating bite than have her mimic me. My dragon would be happier with that. It was our plan all along when we realized there were no other predators with flight capabilities—a way to ensure her complete safety on this mission. I wanted Xavier to teleport her to our ship so we could seal our bond this evening."

My mouth drops open in shock. Did he just tell me he wants to commit to me right here and now? I must have heard wrong, and if I didn't, then I don't know how I feel about it. Instead of acknowledging what Tirrian just said, I change the subject.

"Did the Aaz'axians have problems because you didn't want them to establish a base on your planet during the war?" It's something I've been wondering. So far, the stories of the plants and animals have been greatly overexaggerated. I don't miss the hurt look Tirrian gives me when I don't respond to his declaration of wanting to mate with me, but he hurt me so often, how could he really expect me to fall on his dick with that half-assed apology? Heck, it wasn't even an apology, and he didn't even say it to me, he was telling Zeydan.

Zeydan looks back and forth between us, his mouth pursed in contemplation, but I guess he chooses not to get involved.

"Yes, I didn't want them here, so I encouraged the inhabitants of this planet to make it difficult for them, but don't be lulled into a false sense of security. Everything here is dangerous, and with my waning power, I do sometimes have trouble controlling them."

"Did Xavier tell you who Zeydan is?" I ask the dragon who is happily consuming the bowl of food I gave him. He nods as he swallows his mouthful, a look of determination glowing in his eyes.

"Yes, he filled us in." Tirrian frowns at Zeydan. "But I don't think he has been completely honest with you."

"Like you were honest with her or yourself?" Zeydan rumbles, sounding slightly put out.

"I have learned from my mistakes, and I don't like to keep secrets from my mate." I flinch. It's not the first time he's called me that, but it's still a little jarring to hear since he was always so anti Lila from the start. "I made mistakes, and I don't wish for anyone else to do the same. I also don't see any disadvantage to her knowing the truth."

They both obviously know something I don't, and I'm starting to feel a little annoyed.

I cross my arms and glare at them. "Anyone want to share with the class?" I ask, not holding back on the sarcasm.

"You are my mate," Zeydan says casually, and I feel like I've been hit over the head with a two-by-four.

"I'm sorry, come again?" I say, spluttering.

"You are my mate. I'm not sure what is so confusing for you. Don't you feel the pull between us?" He waves a finger between us.

"Ah yes, but I thought that was my mimic power wanting to add you to the collection," I tell him frankly, shrugging. "It's hard to tell, to be honest."

"Yes. I guess that could be a problem. If it's any consolation, you can't mimic me or any of the gods. It was one of the safeguards Lilessa made when she created mimic powers. We didn't want anyone having more power than us."

"I can see how that could be a problem. So mates… with both of you. I understand the mating process with the dragon, but what about the mating process with you?" I can be calm and mature about these things—at least outwardly. Inside, I'm screaming like a little girl, and I don't know if it's Swifties at a Taylor Swift concert excitement or cheerleader at the start of a horror movie.

I should probably be more upset than I am, but there is a part of me—that slutty, needy, horny shallow part—that is thrilled this gorgeous being is my mate. I already wanted to claim him as mine by licking him, so this makes it more permanent and gives me the option of killing any bitch who looks his way—at either of them, to be honest. I kind of like how primal I feel about claiming them, and I can assure you that I will be stamping my own claim all over them so everyone can see they are mine. Maybe I need shirts that say, "Property of Lila Adams," for all my mates… or a tattoo. Yes, that's even better. I will have them all tattooed with it.

"Lila?" Tirrian's growl has me shaking my head and pushing those possessive thoughts down.

"Sorry, did you say something?" I ask, and he nods at Zeydan. "He was explaining the mating process, and you seemed to zone out," Tirrian scolds me.

"Oh, I'm so sorry." I slap a hand over my mouth, feeling embarrassed. "I was just thinking about ways that I can make sure everyone knows you're all mine. I didn't mean to ignore you."

Zeydan chuckles. "That's okay. I could hear your distracted thoughts. I was just saying that I won't be able to mate with you until I am restored to full power, and we find one of the other gods. They have to carve out a small sliver of my soul and gift it to you to create a mate bond." He sounds sad, and I know the likelihood of us finding them after all this time is slim, which means we will never be mated. I don't like the idea of that at all. A growl rumbles out of me as my kraken makes her displeasure known.

"She could always mate you the Skarrian way. Would that work too?" Tirrian suggests, and I could kiss him. I expected him to be possessive and dismissive of the god, but it really seems like he's trying. That's going to earn him some very big brownie points.

Zeydan's eyebrows furrow slightly as he thinks about it, and his tails seem to vibrate with anticipation behind him. They are curled around him so he doesn't squash them in his seat.

"It might. It wouldn't give her access to all my powers, but maybe some of them."

I wave a hand at him. "At this stage, having less powers is actually a relief. I don't think I would know what to do with life-altering godlike powers. It would probably go to my head, and I'd become Lilazilla supreme overbitch."

They exchange a confused look.

"Lilessa claimed our mates would be a perfect counterbalance for us, able to handle our power with grace and dignity," Zeydan argues, standing up. "I will take my leave. I plan on scouting the death forest, which is quite a distance from here. I have no idea how they got onto the planet without me realizing it. Maybe I was away when they were here. Anyway, you are welcome to use my bed for your mating." His tails vibrate behind him as he stretches, reaching his hands to the sky. That is quite the sight, all his long, lean muscles rippling like they want me to touch them. My hand rises, but Tirrian's snort of laughter has me blushing and putting it down, then I comprehend what Zeydan said.

"What? Ah, no. We won't be mating." I leap to my feet, Tirrian quickly hiding his look of hurt. "You were nothing but aggressive to me for weeks, and now you've suddenly changed your mind. I don't buy it. Did Xavier mess around with your head? What's to say that if we mate tonight, you won't return to being a dick tomorrow and resent me because you're trapped with me for the rest of your life?"

Tirrian winces and also stands up, reaching for me. I slap his hand away, and his shoulders slump. "I'm sorry, Lila, truly sorry for my horrible behavior. God, when I thought you had been taken by the carevasta bears, it was a huge wake-up call." He drops to his knees before me, taking my hands in his. "Please, will you forgive me? I'll spend the rest of our years together making it up to you."

Holy shiitake mushrooms, the dragon is begging me. Did I trip and smack my head? I look around the room, and I notice that Zeydan is gone. Is this a dream? Did I actually dream all of this? Tirrian's hands feel solid in mine. This must be real. But how do I respond? I want this, I really do, but he has proven he has the power to hurt me. Do I put my heart on the line for him to smash it once more?

CHAPTER TWENTY-TWO

Lila

Before I can form a response, he leaps to his feet, sweeps me up into his arms, and kisses me. Whoa, he's forceful and not taking no for an answer. He nips my bottom lip before his tongue sweeps across it, asking for entry. I sink into his embrace and allow him to kiss the hell out of me. Our tongues wrestle for dominance, but one of his hands drifts up to my hair, threading through the strands, and he gives a little tug, angling my head so he has better access to my mouth, and my inner submissive melts. I give myself over to him, my hands running up and down his back as we make out. When he pulls away, my core throbs, my heart races, and I'm breathing heavily.

"Please, Lila, please be my mate. Allow me to

bite you and make my dragons the happiest dragons in the galaxy."

My mouth drops open in shock, and I gape at him. I feel him chuckle, my body shaking with it.

"Yeah, I guess I kind of deserve that reaction and so much more, but I promise I'm sincere. If you don't believe me, switch to your warlock form and read my mind. I will happily give you access to my inner workings." His tone starts to hold a hint of desperation, and as much as I just want to go with the flow, he has hurt me so many times. I know his dragons want me, but I want to know how the man feels.

I'm still wearing Zeydan's robe, so I pull away and let it drop, not wanting to destroy it when I shift forms.

Tirrian's eyes darken, and his pupils elongate as he catches sight of my naked body. "Why are you naked? Could the god man not even create you some clothes?" he growls as smoke drifts out of his nose.

I don't bother answering him as my mimic powers take over, and I assume my warlock form. I use my nakedness as a distraction to slide into Tirrian's brain. It's a little confusing to start with, because there are three distinct voices. Holy crap, no wonder he's a grumpy fuck. Sharing his head with two different creatures must be exhausting, especially two dominant creatures, but as I concentrate, I can separate each voice.

The two dragons are guttural and beastly with animal instincts, and they are shouting, "Mate," and "Breed."

Whoa Nelly, let's ease up on the whole breeding thing. I'm not ready to add any more children to our large brood at this stage. I feel them both pout and retreat as I share my thoughts with them, and I feel a little guilty. *I promise we will one day, just not right now,* I add that extra bit of reassurance, which seems to make them happy, and they fall silent, leaving Tirrian's mind.

God, I was such a fool. I hurt her so many times, no wonder she won't forgive me. Scales, she's beautiful. How am I going to convince her that I have always wanted her, and that I am ready to commit? I can't wait to see what her dragon form looks like. Hopefully she gets both dragons so they can have fun with one another. They are going to be so sad if she doesn't get a form. My teeth ache to bite her. Dad warned me it would happen, but I didn't believe him. I just want to taste her and spend the rest of my life keeping her safe. I wonder if she would like to see my hoard. I have a lot of pretty, sparkly things to tempt her. Maybe that's what I need to do. Dragon women want to know that you can provide for them, they love pretty sparkly gems, so maybe I should show Lila my hoard—or my dick, that would probably work better. I want to chase and bite her like my dad chased my mom.

I pull out of his brain and burst into laughter. Tirrian frowns, looking slightly offended.

"Oh, you poor, poor man. No wonder you're so grumpy, your mind is chaotic," I tell him, stifling my laughter because I really don't want to upset him. It did help me make a decision though. I thought he had his shit together and knew what he wanted, but his mind is just as much of a mess as mine is. The one thing that stands out, though, is that he wants me. Heck, I can feel that he already loves me, yet he was taught that showing love makes him vulnerable, so he hides it deep down.

He steps back and crosses his arms, and I know I upset him, but I'm still naked, and he's a man, so his gaze drifts down my body again. I step toward him, and when he takes a small step back, I smirk.

"Lila, baby, stop there. You're gloriously naked, and I'm a man with two dragons riding me hard. If you want to continue this conversation, I am begging you to put clothes on."

I let my warlock form fall away, returning to my original form, and I take another step toward him.

"Lila," he growls, smoke drifting out of his nose. "I hope you are sure about this."

I look over his shoulder at the bed and wrinkle my nose. I don't want our first time to be in Zeydan's bed. That's not fair to any of us. I did see he'd like to chase me, and I want to give him that. I glance out the window, and I'm surprised to see the forest is still lit up, and there isn't an animal to be seen.

Stay within the lit area, and you will be safe, little one. Have fun, and return by morning so we can find your grand-mother. Zeydan's voice is gentle and encouraging, and I feel a rush of affection for the god. I'm still trying to wrap my head around the fact that he is my mate as well.

I push Tirrian away, and I hate the look that crosses his face, like I'm rejecting him, but I take another step backward and head toward the glass wall, which is still missing a panel from when we first let Tirrian inside. "Prove how much you want me," I taunt him and take off, using a burst of Vilaxian speed to get ahead of him and into the bushes. A roar echoes through the trees, but I don't stop to look, although I do slow to normal speed, a thrill of excitement rushing through me at the thought of being caught.

"Lila!" Tirrian growls somewhere behind me. "You better be sure, because if I catch you, I'm going to fuck you so hard you'll see stars and then bite you, making you mine. I can't stop this, you've triggered my animal's mating drive."

It's sweet that he thinks he still has to give me a choice. I knew from the minute he announced I was his mate that this male would be mine, but I had to make him work for it for all the pain he caused.

I skip over roots and leaves and duck under low-hanging branches. There isn't a path other than the one I'm making. I can see easily with my Vilaxian senses, and I can hear Tirrian slowly starting to gain ground.

"I'm going to make that pussy mine. I'm going to fuck you so hard you will feel me for days," he snarls loudly, announcing his intentions to the wilderness.

My pussy throbs with joy, and my inner voices cheer him on, willing him to go faster as my thighs grow damp. Shit, I wasn't really thinking clearly when I decided to run through the forest naked. I was thinking with my pussy and nothing else. Branches scrape and scratch me, and the slight sting of pain combined with the adrenaline of knowing I'm being pursued by a dragon make the sensations that much more intense, and my whole body throbs with need.

Should I just stop and let him catch me? Would that be fair? I'm totally down for it, but would he be upset? Why didn't I research the mating habits of dragons?

I keep running, but I realize the sound of Tirrian crashing through the bushes behind me has stopped. I slow my pace, my breath a little ragged, and I try to focus on my surroundings. I'm in a little clearing with a small pool of water surrounded by some rocks. It's like a private grotto, and there is steam drifting off the water, the light smell of sulfur in the air. Oh nice, a hot spring. I wonder if the dragon would like to go for a dip with me. Now, where did that dragon get to?

I wait, trying to catch a hint of him, but there's nothing—no sound, no movement. It's like he's gone. Did he give up? Was it too much for him? Or did one of the predators get him? Zeydan said his power wasn't always reliable. I start to move back in the direction I came, worried that maybe he's hurt or worse. No, I won't think about that, I'm sure he's fine.

There's suddenly a tremendous roar, and out of nowhere, I'm tackled to the ground. I scream and struggle, fighting the arms that are wrapped around my waist. "Gotcha," he growls into my ear, his hard length pressed against me as the rough fabric of his skirt rubs over my naked skin. That familiar scent of spicy smoke hits me, and my mouth waters as my fangs drop. I remember what Tirrian tastes like—smoky and spicy—and my stomach rumbles. Using my Vilaxian strength, I break his grip and flip him onto his back, straddling him. His eyes widen in shock. I don't think he was expecting for me to turn the tables on him. They soon narrow again as he reaches for me, but I pin his hands to the ground and tap into my warlock powers. They do as I bid, even though I retain my Lila form, and cause the vines to slither out of the surrounding forest and trap his hands.

"Hey!" He looks panicked as they wrap around his wrists and pin him in place. He thrashes around, but I have him fairly well contained.

I smirk down at him. "Oh, it was fun when I was the prey, but not so fun now, is it?" I run a finger over his naked chest, and I feel his cock twitch underneath me. I wiggle a little, moaning at the friction. "Be patient," I purr. "You will get your turn, but first, I want to have some fun. After all, you did make me wait, so it's only fair that I turn the tables." I lean in and run my nose over the vein in his neck, groaning at his scent. My fangs throb as I whisper, "Tell me no if you don't want this."

"Please, Lila," he stammers, his hips thrusting up into my body, rubbing himself against me. "Bite me," he demands, and a wide grin crosses my lips.

"Yes, sir," I say before I strike. I don't make it painless, I want him to feel my fangs—a bit of payback for the pain he caused me.

He yelps, but then I inject some venom into his blood before I start to draw mouthfuls from his vein. He relaxes beneath me as the venom rushes through his system, and his hips start to work harder against my pussy. I continue to drink as we writhe against one another like teenagers dry humping in the back row of the movie theater. I drink my fill and pull back, sealing the puncture marks with a flick of my tongue. When I look down at him, his eyes are glazed with desire and his teeth are clenched, the muscles in his jaw flexing as my venom works its way through his system.

There's no way to stop his orgasm from happening, and I don't want to waste a single drop of his cum, so I slide down his body, push his skirt up, and lick a long line up the length of his cock. He groans gutturally, and smoke starts to puff out of his nose as his nostrils flare. I'm surprised to see he has a large bulge at the base of his cock like the lightning cats, but it also has a spiked barb in the center of it two finger lengths up from the base. The barb drips with a clear fluid much like my fangs do. I stroke a finger over it, and he grimaces in pleasure and pain.

"What does this do?" I ask him, but he squeezes his eyes shut and pants.

"Please, Lila."

I remember my venom. Ignoring the barb for now, I take his fat head into my mouth. Tirrian's cock is too long for me to take all of it into my throat, even if it didn't have that sharp protrusion. I do my best, hollowing my cheeks and sucking, teasing him with my tongue and letting my fangs scrape his sensitive skin. It's what tips him over the edge, and he thrusts up. I gag in surprise as he shouts and floods my mouth with his cum. I swallow the best I can, but it's copious amounts, and he keeps bellowing as his orgasm stretches out for minutes, his cum leaking out of the sides of my mouth, making a mess of me. I feel the hot liquid dribble down my chin and onto my breast as I pull away, panting for air. His taste is unusual, kind of like a pineapple strawberry with a slightly sour bite. I swipe some of the spilled cum up with my finger and suck it off, watching my mate watch me. His eyes are slits, and there's a continuous rumble from the back of his throat, his wings shuddering underneath him.

He yanks first one arm and then the other free of the vines I had holding him in place. Crap, obviously he was just humoring me. I underestimated his shifter strength. Before I can react, he pounces, flipping me over and pushing my chest into the dirt below me.

My heart skips a beat, the thrill of being dominated sending my senses racing. I feel him run a forked tongue up my spine as his arms wrap around me, and he massages the mess of his release into my body. He's purring and rumbling and mostly beyond comprehension, which I recognize as his beasts pushing to the front.

"Such a pretty, brave, and strong mate. Made us chase her, but we caught her, and now we are going to make her ours," I hear him mutter, his voice completely guttural. I feel the pain of needles pricking my skin, and when I glance at his hands on my breasts, I notice his fingernails have given way to claws. He's dragging them over my skin in a way that has my fear rising, which just intensifies the whole situation.

"Pretty, pretty mate, going to have to make her take our cock, lock her in, and breed her."

I send a little prayer of thanks to the gods that I had Link inject me with species wide contraception. Hopefully it will stand up to whatever plan this dragon has. Otherwise, I will turn him into a set of leather handbags and shoes for me and Magenta.

I start to say something, but my complaint turns to a moan as he lightly drags a nail over my swollen, needy clit. The pain adds an extra bite of pleasure, and I relax, my body becoming pliant and flexible under his ministrations.

"Such a good, pretty girl," Tirrian mutters as I feel him line up his massive dragon dick at my entrance. It's going to hurt if he thrusts deeply, but luckily my pussy is already soaked from our play beforehand, and I like a bit of pain with sex.

His clawed hands caress the globes of my ass before he grabs my hips. His claws dig in at the same time as he thrusts his monster cock into me, and I scream, the sound high and piercing, echoing through the jungle.

"Good girl, almost there," he coos, his nails lodged into my skin, and I feel blood trickle down my body. Fuck, he isn't all the way in. My eyes water from the pain in my hips and in my pussy, but it slowly seeps away and is replaced by red-hot pleasure. No, seriously, it's hot. His hands start to heat up, and so does his cock, my pussy walls giving way to the heat and allowing him to slide a little farther in. His grip on my hips doesn't falter as he starts to slide back and forth, and I groan as I feel him all the way in my soul.

"Little more, and I promise it's going to be perfect," he says encouragingly. "Just a pinch of pain." He pulls back and slams inside again, and my eyes roll back in my head as another rush of pain washes through me, my body almost seizing at the feeling. The sharp barb that was on his dick is now inside me, digging into the walls of my pussy. I writhe under him, trying to push him away as the pain intensifies.

"Stop, please stop," I beg him, and he releases one of my hips to run his hand down my spine.

"Easy, princess, just hold out a little more." The guttural voice of his beast is gone, and it's replaced with the smooth, deep timbre of Tirrian. I'm sobbing, but as his hands soothe my skin, I feel the heat intensify as the knot at the base of his cock starts to inflate, locking him into my tight channel. He leans over me and starts to pulse his pelvis in and out, and that barb, lodged into my upper wall, starts to vibrate. My eyes roll back in my head as the pain does a one-eighty and becomes intense, unbelievable pleasure. My limbs tingle, and my body shudders as I bite down on my tongue and moan a long, loud, beastly noise. Dragon sex is mind-blowing. He continues to pulse his hips, whispering sweet words of encouragement that turn dirty.

"Look at you, taking my whole cock. Your pussy was made for me. It grips me so nicely, and I'm going to stuff you full of my cum over and over again, and when my knot deflates, I'm just going to stuff it back in with my fingers." Damn, these aliens are obsessed with breeding. I'm lucky I have my own animals that feel the same way. My kraken and whisperer side are shouting their encouragement.

He leans in and licks my neck as the vibrating barb picks up speed, and I start to thrash around underneath him. His claws return to my hips, and he holds me still as his thrusting picks up. "Want to feel you squeeze my cock. Come for me, Lila," he orders, and I am helpless to obey. It slams into me like nothing I've felt before.

My whole body explodes into one giant mass of writhing, blissful nerves as I feel it roll through every part of me. I scream out his name as I feel him latch his teeth in my shoulder blade as he grunts. The heat in my pussy becomes blistering as he fills it with his dragon cum. Like his last orgasm, this one seems to go on forever, drawing out my own pleasure for the same amount of time. I'm panting and gasping, and I feel my lower stomach start to bulge with the amount of cum he's filling me with.

Holy shit, that's not normal, but I guess my weird-shit-o-meter has had to grow a lot these last couple of months. Finally, he removes his teeth from my shoulder, and I feel the bond between us snap into place. It's all too much, and my brain short-circuits, and then it's lights out. The last thing I hear is Tirrian calling me his mate.

CHAPTER TWENTY-THREE

Tirrian

My beasts crow in my head when I feel Lila go limp in my arms. Retracting my nails from her hips, I lean down and lick up the blood on her left hip and then on the right. My cock is still firmly lodged in Lila and isn't going anywhere for a while. I'll come at least a few more times before my cock deflates.

Next, I lean in and clean up her shoulder blade. All three wounds are going to scar, showing the world that Lila belongs to me. I can't wait for her to feel her own dragon and return the favor. My cock throbs again, the barb pulses, and she moans. I gather her up and sit back on my heels, wrapping my body around her. My natural heat should keep her warm while we wait this out. I purr to her and stroke her silky hair before brushing the dirt off the front of her body. My hand runs over the small bulge in her lower stomach, which is filled with my cum, and I can't stop the roar that leaves my lips.

My mate is filled with my cum. I will be sad to see it all run out, but one day soon, it won't. One day soon, I will fuck her in our dragon forms, and that cum will fill her womb, fertilizing her eggs and helping grow our babies. Then, when she lays them, we will take turns keeping them warm with our fire. She will be such a fierce mother to our babies, just as she is to the ones we already have.

I freeze. Whoa. I have kids. Three adorable bundles of trouble with four more to arrive soon. My dragons start to purr at the realization. We hadn't even thought about not just gaining a new mate but a family—a family with children. Dragons adore children, and while I've seen Lila's beautiful babies a few times, it took everything I had to hold myself back. My dragons want to gather them up and spirit them away, locking them in our hoard to keep them safe. Now I no longer have to restrain myself. I must find them some gifts. You are never too young to start your own hoard. When we are on Fluxx, I will gift them something from my own. No, I'll show them and let them pick out something. That will be more meaningful. It's what dragon parents do for their own children to start their hoard, and it would show that I consider all of those babies mine as well. Yes, that is a good idea. I'm sure my mother and father will do the same thing. They will spoil those children rotten. Oh well, they have plenty of other parents and grandparents for discipline.

Lila groans and moves a little, and I know she's regaining consciousness. I've tried so hard to stay still. I want her awake and participating during this. I lean down and place little kisses all over her neck. "Are you okay?" I ask her, wanting to gauge how she feels before I start the process all over again. I don't have to claw and bite her this time, I'll leave those marks be, but I'm going to make her feel good again. My barb buzzes, and she moans.

"Holy crap," she rasps, her voice husky from abuse. "That thing is like my favorite vibrator on steroids."

"Do you feel okay? We'll probably stay like this for a while. I have to come a few more times before it will deflate," I tell her gently, although my inner dragons are preening with her praise.

She gives me a thumbs-up before brushing her hair back from her face. She succeeds, but not before she smudges the dirt streaked across her cheek.

"I could really use a bath," she mutters and then looks down. "Whoa. That looks a lot like it did when I was pregnant." She points to her stomach, and I feel her heart start to race, and she squirms with panic. My dragons are hurt, but I understand.

"Easy, it's just my cum. Dragons produce a lot of it. I can't get you pregnant in this form. We have to do it in dragon form," I explain, and she freezes. I feel her pussy contract around me, and my eyebrows jump. Oh, she likes the idea of that, and it makes my dragons very happy.

"In dragon form?" she asks, and her pussy ripples around me as her breathing starts to grow heavier once more.

"Yes, we would both shift and then mate while in flight, where I would impregnate you. You would then lay our eggs, and we would keep them warm by blowing fire over them.

"In dragon form?" she asks again, and I think I may have broken her brain. I stifle a chuckle.

"Yes, princess, in dragon form. We can't wait to see what you look like when you shift. My dragons are dying for you to bite us too," I tell her reassuringly, worried this is all too much for her.

"Oh God. That's what that new voice in my head is." She reaches up to rub her temple, shifting her body slightly, and she moans when my cock pulses inside her. I'm ready to go again, but I need her to be on the same page. "My dragon. It's getting a little crowded up here."

"Is she talking to you?" I ask, curious to know what she's like. Female dragons are fierce and protective, but once they have been caught, they are submissive with their mates.

"She isn't making a lot of sense right now. She's

dicktimitized. Basically, she's praising your giant cock and the amount of seed you have given us," Lila says, sounding a little exasperated, and I can't help but laugh. Poor Lila, it has been such an adjustment for her prudish Earth sensibilities, but she is making such an effort to embrace the more primal parts of her psyche, which are making themselves known.

I wrap my arms around her, cupping each breast with my hands as I lick the bite mark on her shoulder. It's still weeping blood and will continue to until we part. Blood is life and a large part of dragon mating. When two dragons mate in their animal form, there is often a fight before the male can get the female to submit. He has to prove his worth, that he is strong enough to protect their hoard and their family, and female dragons are vicious when they are testing their mates. If I can't subdue her dragon, I won't be allowed to mate her. I can't wait to try.

"Tirrian," she moans, and I love the way my name sounds coming off her tongue. I lean her over, her hands coming down to brace herself against the ground, as I start to thrust once more, no longer able to hold back.

I can't fuck her as hard as I want because I'm locked into place. Next time, I won't use my barb or knot. Normally I can pick and choose when I use it, and I haven't ever felt the need to with any other female before Lila, but I literally wasn't able to stop it this time. Breeding my mate for the first time is indescribable. Next time, I will fuck her long and hard. I'll let her feel every inch of my dick as I drive it into her body.

She thrashes around, but I have her trapped and unable to get away, the barb inside vibrating on her inner walls, sending her flying once more. I reach around and pinch her nipples, and her pussy convulses, the suckers deep inside fluttering like a thousand little kisses on my dick, and I can't hold back. I roar again, and I flood her belly with my seed. My hands slide from her nipples to her stomach so I can feel it bulge out even farther.

"Oh God, yes, breed me! Fill me with your cum!" Lila's voice has a gravelly growl, and I know I'm hearing from her dragon for the first time.

I roar again. This time, she echoes it, throwing her head back and bellowing her pleasure to the sky. My scales ripple across my body as I struggle to hold my form. My dragons want to push forward and meet their mate, but if they do that while I'm locked in her, they will kill her. I beg them to stay calm, and when they realize she might die, they quickly retreat.

I feel her skin ripple beneath my chest, and I pull back, leaving her on her knees in front of me as scales flow across her skin. I watch in horror as her skin splits and wings push out of her back as she screams with pain, and my barb pulses again, turning that pain back into pleasure. I heave out gasps of air as my orgasm continues to roll through my body, and Lila's wings push out through the jagged wounds in her body. They stretch out wide to the sides, and she groans before they tuck in against her back. I guess these aren't her first set of wings, but they are very different from her Celestian and Elementi wings. These are leather, with bony talon protrusions on the ends of each wing.

I run a hand over one of them. Her color is stunning. Just like her hair, she is shimmery white with opalescent orange, blue, and pink veins running through it. She's going to look stunning as a dragon. I know of no other dragon who has the same coloring, and she's all mine. All the other dragons are going to be so envious. I feel a smug sense of satisfaction from both of my dragons, and I roll my eyes.

"Are you okay?" I ask her as she shivers from my touch on her new wings.

"God, yes, so okay. That feels incredible. My whole body is like one deliciously sensitive nerve."

"Good girl," I rumble, feeling so proud of my mate, and she purrs with contentment. "Only two more times." I drape my body over hers again and start rolling my hips, ready to add to the load of cum inside Lila's body.

Time seems to fade away, and I'm not sure how long we've been connected when my knot finally deflates and my barb lies flat against my cock once more. Instead of pulling out, I keep my cock lodged deep inside of my mate as I pet and caress her, praising her for being such a good girl. Lila shivers and smiles softly. My dragons are both satisfied with breeding her. Next time we fuck, it will be for the man and woman without knots or barbs.

"Lila, baby, should we wash off?" I ask her, pointing out the hot spring, and she raises her head, giving a small nod before sagging again. She's completely worn out, and I go into caring mode. I stand up with her still seated on my cock. It's going to be messy when I pull out, because Lila's body won't retain my cum like her dragon form would. I really don't want to wear all of it, but I also don't want it floating around in the springs, so there is no other option.

When her feet touch the ground, I hold her hips and bend my knees, sliding my cock out of her. It's like I pulled a plug, and I watch with detached emotions as all of my cum, my fertile seed, rushes out of Lila's body. My dragons croon a sad sound inside me that has my heart aching. I try to reassure them that Lila will give us babies one day, and remind them we still have three little ones to love on back at the ship, with four more to join them soon. This appeases them slightly.

"Holy fuck. Is your cock a firehose?" Lila gasps in horror as the mess of sticky, thick golden fluid continues to drain out of her, flowing down her legs and onto the ground.

"Dragon eggs require a lot of cum for fertilization. They are thick shelled and large," I explain. "It correlates in human form as well."

"Where does it all go when you're at home? You must have plastic protective sheets on your beds."

I chuckle at my new little mate. Goosebumps break out over my skin at the knowledge that this beautiful woman is my mate. I was an idiot for fighting it for so long. Dylan had me all twisted up inside and feeling guilty. God, I could kill him myself now.

"Well, in dragon form, it stays inside the female dragon. When the male dragon unlocks and pulls his cock out, the female's opening seals until she's ready to lay her eggs, keeping all the cum inside her body to fertilize the eggs. In their humanoid form, most males will carry their female to a bathroom and let it run out into the shower or bath."

She wrinkles her nose as the fluid continues to run out, though it has slowed considerably. "Not in our bath. Everyone bathes in that, and it's continuously full, like a hot tub. It will have to be a shower. Hopefully it won't clog up the ship's waste system."

I burst out laughing, unable to control it any longer, and she grimaces, looking embarrassed.

"Shut up, these are important issues."

I grab her shoulders and kiss her before scooping her up into my arms. "No one is going to care about a little bit of extra fluid, Lila. Your kraken makes a mess too, doesn't he?" I ask.

"They will if they have to lie in the wet spot, because that's going to give it a whole other meaning, and yes he does, but not all at once."

I stride over to the pool, my gorgeous mate in my arms, and step down into the steaming water. It's blistering hot, but I'm a dragon, and we like it hot. It feels amazing on my achy body, and from the indecent moan Lila lets out as I move deeper, I would say she agrees.

"Ugh, that feels so good," she murmurs, and I let her feet drop down while keeping my arms around her body. She embraces me and rests her head against my chest as we float for a moment.

"You are a lot more heat resistant now that we are mated."

She lifts her head and looks up at me, her eyes hooded and sleepy. "But I didn't bite you yet," she argues, and I shrug.

"No, not yet, but my bite when I filled you with my cum was enough to trigger your change. Once we have washed off, we can see if you can shift if you want."

She sighs and snuggles against me, this time wrapping her legs around my waist. "We can. How late do you think it is?" she asks, not moving.

"It's probably middle of the night, so we can wash off, shift, and let our dragons stretch their wings together if you want."

"Will I have a sea dragon form as well?" she asks.

"I don't know. We will have to wait and see. There isn't enough water here to try."

"What about in the Aquilian pool on the ship? Is that going to be big enough for two sea dragons?"

"Dragons can change their size at will. The size of my dragon in the circus show is not its full size. I'm afraid it wouldn't be able to fly like it does in the dome if I was at full size, and I can make the sea dragon smaller than you've seen it before."

"You were the dragon on Fluxx, swimming outside of the mating dome?" She pulls back and looks me in the eye.

I wince and drop my head, not looking at her. "Yes, sorry. I went home to visit my family and needed to take a swim. I didn't realize he headed in that direction until it was too late. He pushed me to the back, so to speak, and was fully in control. I only wrestled it back once he could no longer scent you in the water."

"So you've known all along that I was your mate?"

I expected her to be angry, but she just sounds curious. "Yes. The moment I saw you, I knew, but Dylan filled my head with crap, and I felt guilty so I lashed out—not to mention I always hated the idea that the animals decide for us."

"I can understand that. I've had every choice but Link taken out of my hands, so I understand where you are coming from."

I flinch, her words cutting me, and she quickly shakes her head. "No, I wasn't having a go at you. I really am okay with everything that's happened, but it did take me a while to adjust to fated mates. It's why I don't fight it anymore. My inner kraken taught me to accept it."

I pull her back into my arms, not wanting to let go of her just yet. "When we are back on Fluxx to rescue Silac's family, will you come with me to the dragon stronghold and meet my parents?"

"I'd love to," she tells me, and I feel her smile against my chest. "Are there any others of your family members who are going to try and kill me?"

She snuggles deeper into my embrace. Her wet, sexy body rubs against me, and my cock decides to join the party. I'm only a hot-blooded male, after all, and her tits feel amazing rubbing against my wet chest.

"There's always a chance, but I doubt it," I growl, and smoke wafts out of my nose as my hands drift to her ass. I cup it, lifting her higher before sliding my long length through her folds.

She moans and throws her head back, grinding down on my length.

"Oh well, something to look forward to. Now how about you fuck me when I can watch you?" she asks, her wings spreading out in the water as she lies back, and I slide my cock into her pussy. I'm going to have to work it in there again, but I'm up for the challenge.

"Gladly," I growl and pull my hips back.

CHAPTER TWENTY-FOUR

Lila

Tirrian fucks like a dragon. There's nothing gentle or kind about it, it's beastial and vicious. God, his cock is massive, but we make it work. Somehow, my pussy expands or does something to take it all again. There's no barb or knot this time as he destroys my cunt. I scream and pant, riding the fine line of pleasure and pain when I feel my teeth change, and then I lunge forward, biting his peck. My teeth slide through his tough, scaled flesh until his blood floods my mouth. I swallow it down, gnawing the wound to make sure he's good and marked. He stiffens and floods my pussy with his cum once more. I feel sorry for any beast who wants to drink from this pool in the future. It's probably too hot to drink, but I don't know what kind of creatures are on this planet.

Pulling back, I inspect my mating bite, satisfied when I see I marked him up. It better scar, and he's never wearing a shirt again. I want everyone to see that he's mine, especially all of those needy, thirsty dragon bitches when we visit his family. I won't hesitate to put any of them in their place if they even look at him the wrong way.

Once we finish that round of sex, we actually make an effort to clean ourselves before getting out. I'm excited for my shifting lesson.

"Is this space big enough?" I ask, looking around the small clearing.

"Not for both of us, but I'll shift first and launch into the sky, and then you can do the same thing," he tells me, his eyes shining with anticipation.

"Launch into the sky, just like that," I mutter, snapping my fingers at him, and he nods.

"Yes. Wasn't swimming in your kraken form instinctual? Or being in your cat form?"

"I haven't been in full cat form yet," I argue for the sake of it, my nerves causing me to be petty. "But yes, the kraken inside me just took over."

He nods. "So let your dragon do the same thing."

I look inside and feel her excitement and impatience. "Yeah, okay."

He gives me another quick kiss. "See you in the sky," he says, winking before walking backward into the middle of the clearing. His body shifts and grows, and before me is his beautiful black dragon. In the low bioluminescent light, I can't see his pink shimmer. I still can't wrap my head around this Tirrian. He's so different from the surly asshole I've known for so long. I like it, but I kind of miss sparring with him too. His giant wings stretch out, brushing against the trees on either side of the clearing, before he lifts with a mighty stroke, the rush of air almost knocking me off my feet. I just steady myself when the wings beat again, and another rush of air pummels me. I lock my knees and lean into it to stay standing, because it happens a few more times until he finally clears the trees. He disappears into the darkness, but I can hear him up there waiting for me. His wing beats are slow and steady, keeping him in place.

Come, mate. His voice is growly, and I know his beast is in charge, so I turn to my inner animals. The whisperer and kraken are quiet, but I can feel my dragon's impatience. She surges to the forefront of my mind, pushing me back, and I feel my body start to change. Unlike shifting into a kraken, this one hurts. I feel my bones break and shift before reforming, and my scream of pain echoes throughout the forest. Tirrian's dragon roars, and there's a touch of sorrow.

Only the first time, he tells me as I collapse to the ground, lost to the shift and my dragon.

When I return to consciousness, I'm flying through the darkness. The bioluminescent forest is gone, and I can see heat signatures of animals on the ground hidden amongst the foliage, their bodies undetectable by the human eye. They are the ultimate predators waiting for unsuspecting prey, but to a dragon, they are nothing but prey. There's a nagging urge to hunt, but thankfully my dragon isn't pushing it—unless she already did when I was taking a nap. Not sure I could be in the passenger seat when we chomp on something cute and fluffy.

I look over and see Tirrian flying at my side, his heat signature a blast of color in the darkness. The stars twinkle above us, and the cold air on my face cools my overly hot body. There's a funny taste in my mouth that I don't recognize.

Dragons run very hot, he informs me. *You are doing so well, my beautiful mate.* I can hear how proud he is. I thought it would be terrifying, sharing my consciousness with the dragon, but it isn't. It's thrilling, and I feel free in a way I never have before. Flying in dragon form could be addicting if I'm not careful. *Hunted down our meal like a true dragon queen. You were magnificent. I didn't need to do anything.*

We ate? I ask. That would explain the taste in my mouth. *You know what? I don't want to know,* I tell him, and he chuckles.

Let us return to Zeydan's dwelling. You are going to need to rest. Your first shift is always exhausting. We want to be in perfect condition to go after your grandma tomorrow.

He tips his wing down and angles his body so he turns back the way we came in a large arc. I follow him, my dragon in perfect control. The return flight takes about half an hour, and I can see the biolumi-nescent part about ten minutes out. A dragon's eyesight is amazing.

Instead of landing in the clearing near the pool, Tirrian keeps flying and lands in front of the cabin like he did when he arrived. It's a much larger space, but I wait for him to shift into human form and move out of the way before I follow him down. My wings are tired, and I can feel my dragon's exhaustion as we flap them to keep us hovering. Thankfully, Tirrian's shift is quick. I allow myself to lower, but the last few yards, my wings turn to jelly, and they sort of fold in on themselves. I crash, shaking the ground around me with a giant thud.

"Lila." Tirrian runs over to me. "Are you okay?" he asks me, running his hands over my body. I flop down onto my stomach and pant, a small stream of fire sputtering out of my mouth and hitting Tirri-an's legs. I freeze, horrified that I just burned my mate.

Fuck, are you okay? I ask him, waiting for his

screams of pain, but he smiles and continues to check me over for damage. His hands feel nice on my scales, and I start purring.

"Yes, we are impervious to each other's and other species' flames. It's only flames of other dragons we need to worry about, and to be honest, most of the time they only singe us a little."

I allow my eyes to close as he keeps stroking me. *That's nice,* I mutter into his head. His hands go to my wings, and he grabs one by the edge and starts walking backwards, stretching it out. It hurts, but when he has it fully stretched out, I groan as my stiff muscles loosen under his ministrations. He holds it before walking it back in and then going around and doing the same to the other one.

"You should see yourself, Lila. You are beautiful. Your dragon is the same color as your hair. Look in Zeydan's windows, and you should be able to see your reflection." I hear admiration and awe in his tone, and I'm excited to check myself out.

I crack my eyes open, not wanting to move, and look at myself in the glass. Zeydan walks out of the house and down the steps, coming over to us. "You are magnificent, little one," he tells me, stroking a hand over my muzzle.

Not so little now, I grumble before turning my attention back to my reflection, enjoying both males' hands on me.

Tirrian is right. My body is a shimmery, pearlescent white with orange, blue, and pink veins running throughout it. I bet I would sparkle brightly in the sun. Shiny and I are a matching set. We are going to look so pretty flying together.

"Come on, shift back, and you can fall asleep in a nice, comfy bed," Tirrian cajoles, joining Zeydan in front of me.

Don't want to, I grumble, hoping that Zeydan can hear my inner voice too.

"You know, in all my years, I don't think I've ever seen a dragon pout," Zeydan murmurs to Tirrian, and he chuckles.

"Me either, but Lila worked very hard tonight, so it's no wonder she's tired."

Worked and got worked over very hard, I mutter, and Zeydan snorts with amusement as Tirrian rolls his eyes.

"Come on, change." Tirrian goes around behind me and smacks my rump.

You're lucky I'm too tired to eat you, I growl at him fiercely, turning my head to glare at him. He rolls his eyes again. *Hey, I'm fearsome. Be afraid.*

"Yes, you are terrifying, but I'm also tired, and that trumps being afraid at the moment." The bastard is just humoring me, but I'm too tired to take a chunk out of his ass. Rain check.

I let my shift wash over me. It still hurts, but it's not as bad as the first one. It takes a few minutes, and when I finally return to my normal form, I'm panting and sweating and a few tears drip down my face.

"Come, a bath will help those aches and pains." Zeydan leads the way after Tirrian scoops me up into his arms. I'm naked, but both of them are doing a good job of ignoring it, which I appreciate at the moment. I'm too tired to be upset.

They manhandle me into the rustic bathtub in Zeydan's bathroom. Tirrian blows fire over it to warm the water before submerging me in it, and Zeydan adds a dribble of something from a bottle on a shelf next to the tub. "This will help the aches and pains. I use it after I shift. I don't do it very often now that I don't have all my power, so it's painful every time."

That actually doesn't bode well for future Lila. I can't imagine I will have a reason to shift all that often either. The oil disperses over the top of the bath before sinking into the hot water. The smell is reminiscent of menthol and arnica, and my muscles relax, becoming nicely numbed. It also helps the very real ache in between my legs. His monster cock really did destroy my pussy. Thank God for the resilient Skarrian vagina that Magenta keeps telling me about.

My eyes drift closed, and I hear them talking, but I'm just too tired to pay any attention. Tirrian's hands are both gentle and efficient on my body as he washes me all over, murmuring words of encouragement and praise. He finally lifts me up, and I feel a towel wrap around my body and hair as he dries me before laying me down on a soft bed. Tirrian presses a kiss to my lips.

"I'm just going to wash off, and then I'll join you," he promises me, and then it's lights out. I wake sometime later surrounded by heat. I crack open my eyes. The room is dark except for the bathroom doorway, where bioluminescent vines light the way. How thoughtful of Zeydan. Speaking of the god, he's lying next to me on my right, so it must be Tirrian whose hot as fuck body is wrapped around me. I never would have guessed he was a snuggler. I wriggle in his arms, but he just tightens them like he's afraid to let me go. I give up for a moment and turn my attention back to the god. His eyes are open, and he's watching me.

"Hi." I smile at him, still not completely sure where I stand with him, but I'm willing to find out.

One of his murder puppies next to him lifts his head and growls at me before returning its head to the bed. When I look around, I can see the rest of them spread out on the floor around us.

"They are a little put out because they have to sleep on the floor," he tells me, sounding slightly sheepish.

"Is that why your bed is so big? So your murder puppies can sleep with you?"

"Yes, they guard me when I am at my most vulnerable," he says quietly so we don't wake the sleeping dragon—literally.

"I'll have to give them extra snuggles when we

get up to make it up to them." I feel a little guilty now. Hopefully they don't hold a grudge.

"Are you okay? Can I get you anything?" he asks me, and I wince.

"I need to go to the bathroom, but he's holding on pretty tight."

"Dragons are fairly possessive, and you just became the most important part of his hoard. I would offer to help you, but your mating is too new, and I do not want to get cooked. Even with immortality, burning still hurts, and with my powers at less than half, I probably wouldn't regenerate as quickly as I normally would."

"Why do I get the feeling you're enjoying this?" I ask him, looking at him.

"It has been a long time since I enjoyed company, and the fact that it's my mate and her mates who I hope will become friends is exciting. I like watching relationship dynamics, and I'm eager to see how this all unfolds."

"Is that what we are? Entertainment?" I ask, feeling hurt by his declaration, and his smile drops as he shakes his head, reaching out to touch me, but he hesitates.

"No, not at all. Sorry, like I said, it's been a long time since I had interaction with other sentient life-forms. I don't even interact with the harvesters. I am looking forward to having family and friends again. When we all went our separate ways in search of life and death and what happened to our powers, I never imagined I wouldn't see my family again. They are not dead, I'd know if they were, but I guess they probably decided to protect themselves and found somewhere to lay low. We are immortal, but we can be killed. How we die determines how long it takes to regenerate. Anyway, I miss them, and it wasn't until just now that I realized how much. I may be a god, but I am still a red-blooded male with feelings."

His words appease my hurt feelings, and I wriggle a little more, trying to get my Klingon to release me. "Tirrian, I have to pee," I hiss at him, and he grumbles and releases me. I slip out quickly, not wanting him to latch on before I can leave the bed. I'm still naked, but I'm past the point of caring now, and I hope Zeydan gets a good look as I crawl down to the bottom and climb over the pile of murder puppies, careful not to step on any of them.

I give one or two of them a scratch, making a head start on sucking up, and I get a couple of happy tail thumps before hurrying to the bathroom. I find the toilet in a little alcove and do my business before flushing it. Thankfully there are pipes in this section of the house. I wondered how they filled the bath so quickly.

When I return to the bed, I stop abruptly, trying to figure out what I'm seeing. In my absence, Tirrian shuffled into my spot. He must have been attracted by the heat, and he wrapped his arms around Zeydan. I slap my hand over my mouth at the look on Zeydan's face. He seems bemused and slightly panicked. What's even funnier is Tirrian is rubbing his face against Zeydan's chest and petting him.

"Would you like some help?" I ask him, smothering the laugh that wants to bubble up.

"If you wouldn't mind. I think your mate would be perturbed if he woke up and saw that he was grinding against me, especially since he's naked and erect."

"Oh? Oh!" Intrigued by this but unsure where Tirrian or Zeydan sit on the bisexual spectrum, I decide to help him out, not wanting him to feel uncomfortable. I mean, he's a god, so I'm sure he's probably experimented, but he did say it has been some time since he has been around people, and I don't want either of them to feel uncomfortable. Also, being humped by a dragon probably isn't the best way to start a friendship, even if they have been playing nicely up until now, much to my amazement.

"Come on, lover boy." I drag his arm off Zeydan and shove him, trying to move him back onto his side of the bed so I can slip between them. It proves impossible, so I climb into the spot Tirrian was in previously. That's all it takes. He must smell me, because he releases Zeydan and rolls over, wrapping himself around me once more. His weight draped over me and the heat he puts off warms me quickly. The trip to the bathroom had been cold, and I'm happy for my heater.

"Thank you, and sleep well, little one," Zeydan says.

"Night, Z," I call back. "And thank you for everything." I reach over Tirrian, and I feel Zeydan give my hand a squeeze. A spark lights up my nerves.

"Whoa, what was that?" I ask him, snatching my hand away quickly.

"That's my soul reaching out to yours. I'm sorry if it scared you. It's quite excited about you," he answers calmly, his tone belying what his soul told me. That little spark was a small shot of joy and celebration, and I can't believe that's what he feels without even knowing me, but I'm also thrilled about it.

"It's okay, I liked it," I tell him.

"Good." He sounds pleased now, and I feel a smile drift across my lips as I fall asleep again.

CHAPTER TWENTY-FIVE

Lila

The next morning, I'm woken by what I'm sure they think is a quiet conversation, but it sounds like a bunch of pissed off cats hissing.

"A large craft just appeared in the orbit of Husadavia. It's cloaked, but I can feel its presence," Zeydan tells my dragon. He sounds worried, which is a concern in itself, considering he's a god.

"Were you expecting anybody?" Tirrian asks calmly, and I'm impressed. I thought he'd hit hyper-drive on panic.

"No. No one visits this planet except the harvesters I employ. The only reason the carevasta bears got onto the planet was because I was on Z68, gathering the crew. I'm surprised they got as far as they did—unless they beamed directly to the spot where they left Lila's grandmother's stasis box, which should have been impossible. They must have had intel from someone who knows the planet, and the only living people would be my fellow gods."

"Do you know where it is?" Tirrian asks as I stretch, deciding I need to be involved in this conversation as well. I look around for some clothes as Zeydan answers.

"Yes, I searched for it last night while you were otherwise occupied. The bears' bodies are nothing but bones scattered around it, but I couldn't penetrate the box. It has a signature I recognize on it though, which makes me think one of my fellow gods is definitely involved, but I have no idea why. What would be the benefit of keeping Liliana Adams in stasis?" Zeydan sounds aggrieved. "If I were at full power, opening it would be child's play, but I don't have access to all of my powers."

I hate how defeated he sounds. I spy Zeydan's cloak on the end of the bed. He must have picked it up after I dropped it to run from Tirrian. I snatch it up and pull it around me, my movement drawing the males' attention.

"Lila, you're awake." Tirrian's worry drops for a moment as he smiles gently at me.

I crawl down the bed and join them on the seats we used last night. Outside the glass, I see Zeydan's murder puppies all on alert. Their ears and tails are up, and their eyes are on the dark forest.

"Yeah, why didn't you wake me? I definitely

overslept. I bet the harvesters returned. We need to meet them at the next field."

Zeydan shakes his head. "They can't without me, otherwise they will die. They don't come down until I send them the okay," he reminds me, and I feel a rush of panic for Brannock and Xavier.

"Shit, we better get going then." I look around for the little dress I wore in my other form. I can't return naked.

Zeydan puts up a hand. "Don't worry about the harvesters now. Lila, we have another problem. There is a ship in the atmosphere other than the circus's and the harvesters' ships."

"Do you know who it is?" I ask, and he frowns.

"It has a Madovian energy signature."

I gasp and shudder. That isn't good. "Do you think the Syndicate sent them? How would they know we were trying to rescue Grandma?"

"I'm guessing that's why they are there. There is no other reason for them to be in orbit." Zeydan sounds unconcerned, but I'm starting to panic.

"But how would they know we are here?"

"We weren't very quiet about what we were doing. They could have found out any number of ways," Tirrian suggests. "Will the flora and fauna attack them?"

Zeydan nods decisively. "Yes, but Madovians are fairly hardy creatures, much like dragons. Their skin is resilient. If I was expecting any creature to have a chance on my planet, it would be them."

"I don't know. Laser beams do a fairly good job of killing them." I remember what the one we killed on the circus ship looked like after the gun did its job.

"Why don't we just teleport the stasis box straight back to the ship?" I ask, and Tirrian and Zeydan shake their heads.

"They need specific coordinates to be able to beam it aboard, which means one of us has to be touching it," Tirrian explains.

"Okay, so we teleport directly to it, slap our hands on it, and then we're back on the ship." I'm grasping for ideas at the moment, but I seem to be the only one.

Zeydan shoots me down once more. "The surrounding forest is too dense to teleport in. We're going to have to walk until we get to the clearing the box is in, which is in the very middle of the forest. There was a funny forcefield on it too, which may not allow for teleportation."

"We're definitely going to need Ghosie," Tirrian grumbles, not sounding thrilled with the idea. While he was welcoming and thankful he saved me, Tirrian is still wary of his intentions, especially after Brannock's bombshell.

"For fuck's sake, do either of you have suggestions instead of just shooting mine down? What about shooting the Mordovian ship out of the sky? The circus ship has weapons!"

Tirrian grimaces, and I know I'm not going to

like what he says. "It's cloaked, and they have to be able to see it to shoot it down."

I feel a wave of dejection before a burst of confidence. "Right then, I guess we're going to have to fight. Tirrian and I can shift into dragon form and burn them all."

Zeydan winces and shakes his head. "You'll set the whole forest on fire, and it's too dense for you to land."

"But we can make our dragons smaller," I argue, remembering what Tirrian told me.

"Not that small." Tirrian shoots another idea down.

"Agh!" I scream, and the murder puppies yip and run inside to see what the problem is. They surround me, whining and pawing at my legs. I reach down and give them little scratches. "It's okay. I'm just frustrated," I tell them.

"We're going to have to call in reinforcements. Can you protect more of us from the creatures?" Tirrian asks, and Zeydan finally gives a positive answer.

"Yes, as long as we don't drift too far apart, but it isn't the actual creatures that's the problem in the death forest, it's the trees themselves."

"Was the green circle of magic yesterday your limit?" I ask him, standing up, and he gives me a decisive nod.

"It was about a hundred feet in diameter. Plenty of space for a few others."

"I don't know this feet measurement, but I think it's time to invite some of the others to the party." Tirrian lifts a piece of cloth that was under his arm on the chair. I'm surprised to see it's the dress I was looking for, and the communicator that was in the hem is now ripped out.

"I spoke to the ship last night to let them know you were okay," he explains when I give him a quizzical look, wondering why he pulled it out.

"Oh, thank you, that was nice of you." That was super thoughtful. Of course the others would have been worried.

"Don't worry about radioing them. I'll go get them." Zeydan doesn't wait for a response. He stands up and whistles, and his foxes flow back into him, appearing as his tail behind him. He magics up another cloak and quickly disappears.

"Well, I guess his idea of low powers and ours is slightly different," I say in amazement, staring at the empty space.

"I'm afraid he's going to use up a good portion of them retrieving our friends though." Tirrian's brow crinkles.

My stomach rumbles, drawing his attention.

"Zeydan made breakfast," he says, getting up and moving over to the kitchen. He spoons something into a bowl for me and returns, handing it to me. It's a thick, black grainy substance. I wrinkle my nose, and Tirrian chuckles. "Try it, I think you'll be surprised. Even my dragon enjoyed it."

I scoop up a spoonful and take a small amount into my mouth. The flavors hit my taste buds, and my eyes widen in surprise. It has a slightly chewy texture, but it tastes like honey oats with dried fruit pieces mixed in.

"It's good," I tell him as I quickly devour the rest.

"Lila." Tirrian sounds hesitant, and when I look up, he's biting his thumb nail, his eyes unfocused like he's thinking hard. "I think you need to mimic Brannock and go into berserker mode if the Madovians try to stop us from getting to your grandmother."

"Why that form? What about my Madovian form? I'd be at an advantage," I ask him, and he quickly shakes his head.

"No, you remember how hard it was to control. We may never get you back. At least the Aaz'axian berserker is lethal, and Brannock should be able to coax you back."

"Well, what about the warlock or the Barcoa?" I argue, and this time he focuses on me.

"Why don't you want to mimic Brannock? And the truth please, I think I deserve it."

I sigh and try to put my thoughts into words. "Because I don't want to be seen as just a baby factory. I want them to like me for me, and not the fact that I am their only option."

"You said them. Do you mean Brannock and Ghosie?"

I wince, I did say them, didn't I? "I'm not there with Ghosie yet despite being attracted to him. I barely know him, but I mean Silac too."

"Yes, you are a chance for all of them to flourish again."

I shake my head vigorously. "Maybe the Aaz'axians and the carevasta, yes, they have more bloodlines, but from what I understand, the nagas are only Silac's family. Any children he and I might have will be his brothers' nieces or nephews. That doesn't help in the long run."

He mulls over my words. "No, you're right, but I don't even think that's what we need to focus on. We need to focus on the fact that you think they want you to breed babies for them. Why wouldn't they want you for you? Hell, Silac was attracted to you before we even knew you were a mimic, and Brannock certainly isn't that shallow. He had an Earth female for a wife. He already has a child who needs us, so he may not want any more."

I fiddle with Zeydan's cloak, not wanting to look at him. "Yeah, you're right. I guess I'm just being silly."

He slides off his chair and shuffles over on his knees. He's wearing the skirt Zeydan gave him and nothing else, and in the light of day, the shimmer on black scales is distractingly pretty. All the exposed flesh doesn't help either. When he gets to me, he's smirking, but he grabs my hands and gives them a squeeze.

"And don't forget this isn't being forced on you. You can do it the Skarrian way, so if you find you're unable to control your urges in that form, then one little fuck fest won't seal you together for all eternity." He pulls me close and gives me a kiss before pressing our foreheads together, looking me straight in the eye.

"I love you, Lila. I don't think I told you that, and being bonded to you for all eternity is a blessing. The others will feel the same way, trust me. Take the Aaz'axian form and keep yourself safe."

I slide off the chair and onto the floor. He wraps his arms around me as I hug him tightly. Who would have thought the dragon had a romantic bone in his body?

My hands brush across his wings, and he shivers. I feel his cock press against me as he pulls me harder against him. I slide one of my hands up and under his skirt and find him, stroking the hard flesh.

"How long until they return?" I ask as he parts my robe and fondles my breasts, smoke drifting out of his nose.

"Not long enough," a dry voice remarks, and Tirrian jumps to his feet, growling and spreading his wings to protect me.

I blink to clear the lusty fog from my mind, pulling my robe closed again before peering around his legs. Xavier, Brannock, Saxon, Silac, Ghosie, and Maxsim are all with Zeydan. All but Maxsim are wearing black leather-like armor I saw

Xavier in the first time. Shit, It's too hot here for Maxsim.

"What are you doing here?" I ask, scrambling to my feet as I try to keep my large robe closed but failing, if the interest in their eyes says anything. "You're going to get sick or die from the heat." I hurry over to him and run my hands up and down his arms. "Take him back now," I plead to Zeydan.

"Lila, it's okay, Xavier gave me this." Max holds up the necklace I noticed around his neck. "It's a permanent protective charm. I can go anywhere now."

I sigh with relief and throw my arms around him, hugging him hard.

"Fuck, I was worried, but I'm glad you're here." I give him a kiss before turning and stomping over to my warlock. "I love you," I tell him, and he smirks and pulls me in for a kiss.

"Of course you do," he says smugly, and I hear the rest of them mutter under their breaths.

Tirrian doesn't hide his scoff.

"Nice skirt." Xavier smirks at the dragon as I pull away from him. Tirrian just flips him off as Xavier waves a hand and puts him in the same armor as the rest of them.

"I'll need to shift," Tirrian says, shaking his head.

"It will shift with you. It's like the performance outfits." He waves his hand again, and weapons appear, floating in front of him. Tirrian grabs two laser guns and sticks them into the holsters built into the leathers. All of them are armed to the teeth. "Now let's deal with you two." He turns his attention to Zeydan and me.

"Do you want me to outfit you?" he asks the god carefully. I'm surprised he's being delicate, since he's usually tactless.

"No, there are a lot of things I can't do, and my power is reduced, but I can still conjure. I am going to scout ahead anyway. There's nowhere in that forest where they can hide from me, and I will let you know if you walk into an ambush." Zeydan strips off his robe, and I have to hide a chuckle when the others' eyes widen at his form.

"Damn," my horny warlock mutters.

"You have a little drool," I tell him, pointing to the corner of his mouth.

He rolls his eyes and slaps my hand away, and I giggle, admiring my supposed new mate.

"How are you all here so quickly?" I ask as we follow Zeydan out onto the patio.

"I sensed the ship when it dropped out of hyperspace, and Brannock and I returned to the galaxy ship. There was no need to keep up the farce any longer," Xavier explains, not hiding his admiration of the half naked god in front of us.

"What about the harvesters?" I ask Zeydan as his hands go to the waistband of his skirt.

"They will wait. I will cast the repelling spell out here and link it to you, Lila. It will give you protection when I leave and follow." He holds up both hands and mutters something, and the house is surrounded by the same ring of green magic as we were in yesterday. "Be careful. I will speak into your minds when I have news." He pulls his skirt off with a flourish, and his body starts to shimmer, but not before I catch an eyeful of what he's hiding under his skirt. Holy hell, he gives the dragon a run for his money, and it has a twist in it. I turn my head to the side a little to see if I can work out exactly what I'm seeing.

"Double damn," Xavier mutters again, also tilting his head slightly, and this time, I elbow him. We watch as his body contorts and shifts until a huge foxlike creature with nine tails stands before us. I mean, he's almost as tall as an elephant. Three of us could ride on his back. I walk down the steps and reach out to stroke his pointy nose.

"Be careful," I tell him, and he clicks at me, before his large tongue lashes me, leaving behind a trail of slobber.

"Eww." He makes a laughing, chattering sound before shimmering and disappearing.

"Lila, let's get you outfitted." Saxon is the one to approach me. "This is the one coded to your blood, but I bought another for you to activate," he tells me, holding guns in each hand.

"And you're going to need a whole new outfit. As much as we would like to see you run through the jungle naked, it isn't going to work for this." My warlock starts to wave his hand, but I snap my own out to stop him.

"Hang on please. There's something I need to do first." I look around. Tirrian, Ghosie, Brannock, Max, and Silac stayed inside the house while Zeydan changed. Only Saxon and Xavier followed us outside.

Xavier gives me a nod, following my gaze inside. "We'll just wait here. Don't be too long, the sooner we get moving, the sooner we can be back on the ship. Your grandpas are stressed, and so are your mates we left behind."

A wave of guilt washes over me. *Woman up, Lila, it's just mimicking a new form. Stop overthinking it.*

I take a big breath and let it out, then I march inside to ask Brannock if I can mimic him.

CHAPTER TWENTY-SIX

Lila

"Can I talk to you for a moment?" I ask Brannock when I reenter the house. Tirrian must see the determination in my eyes, because he herds the others outside, leaving me alone with the Aaz'axian.

"Of course, Lila. What do you need?"

"Will you allow me to mimic your form, please?"

He doesn't say anything for a moment, and my stomach drops.

"Tirrian thinks it would be the safest form for me to take with the Madovian threat hanging over us," I explain in a rush. "He thinks that going berserker if I need to will be effective against them."

Brannock slowly nods his head. "Yes, I have fought the Madovians before, though they were on our side during the war, but unlike the Aaz'axians who were forced to be there, Madovians reveled in the slaughter and used their victims for breeding. They are vile creatures, and there were constant fights between our troops because they kept trying to seduce the Aaz'axian forces. It worked for a little while, especially once our females got sick and died off. A lot of our males took them up on the offer because they were desperate, and Madovian females seemed to enjoy our barbed cocks, but then we realized what they were doing—implanting their eggs to use us as incubators."

I shudder at the thought, remembering what the one on the ship did to one of the crew.

"Our thorns will penetrate their skin, and the poison eats away at their flesh."

"Your thorns have poison in them?" I don't remember him saying that before.

He nods. "Yes, it's what makes us so lethal in that form."

"Do the females have the berserker form?" I ask.

"Yes, our females were just as lethal as the males until they started to get sick. I would very much like it if you mimicked my form, Lila," Brannock says carefully, his eyes on mine, and I feel his excitement, though he's trying desperately to lock it down.

"Alright, well, I have to get naked to do this so I

don't destroy Zeydan's robe," I warn him, and his eyes sparkle with amusement as one corner of his mouth kicks up, but he manages to keep a straight face. "I wonder if Xavier can create a spell that will allow clothes to shift with my mimic forms like he did with the kids."

"It's really no hardship for you to get naked in front of us," Brannock says calmly.

"I know, but my mates aren't the only people I'll ever shift in front of," I say as I drop the robes, and his eyes go from amused to hooded and heated with desire.

"Are you saying you would like to mate with me?" he asks slowly, and I think about what I just said. Oh, I guess it could be taken that way.

I don't answer him immediately, instead studying him so his form will sink into my mind. I feel my mimic powers take over, and lavender mist surrounds me. Unlike my dragon shift, this one doesn't hurt as I feel my body start to change. I get taller and broader, and spikes burst out of my skin, down my spine, and over my shoulder blades. Ridges and bumps appear on my arms, and I feel more spikes push out of my skull, creating a crest on my head. I reach up and touch my skull. My hair is still there, but the spikes have pushed out through the middle. I'll need to braid it out of the way.

The mist clears, and I look down at myself. I'm the same opal blue color as Brannock, unlike the white opalescent color of Shiny or my dragon. I'm completely hairless apart from my head, my breasts are slightly smaller in this form, and my arms have spikes on them. My pubic mound is fleshy and a little more rounded than it is in human form, like there's a little more padding down there. I reach up and touch the spikes on my head. Like Brannock's, they are flexible to my touch, but if someone else were to touch them, they would find them razor sharp.

"You're beautiful," he murmurs, and I drop my hands and meet his gaze. There's a sheen of wonder in his eyes, and he walks around me, getting a good look. I should feel embarrassed and exposed, but instead I feel like preening at the way he looks at me, like I'm the most precious thing in the world to him. I feel my spines bristle, and the membranes between the ones on my back shimmer.

"You need to stop that, Lila." When he steps in front of me, I see him gritting his teeth and clenching his hands. "Females would shimmer their spines to attract a mate. It releases a scent to bring eligible males to her side to fight for the right to mate with her. It's all I can do to hold myself back."

I freeze. "Oh my god, I'm so sorry. It just started to happen without any help from me." I slap my hands over my face, completely mortified. Yes, I'm attracted to this man, and I would like to ride him like a pony as Xavier suggested, but now is not the time.

"It's okay." I see him heave out a breath and step backward. "Maybe just use the robe to cover up until Xavier can find you something to wear." I see him adjust himself behind his combat pants. His armor is slightly different from everyone else's, allowing all his spikes and ridges to be free.

I bend down and grab the robe, pulling it up and over myself, glad it's large enough for Zeydan's tails and now my spikes. I can't even look at him as I hide myself within the hood, but I feel him step in front of me, and he lifts my chin with a finger when I won't look at him.

"Don't be embarrassed. I have never in all my life smelled anything as intoxicating as you. My mouth waters to get a taste, but we have a few pressing matters to take care of first. I assure you, Lila, when we return to the ship, I would like our Aaz'axian forms to become very well acquainted. I promised you something earlier, and I fully intend to keep my promise."

He walks away, leaving me confused. What did he promise me? Oh. Oh! He promised to shred my pussy. Yes please.

Brannock must send Xavier inside, because he appears in my line of sight, smirking. "Are you thinking naughty things, *phoeall*?"

"No," is my swift response, and I can see he doesn't believe me. Damn warlock and his emotion feeling powers.

"Let's outfit you so we can get this show on the

road." He pushes the robes off me, and I watch him scan me from head to toe. "Well, I guess I understand the raging lust coming from Brannock now." He reaches out and runs a finger down between my breasts and my stomach to just above my clit. "You are a fucking feast for him. I'm not sure if this is the best idea you've had or the cruelest."

"It was Tirrian's idea. He thought this form would be the safest since we can't land in dragon form in the clearing, and while I'm okay with warlock powers, I'm not as fast, and they drain my energy quickly." I bite my lip as he waves his hand, and the same outfit that Brannock wore covers me from head to toe, leaving my arms exposed.

"This should let you change into your berserker form, and yes, I agree. While I would like to see you use your warlock powers, this is a safer option."

"But how do we launch our thorns? Brannock was able to launch them from all parts of his body."

"I think it would be safer for you and all of us if you just launch them from your arms and hands, keeping the rest of your body protected so there isn't a chance of a stray one hitting one of us."

"That seems fair, but how am I supposed to fire my guns and shoot thorns out of my hands?"

"Start with your weapons. Once they run out of juice, go with the thorns," he suggests, sounding unconcerned.

"They run out of juice?" I feel a moment of panic. "We didn't get that far in my lesson because the smell of my blood triggered Saxon. To be honest, I'm probably more of a liability with them than without."

"Pfft," he scoffs. "It's point and shoot. Just make sure you're not pointing at any of us when you pull the trigger. It has a hundred shots, and then the laser will need to be repowered. Just move to your second weapon, and then once that's empty, use your thorns. Hopefully by then we will have taken care of all of the Madovians. I can conjure more weapons, but they need to be calibrated to your blood, which will take precious time we won't have."

"How are you so calm?" I ask him, beginning to freak out now that this is becoming more real. My palms are sweaty, and there's a funny taste in my mouth.

"I've been in battle before. Don't forget I have a few years on you, Lila. I couldn't remember how old I was when I first met you because my parents stole that memory, but now I know I was ten. It wasn't long after that when my dad first took me into a firefight. It was against a group of warlocks who were trying to overthrow the crown. He thought it would be a good experience for people to see how ruthless the warlock crown prince was even at a young age. It's how I ended up with the reputation I have. It also helps that I have the power to back that reputation up," he explains as he takes my arm and leads me outside.

"If you touch my spikes, does it hurt?" I ask him, and he reaches to run his hand over one of them. Instead of stabbing him like I thought they would, they bend just like they do for me.

"They only become rigid if you feel fear," Brannock explains, overhearing me talking to Xavier.

"Whoa." Saxon scans me from head to toe, nodding with approval. "That was a good idea."

Tirrian nods, looking smug. "I thought it would be best, considering we don't know what we are walking into."

"Surely the great warlock will be able to protect you from anything, but just in case, we are here as backup." Silac speaks up for the first time, being sassy and giving me a wink. I'm kind of happy to see it, even as Xavier flips him off, because he's been so worried about his family. At least this provides a distraction.

"But how are we going to find our way to the center of the death forest if the god has already gone ahead?" Maxsim asks, and he sparks with impatience. I'm so happy he's here, but I'm worried too. Echo will never forgive me if something happens to him.

"Why is it called the death forest?" I ask, looking into the lush green foliage stretched out in front of us.

"That's not the death forest," Ghosie says, shaking his head. "The death forest is on the opposite side of the planet. We need to teleport there, just like the god did."

"Oh, so that's where he went. I'm glad one of us knows what we're doing. How do you know that?" I ask him, and I see him blush, his furry multicolored cheeks darkening.

"Because the carevasta bears are space pirates. Raping and hoarding women is the least of our bad habits. Murder for hire is another thing that some of the bears would contract out for. It's easy to slit someone's throat when they are trying to rub their body all over you. The death forest is a good place to dispose of any bodies you don't want to be found. It's even better than letting them float through space, because no one is game enough to go searching there. I can assure you, I did not take part in these practices, but all bears know of it."

"Right then, gather close. It will be easy for me to teleport everyone together if we're all touching one another." Xavier waves at us.

Saxon hands me my guns, and I stick them into the holsters in my leathers and put my arm on his to link us.

"You've got this. Just point and shoot. Head-shots if you can, because that will kill them, but body shots will slow them down," he tells me, patting my hand before reaching out to touch Silac who is next to him. He gives me a wink, and I watch as he changes to his half form. His body rises higher so Saxon has to stretch to reach his arm.

Maxsim strides through the half circle and kisses me.

"Take care of yourself. Our omega will be upset if we get hurt," he growls at me.

"Same goes for you." I'm kind of shocked that he kissed me in this form, but I'm just rolling with it.

He steps back, and his body blurs, changing into his cat form. It isn't quite as large as Zeydan's fox form. Where he's the size of a small elephant, Max is probably the height of a rhino. Between the two of them, they are intimidating creatures and could probably skull stomp the Madovians. I don't know how big they are in their shifted form. If they are like Silac, then they are considerably bigger than their humanoid form.

Ghosie steps up on my other side and holds up his arm. His fur is covered by protective leathers, so I can put my hand on his arm without worrying about becoming infatuated. "Are you going to be okay?" I ask him. I'm not sure what abilities he holds apart from the mesmerizing fur and matter disrupter.

He gives me a small smile. "I'll be fine. This isn't my first raid. In fact, I probably have the most experience in stealing something from under the nose of others, and I'm fairly handy with a laser gun."

Tirrian and Xavier complete the circle— Xavier on Ghosie's other side, with Maxsim between them, both of them shoving a hand onto his fur.

"Let's make this quick, Maxsim is freezing my balls off." Tirrian's teeth start to chatter, and Xavier chuckles as we dissipate, reappearing a few seconds later. I cough and stumble, but Ghosie and Saxon hold me upright. I look around to get my bearings, and I notice the green magic circling us.

"Don't go beyond the green barrier. We are only protected inside it," I warn the others as I get my first look at the death forest.

"Holy fuck." Fear washes over me, and I shiver. "This is going to suck."

CHAPTER TWENTY-SEVEN

Brannock

I heave out the breath I'd been holding and drop my hands to my sides, pulling out both of my weapons now that we've arrived at the location. The site is eerily silent, much like when we were harvesting yesterday. The magic circle must deaden the noise around us, which is hardly ideal for the ambush we know is waiting for us.

"Are we sure the Madovian's are hiding somewhere in there? They don't have a circle to protect themselves with." Lila sounds skeptical as she studies the forest in front of us with a frown.

I don't look at her. Seeing her as an Aaz'axian is doing things to my body that I haven't felt for a very long time. When she shimmied her spines earlier, I almost attacked her and forced her to ride my cock, desperate to allow my spikes to pierce her body, fill her with my seed, and watch her body round with my child. I pride myself on my self-control, but it's frayed to its very edges. I loved my wife, but not being able to fuck her to completion was devastating. I was constantly lying to her, and I felt so much guilt. It's part of the reason I agreed to the IVF, thinking it would never work. Hearing Lila refer to me as her mate was nothing short of a miracle, even though I don't think she meant to say it out loud.

Lila is gorgeous as an Aaz'axian. She's gorgeous anyway, but seeing a female of my species is something I never thought I would ever see again. There are supposedly one or two still alive in the galaxy, my daughter being one of them, and I've hoped and prayed every day since she was born that being half human would be enough to save her from the curse that decimated the female population. If not, then I will beg the Celestians or Lila for another flamegem flower to save her. Thankfully she has shown no signs of being unwell up until now. I can only hope it's the same since I've been gone. I'm dying to get back to Earth. Thankfully she is too young yet, but Smith has plans to breed her and create their own army when she becomes of age. I will see them all dead before that happens, especially that traitorous member of my old team. I will make him suffer for what Chloe has had to endure.

A rush of desire floods my body as my eyes drift

to Lila again. Fuck. I shake my head and assess the terrain in front of us.

"I doubt they care if one or two get picked off," Saxon mutters as everyone spreads out with Lila strategically located in the center.

The forest before us is black and dead. A thick fog covers the ground, concealing anything that may be lying in wait for us. The sky-high trees are withered and gnarly, bent at odd angles which makes it difficult to walk in a direct line. It's going to involve us dipping and ducking to get in and around the dense jungle.

I watch as Lila steps toward a waist-high bush and brushes a curious finger over the strangely charred leaves. It turns to ash and crumbles into dust, disappearing into the fog at its base.

"It's dead," she says, looking toward us in amazement.

"The whole forest is." A voice behind us has us whirling and holding up our weapons.

"No!" Lila screams, but luckily no one gets off a shot at the god who is now back in his humanoid form.

"A little warning would be nice. We're all a little jumpy," Silac hisses, and the god inclines his head.

"My apologies. I wasn't thinking. Do not allow the residue to rest on your skin, or you will feel fatigued."

"I thought you said it would burn if we used our dragon fire. That's already dead." She sounds confused, pointing at the bush that just disintegrated.

"Everything beneath the canopy is dead, but the canopy itself is very much alive. Those large trees are what suck life out of everything beneath it. They are what will kill you if you go too slow. No animals will live in the forest, or they get the life sucked out of them as well."

"Right, trees are bad. Do not stop long enough for the trees to get you." Lila nods her head, and her voice rises with a touch of hysteria. "What were you thinking when you created this planet? Everything is out to kill everything else."

"Actually, as far as a natural ecosystem goes, it's fairly harmonious. It's only intruders that get targeted without prejudice. This was my safe haven. We all had one. While I did create this planet, this forest is a product of the goddess of death. She is basically my sister, but she is also a slave to her nature, and over the years, instead of celebrating the rebirth facet of death, she wallowed in its destructive nature. She liked to leave her mark on any planet that has too much life. We permitted her to do things like this, because it was a way of managing her. It didn't hurt anyone unless they ventured into it, and very few do, except if they were looking for death."

"What about the green circle of magic surrounding us? It repels the creatures on this planet, so will it repel the Madovians?" Lila asks, but Zeydan only shrugs, disappointment in his eyes.

"I do not know. I have never tested it on other species except for the ones native to the planet. I've never needed to."

Lila bites her lip, which seems to be a bad habit when she worries about things. I see a smear of blood appear, and she grimaces, wiping her mouth with the back of her hand. She must have forgotten she has fangs in this form as well.

"Shall we stop yapping and get on with it?" Xavier asks as he holds out his hands, and two balls of magic appear in each palm. "I'm ready to get back to our normal lives where all we have to worry about is keeping our children alive and making sure Lila's kraken is well satisfied." The guys chuckle as he winks at his mate, and I see her shoulders relax slightly.

"I will shift and take point. The snake and lightning cat can flank me, leaving the rest of you to follow behind. I have seen no signs of them yet, but the forest has a soul, and for all I know, it may be assisting our enemies," Zeydan says, and we all concede to his plan. He knows this terrain best, so it would make sense if he was out in front.

"Stay behind us," I instruct the bear. "We need you to get to Lila's grandma, and you can't do that if you're dead."

He rolls his eyes. "Glad to see you care," he mutters but does as I say. The warlock said he was to be trusted, but I know firsthand how easy it is to hide true motivations, though he did allow the warlock to search his mind. He wasn't able to get into mine. It's the one reason I am grateful for the chip in my head. It gives off a low frequency that makes it seem like there's a steel wall around my thoughts.

"We will watch our backs." The dragon drops back, giving me a knowing nod. I know he was pissed at me, but learning that it was because of my child made him more inclined to forgive me. He was more welcoming to the bear. He saved Lila, after all, but he is still on high alert, especially after my confession. It's going to take a bit for the men mated to Lila to trust the rest of us.

The nine of us make our way through the forest. It's slow going for most of us, but the three shifters in front seem to have no problems navigating the awkward terrain. Their animals are just that much more agile than us. Silac changed from half form to full now, and he is somewhat terrifying. Hopefully his ability to capture someone with his gaze will be able to stop some of the Madovians on the spot.

The light doesn't penetrate the forest, and the farther we get in, the more Zeydan's fox form seems to glow with an inner fire that lights the way. The green circle of protection surrounding us also gives the area an eerie glow, but it's much better than black as night.

The forest is unnaturally quiet, but whether that's because nothing lives in here or because of the magic protection, I don't know. It's only the sounds of our breaths and the occasional crunch of an unseen twig underfoot that breaks it up.

Zeydan suddenly stops, sniffing the air. Maxsim's tail comes up, and his lightning fizzles, the scent of ozone erasing the dank smell of decay that permeates our noses. Silac hisses, and his hood spreads out as he rises up on his tail.

"Lila, be ready," I whisper as Saxon and Xavier both become even more alert than they were. Saxon has his finger on the triggers, and the balls of energy in Xavier's hands grow bigger.

The smell of smoke joins the scent of ozone, and when I turn to look, both Ghosie and Tirrian are also scanning the area behind us for what set off the shifters. I feel better knowing they are guarding our backs.

"Just burn this fucker down if you have to," Lila mutters quietly, but I hear the dragon grunt his response.

"As long as everyone else is safe. It's likely to go up like an explosion if anything does catch on fire."

He's not wrong. There doesn't seem to be any moisture in this forest at all, it's a lightning strike away from a fire storm. Shit, lightning!

"Max, make sure your hits strike the reptiles and not the trees, otherwise we're all going to burn," I warn quietly, knowing his shifter ears will hear whatever I say.

He turns his head and gives me a quick nod of acknowledgement, and that's when they strike, but we miscalculated. We were so worried about what was in front of us, none of us thought to look up. Something shoots out of the trees, and Xavier is encased in a sticky web-like net, pinning his hands to his sides, gluing his lips shut, and wrapping his body in a cocoon. He topples over, effectively removing him from the board.

"Xavier!" Lila screams as I look up to where the web came from, my heart sinking.

"Fuck, Nelecs." Up in the tree above me is the ten-legged, two-headed, multi-eyed alien that is very similar to an earth spider crossed with a scorpion. Its barbed, serrated stinger sticks up high in the air, waiting to strike its netted prey to inject its venom. They aren't particularly intelligent, but they take orders well.

I raise my gun and shoot the one that entrapped Xavier. The laser pierces its tough outer shell, and it falls to the ground, making a squelching sound as its insides splatter everywhere. As I look around and tune back into what's going on around me, I realize it wasn't the only one. Zeydan is down too. He's struggling more than Xavier is, his form jerking as he tries to remove the sticky substance from his body, but it seems to make it worse.

Saxon aims and takes out another one as I hear

shots behind us as well. Instead of joining in and firing into the top of the trees where the Nelecs are, I keep an eye on the bushes surrounding us. The Madovians are here, they just sent the Nelecs to be cannon fodder and to take out our strongest. It's a smart battle strategy, but they don't realize we're all weapons in this fight.

Silac must sense them at the same time I spot the first one approaching us. He lunges forward, growing even bigger, latching his fangs into the reptilian creature. They are in their beast form, which is a cross between a snake and a water dragon. They have a long, undulating body with a hooded head, and small limbs and wings that help them climb surfaces they may not otherwise be able to. Their fangs drip with poison, and although Lila has healing powers in her Celestian form, it would be better for none of us to be bitten or spat on.

Silac yanks back, tearing out his victim's throat and spits, blood from the Madovian he attacked flying from his mouth. She starts screaming in pain, his venom already killing her. I see one of them approach Lila, who is desperately trying to remove the web from Xavier. I can't stand around and watch anymore, I need to join in. I fire my gun, and it rips the one behind Lila in half.

"Leave him. He will be okay. You need to fight back," I shout at her before I turn, and my eyes widen at the sheer number coming toward us.

Tirrian roars and races forward as Ghosie approaches me and Lila.

"Go, I've got this," he shouts. "Lead them away, and I'll make sure the warlock and god are safe."

Lila and I exchange a glance, and we both get up and race into the fray. I fire my gun at anything that's black and red and moves, taking out three more of our enemy.

"We need to move. We need to draw them away from Xavier and Zeydan so Ghosie can do his thing," I shout to Saxon, who is covered in a thick black substance that I know is Madovian blood. His eyes glow with bloodlust as he gives me a nod and starts to run. Maxsim joins him. He's limping slightly, and his mouth and chest are also covered in the thick black substance. I fire at the one that attacks him from the side that he missed in his impatience to keep up with Saxon. It goes down with a thud, and Maxsim jumps to the side. Tirrian puts another shot in that one just to make sure before he, too, follows behind them.

"Come on, Lila," Tirrian growls. "We need to go." He grabs her arm and tugs her away, urging her to follow the others.

"But we don't know where we're going. I can't leave them," she chokes out, stumbling, torn between staying and following the others.

"I know the way. Zeydan showed me in my mind. Now hurry," he argues. There's a piercing scream, and Lila watches with horror as a

Madovian catches up to Maxsim, his limp slowing him down. He goes down in a tangled heap, the godawful screeching echoing through the forest.

"Max, no!" Lila's form pulses, and I feel her berserker mode push its way forward, triggered by her injured mate. Her body changes, getting larger and broader, her spikes retract, and her color changes to red and green. She growls and starts racing toward the melee. My excitement spikes, and I let my own berserker out. There will be no more damage to any of us, Lila and I will make sure, but I hope they can pull us back after we take care of this mess.

CHAPTER TWENTY-EIGHT

Lila

A wave of pure fury batters at my body unlike anything I have ever felt before. I rush toward my cat and that bitch who better enjoy her last few breaths. A red haze washes over my sight, my emotions lock down, and the need to kill rides me hard. I feel my body change, but I don't stop my forward movement. Nobody touches my mate and gets away with it, especially not a parasitic whore.

I race forward knowing I can't fire my guns or use my thorns until Maxsim is clear, so I tackle the two beasts, joining the rolling ball of fury, then I grab Maxsim by the scruff and hurl him to the side where he lands on his feet, but he falls to the ground, one of his legs unable to hold him up. I curl my arm back and launch my fist into the

Madovian's mouth, and before she can react, I fire thorns from my palm. They fly out and rip her insides to shreds, killing her in an instant. She sags, and I quickly remove my hand from her mouth so she doesn't drag me down with her.

I turn my attention to the next one, our attempts to lure them away from our injured and trapped working as Tirrian takes the lead, and we move farther into the forest. I have a brief moment of worry about the circle of protection staying with us, but Zeydan will be able to protect those we left behind. Hopefully Ghosie gets him out of those webs quickly, and he can rejoin the fight. My attention turns back to the fight in front of me, and out of the corner of my eye, I see that Brannock has turned berserker too. A smile crosses my lips, and I let myself fall into the slaughter. I kill over and over, ripping off limbs with my bare hands and filling their bodies full of thorns, smiling when they scream in agony as the poison eats away at their flesh like acid.

I feel another berserker at my back, and I take a moment to admire his form. He's fast and decimates the Madovian forces. His muscles bulge and ripple, and the strength in his thighs is mesmerizing as he takes on each bitch and makes a mess of them. Between the two of us, we have led them far away from the others, leaving them behind to mop up any we left injured but still alive. A slice across my arm drags my attention from the gorgeous man beside me and back to my target. I lift a hand and fire more thorns. They rip through the Madovian's body, shredding her like Brannock wants to shred the inner walls of my pussy.

There's a somewhat detached thought in my mind that I hope they get Max to the ship to heal before I turn my attention back to the last few remaining Madovians. None of them are leaving this planet alive, but we could get a few answers out of them. I think about stopping, maybe saving one for questioning, but then I quickly throw that idea away. I like how it feels when I watch the life leave their eyes, and their cries and screams are music to my ears.

I watch as the one I'm approaching turns to flee, but I don't let her get far, filling her retreating back with my thorns. I smile when the poison eats away at her flesh, melting it like she's a candle. The tables have turned, and instead of trying to attack, they are fleeing like the ragged bitches they are. They should have known better than to run away from us. I look around, trying to find my next target, and feel sad when there is no one left but my fellow berserker. We're both breathing heavily and are covered from head to toe in thick, black Madovian blood. My tongue flicks out, and I taste the blood smeared across my lips. It tastes like tar and ash, and I grimace.

My adrenaline is still pumping, and the urge to kill is riding me hard. A noise back the way we came has my ears perking up, and I turn my focus in that direction—something else to kill. I growl and head back the way we came, ready to continue our killing spree, but then I'm tackled.

"No, Lila. They are our family," the other berserker shouts, and my attention turns to him. I punch him in the jaw and buck my body, trying to get him off me. How dare he stop me from going after my target?

I shove him off me, and he goes flying backward, his back smashing against one of the trees. I jump to my feet and continue back the way we came, but once again, I'm tackled to the ground and pinned.

"Lila, stop." I shake my head and growl at the being stopping me from reaching my target. "If you want to kill, kill me. That's if you think you can," he taunts, jumping to his feet. I hurry after him, holding up my hands and readying my thorns, but before I can fire them, he takes off, triggering my instincts to chase. I follow him, pumping my arms and legs as fast as I can, the thrill of the chase rushing through my veins. I finally have a challenge, unlike those Madovians who we cut through like butter.

He ducks and weaves around the trees, always just out of reach. The air rushes past me, but I don't feel any of the branches scrape my face as I fire a few half-hearted thorns from my hands. They don't hit their target, running making it harder to aim. I'm not too worried, though, because I want this kill to be hands on. I want to see the life drain from his eyes as he takes his final breath.

The forest opens up ever so slightly, a craggy outcrop of rocks interspersed throughout the large trees. I watch as he ducks behind a particularly large boulder and smirk, slowing slightly as I try to get my breathing under control. As I get to the rock, I pounce, expecting my target to be behind it, but he isn't. There's just a rock face and nothing else. I look around in confusion, disappointed at allowing my prey to escape.

A pebble rolls down the face of the rock, and I look up, but it's too late. A figure drops down from the top of the stone structure. Damn it, why didn't I think to look up or use my senses to sniff him out? I was so focused on what I was going to do to him, I didn't pay attention to those things, and I'm going to pay for it. A large rush of air escapes my lungs as he lands on me, driving my body into the ground and pinning me below him. His weight anchors me in a way I can't escape, and my hands are trapped by his larger ones, a menacing growl rumbling from his chest.

"Now we can either fight or fuck to bring you out of your killing rage, and I know which one I would prefer," the berserker on top of me says, proud of getting the drop on me, but it only makes me madder. I scream my frustration and thrust up with my hips, trying to dislodge him, but instead of moving him, I rub myself against his hardened length, and my pussy throbs. Some of the red haze fades, and I return to my senses a little.

"Brannock?" I look around, slightly confused. "Where is everyone?"

"I thought it would be a bad idea to let you kill them in your berserker rage, so I led you away from them. You seemed to be on a killing spree, my little psycho." He smirks at me. "Berserker rage is hard to control the first few times, and we practice with our teams to be able to turn it off, or we could turn on one another."

I hear what he's saying, but there's still a part of me that wants to do damage, and the male in front of me just became the target for my excess rage. I snap my teeth at him and struggle to get free, but he just chuckles, which makes me even fucking madder.

"I see we're going to have to do this the hard way."

He hauls me up and spins me around, pinning me between his body and the solid rock at my back, my spines lying flat with the movement. Without saying anything, he strikes, his fangs sinking into my neck. I scream in anger and thrash about, but I can't move. I hear him swallow mouthfuls of my blood, but I can't push him away because he has my hands in his, and his strength far exceeds my own. I feel my anger start to fade, almost like he's sucking it out of me.

My body sags against his, feeling a little light-headed from the amount of blood he took, and I feel my berserker form ease away as I return to the mundane Aaz'axian form.

My body shrinks, so I am left dangling in Brannock's grasp with his fangs still lodged in my neck. "Brannock," I gasp, trying to push him off me. He hears me and removes his mouth, blinking owlishly at me before a goofy smile crosses his face.

"Huh, that worked. I've never tried that before." He lowers me to the ground and stumbles back, his own berserker form receding, although he's still slightly taller than me. He reaches out and pushes a stray tendril of hair back from my face. "You're so pretty, and you smell and taste so good." He leans in and sniffs me, his spines and membranes shimmering. A scent fills the air, sort of like wildflowers after rain, and my core throbs again as my nipples tighten.

"Are you drunk?" I feel my shoulder spines ripple in response to seeing Brannock's do it, and he groans and crowds against me, placing kisses on my neck and grinding his hard cock against my center.

"Drinking blood makes us drunk, but I couldn't think of any other way to stop you short of fighting or fucking you, and I didn't want to hurt you or fuck you when you weren't in your right mind."

My mouth drops open at his admission, shocked that he was coherent enough to reason. I was like an unthinking killing machine. I wanted his death, and nothing was going to stop me. "I'm so sorry," I apologize, feeling ashamed, but he just shakes his head, weaving slightly before putting a finger against my lips.

"Shh. It's okay. Everyone is like that the first few times. What matters is that we defeated the enemy, and you didn't hurt me. I will look after you." He slurs his words and wobbles before leaning against me. "Ugh, you feel so good." He rubs against me like a cat, and I feel a smile start to stretch across my lips. Brannock is adorable when he's hammered. "I want to touch you so badly, but I don't want you to think it's for the wrong reason. I wanted you before I even knew you were a mimic, from the moment I saw you fucking Xavier on Earth, even though I knew we wouldn't be compatible. At least I didn't have to hide myself from you."

Oh dear, I don't think he knows his inner thoughts are outer words, but it reminds me how sweet he is, and I wonder why I'm fighting this connection. I know now isn't the time, but fuck, I want this man, so I haul him against me and kiss the hell out of him. My fangs graze his lips, and my mouth fills with his blood. It has a spicy but sweet flavor, like sriracha peanut butter cookies, and it fizzes on my tongue. I sip it as I explore his mouth, my tongue caressing his as his hands wrap around me, pulling me tighter against him. I lift my legs and wrap them around his waist to give me better access to the hard length pressing against me.

He groans, and I feel him lift my top, peeling it up and over my head. Our mouths separate only long enough for him to do the same before his body presses against mine, a hand snaking between us to cup one of my breasts while the other slides into the waistband of my pants.

I probably shouldn't be taking advantage of him, but I'm trying to grab every precious moment when I can. I know I should be worried about the others, especially Maxsim, but I'm sure if anything was serious, they would have found us by now. My mates are giving us this brief moment to just be before we continue with whatever is to come.

His hand is rough against the delicate skin of my breast, but it feels amazing, and when his fingertip brushes my clit, I jump, surprised by the sensations it invokes. I feel liquid drip out of my center, way more than normal, almost like the slick of my lightning cat form. He inhales deeply, pulls back from our kiss, and looks me dead in the eye. Gone is the goofy, slightly drunk man, and in his place is a focused male, hot with desire.

"Your pussy is getting ready to take my cock. It's getting nice and wet so I can stuff you full and rip it to shreds." His words are low and growly and do things to me, but then I realize what he said, and I freeze.

Rip my pussy to shreds. Holy fuck, his cock is lined with barbs, and not the fun one that vibrates like Tirrian's. Brannock's is like a fucking cactus.

"Easy," he croons, reaching out to stroke my spines on my head before touching the ones on my shoulders. It feels like he's stroking my clit, and my pants get even wetter. "I promise it will feel amazing. It's designed to take those barbs, and when they lock into your pussy walls, they will inject you with a pleasure toxin that will have you flying high. Every drag of them against your walls will send you higher as I thrust in and out."

He pauses like he's waiting for me to give him permission. Fuck it. Yolo, right? I give him a little nod, and he strokes his hands over my spines once more, a pleased smile stretching across his mouth.

"Good girl," he murmurs, and my eyes roll back in my head as I shudder. I do like to be called a good girl. It just hits in a sexy sort of way. He drops my legs from around his waist and strips off my pants before doing the same to his own. His cock sticks out, and I watch as he takes it in his hand, stroking it up and down. I can see the little barbs lying flat, rippling with the motion. "They will stay flat until just before I fill your pussy with my seed. The barbs will activate, slicing through your pussy walls and injecting you with the toxin. Then, when we come together, your eggs, which lie within those walls, will release, and my seed will flood them, fertilizing them to create a baby."

My eyes widen, and I shake my head to apologize that this baby factory is closed, but before I can, he presses his finger against my lips again.

"I know you are protected. It's okay, I won't be sad. It is all I can do to control myself now. Just the thought of filling you with my seed is enough to send me over the edge," he admits as he lifts me and pins me against the wall again. The rocks are rough against my naked skin, but his body is a soothing contrast pressed against my front.

"Babies can be discussed later down the track—way later. We have enough to keep us busy for now, and I want to focus on getting my Chloe back." My heart aches at the thought of his child back on Earth with no one to care for her, and I vow to get her back, come hell or high water.

He kisses me and eases his cock in a little, and I groan at the feeling. Like all of my mates, he is large, and it takes a little bit of working it back and forth to get it in. Don't get me wrong, it fucking feels amazing, but every time he slides out, there's a small scrape of pain as those barbs rough up the walls they slide against. It's a push and pull of pleasure and pain, one never dulling the other. I beg for him to go harder and faster and deeper.

"Ugh…" I grasp his shoulder before running my hands over his spikes. They shimmer under my touch, and he groans, thrusting harder.

"You feel so good, so tight and wet and spongy, ready for me to burrow in and implant myself." He thrusts, each one punctuated by a grunt of pleasure. "Not going to last. Need to fuck you harder." He picks up his pace, and I hang on, my body tight with the anticipation of the impending pain and the intense pleasure burning deep inside me.

I seem to plateau. Just when I thought I was going to tip over the edge, I ride the crest with nothing to push me over, and I become needy and desperate.

"God, Brannock, I need more. I want to come, but I can't," I whine as I feel tears well in my eyes, the unreached pleasure causing me to ache.

His thrusts speed up, becoming harder and more demanding, somewhat animalistic. "Going to fucking breed you," he growls, and his eyes turn pitch black while his features become sharper.

"Yes, yes, breed me," I plead, desperate for something, anything, that's going to push me over, my body caught on that fine line of pain and pleasure, tipping over to uncomfortable now.

"Are you ready?" He comes back to his senses and checks, and I nod, not even caring that this is about to hurt. I already ache something fierce.

"Come, Brannock. Come inside me now," I beg, and he roars. I stiffen as his barbs activate, and the minute they pierce the walls of my channel, fire rips through my body. I scream, the pain like nothing I've ever felt before.

I push him away, desperate to do anything to stop this, but he wraps his arms around me and pins me against the rock, thrusting in and out and tearing my pussy to shreds. Just as I think I'm going to pass out, that fiery pain turns to a pleasant burn, and it's like I'm injected with a hit of ecstasy and my body starts to roll. Mind-numbing pain turns to intense pleasure, and my screams become moans.

"Oh yes, oh my god, yes!" My mind and body become weightless, and I fly to the sky with the most intense sensations I've ever felt. This isn't an orgasm, this is like an acid trip to heaven. Every long stroke of his cock seems to inject more toxin, and my pussy eats it up like it's crack before he stills, and I feel his cum flood my inner walls, coating them. I can almost feel it seeping into the long channels his barbs have torn into the flesh lining my pussy.

"Oh my god," I mutter as I close my eyes and just float. I hear him muttering words of praise, but they sound far off and warped. I tried ecstasy once, and this is nothing like that. It's better, and I don't think I ever want to come down.

CHAPTER TWENTY-NINE

Ghosie

Earlier

Laser bullets fly all around me. I duck and take out the two Nelecs in the trees above the dragon and me before looking at the warlock, who is wrapped up. Lila is trying to untangle him, but I know it isn't going to work. Nelec web is one of the toughest substances in the galaxy. Every little piece she manages to remove grows back stronger. The only way to untangle him is for me to disrupt it and drag him out.

I watch as Brannock tries to get Lila to move, and she stubbornly refuses. Cursing drags my attention to the front of the fight. Zeydan is down too. Both of our most powerful players were taken out.

We need them back in the fight if we are going to win this, and only I can help with that.

I hurry over to them. "Go, I've got this," I shout at them. "Lead them away, and I'll make sure the warlock and god are safe."

They pause for a split second, exchanging a glance, but I see the moment they decide to trust me. They race to join the others, the dragon also leaving my side to follow.

"We need to move. We need to draw them away from Xavier and Zeydan so Ghosie can do his thing," Brannock shouts at Saxon, who is quick to follow his lead. He takes off, drawing the Madovians away. The cat and snake change course and follow, and it works—the temptation to chase too much for the Madovians. They follow the rest of my friends, taking the green circle of protection with them.

I breathe a sigh of relief, looking around to make sure all the Nelecs and Madovians left behind are actually dead. I don't want any of them sneaking up behind me while I'm trying to free the other two.

I take a moment to use my gun on them, putting a couple of shots in each head and body just to make sure nothing is going to leap up and attack us, then I shove my guns back into my leathers and approach Xavier. His eyes are wide, but he's still unable to move, the web causing his body to become numb. The sounds of the fight fade into the distance, leaving the surrounding forest eerily quiet.

I crouch down next to the warlock. "We have to be quick. We don't want the trees to start draining you of your life force," I tell him as I watch a root start to snake out from the closest one. "This is going to be a little uncomfortable for you because I need to touch you, and my fur is going to make you happy to see me," I tell him, slightly ashamed, but there's nothing I can do about that now.

It's fine, just get me out of here. We need to catch up with the others.

I blink in surprise at hearing his voice, but I really shouldn't be surprised since he's a warlock.

My hands start to vibrate, my matter disruption powers causing them to blur and pass through the sticky web, wrapping around the warlock's body. I need to be careful, I need to use the same power on his body to make his matter disrupt enough to pass back through the web without breaking apart. I watch as his body starts to vibrate, and his eyes roll back in his head. I hear him groan in discomfort as his body reaches the right frequency, and then I drag him through the web, the sticky substance passing harmlessly through his disrupted form.

I drag him forward so he isn't caught in it again and allow my powers to sink away from him. His body reforms in front of me before I remove my hands. He stumbles a little, the numbing feeling fading instantly. He clenches his hands, and his jaw is tight. I reach out to steady him.

"No!" he shouts, holding up his hands and stumbling back from me. Hurt stabs at my chest, and I guess he must feel it, because when he looks up, his eyes are foggy.

"Whoa, no. Thank you, but I was fighting my need to rub my body against yours. If you touched me again, I would have succumbed and climbed you like a tree," he rasps as I see him impressively fight off the effect of my fur. "Although I reserve the right to try this again, now is not the time."

I chuckle and leave him to recover as I move over to do the same thing to the god. When I get to him, I drop to my knees, and a wave of panic rushes over me. There are three tree roots wrapped around his legs, and they are pulsing. I can literally see them sucking the power out of Zeydan, his fox form fading in color before my very eyes.

"Whoa." Xavier approaches me. "Those trees are no joke." He reaches out to grab one to rip it off the god, but I hold up my hand.

"Stop. It's probably better that we don't touch them either," I tell him, pulling out one of my guns and checking the charge. It's half full, so I aim it at the tree root farther back so I won't risk hitting Lila's future mate. I think harming a god is probably bad for one's own karma as well. Carevasta bears used to worship the old gods, but Markit, the god of air, was our patron god. Regardless, I want to stay on his good side if I have hope of exploring what Lila and I could possibly have.

The sound of the laser firing is a sharp ping in the air, and it hits the first tree root, severing it. It lets out a piercing sound, almost like a scream, before it slithers back toward the tree it came from. The remaining part around the fox's leg shrivels up and falls off, turning to that black dust the minute it hits the ground. Thankful it was successful, I make quick work of the other two roots, watching as they both react the same way. I pass my gun back to Xavier before reaching for the god. He's unconscious, so I can't apologize for the effect of my fur. Then again, I don't know if it will affect him. His body blurs, and I drag him through the surrounding web, his much thicker than the one that had been around the warlock. I'm assuming more than one Nelec attacked him.

When he's clear, I lay him down on the ground. "What are we going to do with him? We can't leave him here without any protection, the trees would be on him again in no time."

"Lila would never forgive us," Xavier agrees before waving his hands, his powers unaffected because the tree roots hadn't gotten to him yet. The large fox rises into the air and hovers. "This is going to suck for him, but it's better than leaving him behind. Come on," he calls and starts to follow the path the fight went. I watch in amazement as the unconscious floating god bobs along behind him, occasionally smacking into a branch when the gaps are smaller than he can reasonably fit through.

"He's going to be covered in bruises," I mutter, taking up the rear to guard him. I pull out my gun again, almost certain there is nothing left alive behind us, but I don't want to make an assumption and have it bite us in the ass.

"Better than dead," is his flippant response, and I guess he isn't wrong.

We pass an occasional dead Madovian, both of us putting laser shots into them just to be sure, but when we finally catch up to everyone, the two of us stop and stare at the sight in front of us. Saxon and Tirrian are crouched beside a whimpering Maxsim while Silac, back in his humanoid form, albeit covered in Madovian blood, is doing the same thing I did and making sure everyone is dead. It looks like a massacre. There are Madovian body parts strewn everywhere, some even hanging from trees, with their blood on almost every surface.

"Holy fuck," I mutter, taking in the carnage.

"Aww, man, we missed it." Xavier pouts. "I didn't get to kill a single one."

Saxon chuckles. "That's because they got the drop on you. You snooze, you lose," he jokes, and Xavier flips him off.

Tirrian rolls his eyes at the Vilaxian. "Don't lie, we didn't do this either."

"Who did then?" Xavier asks, sounding as

confused as I feel, but then I look around and notice people are missing.

"Where are Lila and Brannock?" I ask when I don't see either of them.

"They did this," Tirrian says as he strokes his hand over the lightning cat, trying to soothe him. He's dripping blue blood from a significant gouge in his side.

"Just the two of them?" I can't believe those two could cause this much mayhem.

"Maxsim went down, and Lila lost her shit, going into berserker mode, and Brannock followed her down the path. When all of the Madovian's were dead and she turned her attention to us, he distracted her by making her chase him. I'm assuming he's trying to get her to switch back out of berserker mode." The dragon doesn't seem too worried as he pulls a communicator out of a pocket of his leathers.

"She was going to kill us." Silac sounds a little perturbed, but Xavier waves a hand.

"She wasn't herself, and she will get better. Brannock says the older they are, the easier it is to switch off. They'll either be fucking or fighting to cool the berserker mode. I'm personally hoping for fucking."

I blink, stunned at what I'm hearing.

"You're okay with your intimate fucking him?"

"Not only am I okay with it, I encouraged it. Poor guy hasn't had a release in over seven hundred years. That has to be causing some pent-up emotions."

Saxon scoffs at his friend, dragging our attention back over to the injured cat. "I'm going to return to the ship with Maxsim and get him to Link so he can heal him. I don't know how long Lila is going to be, and he needs medical treatment now. Link should be able to patch him up until Lila can return and use her Celestian powers on him."

We hear the dragon radio the ship and give them the details. There's a reply, but I don't pay attention because I notice the god start to twitch.

"Xavier," I call to get the warlock's attention. He turns back as Maxsim and Saxon disappear, leaving behind the dragon and the snake to help us find Lila and then her grandma.

He lowers the god to the ground, and we watch as his whole body shivers before he reforms into his humanoid form. Xavier waves a hand, and he's clothed in one of those skirts he was wearing earlier.

"Ugh." He groans, rolling into a sitting position before pulling up his knees and grabbing his head. "What the fuck happened?"

"It wasn't just the Madovians, they had Nelecs too," I explain, and he hisses aggressively.

"They took out you and the warlock before we even noticed they were in the trees," Silac explains.

"Lila?" Zeydan's head whips around as he looks for her and struggles to his feet when he doesn't see her. I put out a hand to help him but stop myself, cursing the effect of my fur. Silac takes my place, steadying the god.

"She's fine. We'll catch up with them soon, I'm certain," Tirrian assures him.

"She and the Aaz'axian are just working off the aggression." Xavier winks suggestively, and I can see the exact moment the god comprehends.

"Ah. Well, good. Okay, let's go, it isn't far." He stumbles slightly and groans, grabbing his head again, but he leads us away from the site of such cruel destruction. I heard rumors and tales about the Aaz'axian forces, but seeing it certainly hammers home how deadly they are. It's no wonder the Una's race was decimated in their war.

We follow the god, and while he said it wasn't far, it's still at least an hour of us stumbling through the forest, which seems to get even thicker the closer we get to the middle.

About twenty minutes into the walk, a piercing scream echoes through the forest, the first noise I've heard apart from our own breathing and occasional quiet curse. I think we're all just subdued, thankful we survived the fight with the Madovians. We may not have if Lila and Brannock hadn't assumed berserker form. There were way more than we anticipated, not to mention the Nelecs.

"What is that?" I ask as we freeze. Zeydan's brows furrow in concentration as he scans the tree line, but Xavier just chuckles.

"Lila has a good set of lungs on her, and I hear that Aaz'axian sex is kind of brutal. I've seen the barbs Brannock has on his cock, and I'm not surprised we can hear her." He slaps the god on the shoulder. "Trust me, she's fine."

He keeps walking, and Tirrian follows after him. Silac hisses, and his forked tongue darts out like he's tasting the air, his nostrils and hood flaring before he follows them.

I clench my fists, the urge to find them and save her riding me hard. That scream sounded like she was in agony, but I have no doubt if Xavier was worried, he would have disappeared in a flash to find her. I grit my teeth and hurry to catch up to the other three, hearing the god behind me muttering something under his breath. I'm not certain, but I'm almost sure I hear him mutter about making her scream even louder when he gets his chance.

I'm panting, and my fur is soaked with sweat when we finally make it to the location. We have literally had to squeeze between trees for the last five minutes, but it opens up into a space big enough to hold a large sarcophagus that glows with a grayish light.

Xavier conjures up bottles of water and hands them out. I take one, nodding my thanks before guzzling it down. The others do the same before they all take a seat around the clearing.

"We may as well rest and wait for Lila. A few

more minutes isn't going to hurt." Xavier leans back on his hands.

I don't join them. Instead, I walk around the enclosure, trying to get a feel for its frequency. I know everyone is counting on me to save the day, and I really hope I don't let them down. I reach out and lay my hands on it, allowing my powers to try to sync up with whatever magic is running through the box. I smile and heave out a relieved breath as my magic and its frequency align, and my hands start to push through whatever the substance is.

"Should I wait for Lila or keep going?" I ask, unsure if I should proceed or not. I thought it was going to be harder than this. I turn to look at the others who are all watching me with varying degrees of shock and surprise, but a noise in the forest behind them has them all jumping to attention. I stay where I am, not wanting to cut my hands off by yanking them out, and hold my breath.

Please don't let it be another Madovian, and if it is, someone kill that bitch because I can't move.

CHAPTER THIRTY

Lila

I don't know how long I float for, but when I come back down to Earth, Brannock is holding me like I'm the most precious thing in the world to him. He whispers words of praise and wonder as he strokes my shoulder and head spines. His touch causes goosebumps to break out over my body.

When he sees me looking at him, he smiles, his fangs gleaming brightly. "You're back with me, my lovely. Are you okay?" he asks, concern in his eyes.

I nod and swallow, my mouth super dry. "Yeah, I'm great," I croak, feeling slightly hungover but relaxed as fuck.

"You did so well. Your body absorbed all my seed. If you weren't on birth control, we would be having a baby. Our bodies are compatible." He beams as he lowers my legs.

I wince and stiffen up, bracing for the pain, but there is none. "My seed numbs everything to allow me to pull out without hurting you," he tells me and pulls free of my body. His cock is still hard, but I watch in amazement as the barbs, which are sticking out like a fucking pissed off porcupine, sink back into the grooves in his shaft. I wait for his cum to drip out of my body, but none does, and I frown.

He must see my confusion. "Remember, I said your body absorbs it."

"No wet spot?" I ask, my eyebrows jumping, and he chuckles and shakes his head.

"No."

"Well hell, that's certainly a bonus," I say, winding my arms around his neck and kissing him. "While that was certainly a different experience, I enjoyed it and can't wait to do it again," I tell him, pulling away and looking around for our clothes. "As much as I would like to stay and do it again, I need to find the others and my grandma and get out of this creepy as fuck forest."

"Yes, of course. Let's not keep your grandpas waiting any longer. I hope maybe next time we can do this without activating berserker mode before-hand." He sounds a little unsure, and I stop what I'm doing and throw my arms around him, giving him a big hug. I want to rub my face against his naked chest, but I'm worried I'm going to stab him with my head spikes.

"This body is going to take a little getting used to," I grumble as I pull away. "I hope I never have to use berserker mode again, so I can definitely say this will be happening again without it." I wink and pull away, quickly putting my shirt on as he does the same, covering up the body I really didn't get a good look at.

I will be rectifying that at the soonest possible convenience, but now I need to make sure the rest of my mates are safe, as well as my grandma. A rush of excitement flows through me, and I giggle at my thoughts.

Using my warlock powers, I stretch out with my mind, looking for Xavier's, and when I find it, I realize he's distracted and doesn't notice me, but it gives me a direction to go in. I grab Brannock's hand and drag him quickly through the forest. The two of us move over the gnarled branches, stumps, and roots with ease. The Aaz'axian form is flexible and fit, and we cover the distance in no time.

"They should be just ahead," I tell him. We'd been quiet and alert, on the lookout for more enemies while we traversed the forest, but I can hear the others talking and pick up my pace, wanting to make sure everyone is okay. I remember Maxsim was injured, which triggered my berserker mode, and he may need to be healed.

When we break through a small gap in the trees, everyone but Ghosie is pointing a gun at us.

"Whoa." Brannock steps in front of me and holds up his hands. "It's just us," he cautions the others, but I can't see my lightning cat.

"Where's Maxsim?" I ask with a rush of panic, feeling ill, then I realize someone else is missing. "And Saxon?" I fall to my knees, heartbreak zapping me of my strength. "Tell me they aren't dead," I sob loudly.

"No, baby, no." Tirrian is the first to reach me, gathering me in his arms and scooping me up. "They are both fine," he reassures me.

"Saxon went back to the ship with Maxsim. He was injured and needed Link to patch him up until you can work your magic. It wasn't life threatening, I promise." Xavier picks up my hand and gives it a squeeze, and I feel myself sag in Tirrian's arms. The nausea is still there, but it's tempered by relief.

"Ah, guys, should I keep going? I can't stay here all day," Ghosie calls, and Tirrian lowers me to my feet as we all gather around the stasis box.

It's way bigger than I thought it would be. I was expecting coffin-sized, but this thing is chest height and probably wide enough to fit two people inside it. It's glowing this weird, grayish light and has strange symbols carved onto the side of it. Zeydan runs his finger over one of them, tracing the symbol. He mutters under his breath, a frown creasing his brow in thought.

Ghosie is elbows deep, his whole body vibrating at a frequency that must resonate with the sarcophagus. He looks to me for a response.

"Yes, pull her out. Don't let her wait any longer," I urge him, my body tense with anticipation. I hold my breath, the eerie silence surrounding us only broken by a slight humming sound that Ghosie emits. His entire body disappears as he reaches down. After what seems like hours, but is probably only mere seconds, he steps back, bringing a small form with him.

He moves away from the stasis box with a woman cradled in his arms, and they both appear solid, their bodies no longer vibrating. My first impression of my grandma is confusing. She doesn't look like the photos I saw of her in my grandpas' suites. She had long, straight dark hair and tan skin. This woman is just as petite as the photo had been, but she is pale, with colorless hair that almost looks like it's glowing.

"That's not my grandma," I bite out, disappointment shattering all of my hope that I was going to be able to reunite my grandpas with their mate.

A shocked gasp has me turning my gaze away from the strange woman.

The words that come out of Zeydan's mouth have me frowning with confusion.

"Lilessa?" He steps toward Ghosie, taking the small woman from his arms and cradling her against his chest like she's the most precious thing in the world. Stabbing jealousy flows through my veins, and I clench my fists, berating myself for feeling such a stupid emotion.

No one says anything, so I ask the question we all want to know the answer to.

"Why is the goddess of life in the box instead of my grandma?"

Whoop there it is.
Another fudging cliff hanger.
Not sorry!
Anyway, don't despair I'm working on the next
book as you read this. I'm hoping to have it out
sooner rather than later. I won't leave you hanging.
Is it the last book you ask? I really don't know, but at
this stage, I'm going with no. There are too many
things to wrap up still so I'm leaning into 2 more.
Please if you love Galaxy as much as I do, review it
and smother it with love.

In the mean time why don't you check out one of
my other series. You can find everything you need
to know here.

AFTERWORD

www.lexiewinston.com

ACKNOWLEDGMENTS

To my cover designer Jessica, of Raven Ink Covers. Thank you for making the covers exactly what I envisioned, you nailed it and all of them.

Thank you to Jess at Elemental Editing. My book is pretty and readable thanks to you.

My ever reliable and faithful beta readers Kerry and Tegan… You da bomb xxx

Galaxy Circus is a real passion project for me. I love writing it and I hope to keep working on it for a little while longer. Keep an eye on my Facebook Group - Lexie's Ladygarden for news of when it will release.

And lastly to you guys the readers. I love what I do, and probably would do it regardless if anyone read them or not, but you guys make it that much sweeter so thank you.

Until next time, happy reading

SNEAK PEAK

Coming in 2025

Summertime Scorecard
(Blurb subject to change)

That's it, school is done and dusted, and I just walked with my graduating class. I just need to make it through the summer and I'm off to college.

But now it's time for the Summer Scorecard. A stupid game the local boys in my town like to play during the summer when we get inundated by wealthy holiday makers. A point system for every one they score with, the winner getting bragging rights for the following year.

Last summer my twin brothers reigned supreme. Teaming up and scoring big time. Making every girl's dream come true to be in the middle of an Andrews brothers sandwich. They of course

369

won by a landslide and went off to college as town heroes.

But this year is a little different, the girls have been invited to play and I'm expected to follow in my brothers' footsteps. Sure, I like sex but I have no interest in keeping score. I just want to spend my summer having fun, before I leave this town behind to spread my wings.

That is until my arch nemesis throws down the gauntlet and everyone knows that Oaklee Andrews never backs down from a challenge.

Game on!